# Rayne's Return

## LOVE IN MISSION CITY BOOK 4

## GABBI GREY

E verett

After my infamous half-a-night stand with the mysterious Rayne, I moved on with my life. Success as a lawyer demands long hours and giving a hundred and ten percent to the job. I do carve out enough time to hang out with friends some weekends, but it's depressing to watch them pairing up while I'm relentlessly single. Then, one morning, the man I can't forget shows up bruised and bedraggled at my office door. Rayne has a whopper of a story to go with the bruises, and seeing him again strikes wild sparks I can't deny, but can I trust a man who ditched me without a word? Or will he be gone again by morning light?

Rayne

As a private investigator, I've done some dubious jobs for some very questionable people. The assignment that brought me into Everett's world was one of the worst. Now, someone's trying to kill me, and until I figure out who and why, I need a safe place to hide. All I can think of is Everett. The hot, by-the-book lawyer I hooked up with once doesn't owe me a thing, but he's the only person I trust. I'll do my damnedest to keep danger from reaching him, and hope like hell I can walk away with my heart intact.

*Rayne's Return* is a gay romantic suspense novel with an uptight, by-the-book lawyer and a PI who never manages to stay out of trouble. This age-gap, opposites attract novel is the fourth in the Love in Mission City series.

# Dedication

Dad

You were my first fan, and your support has been unwavering and profound. Thank you.

multimedia, audio, or other medium. We support the right of humans to control their artistic works.

No generative AI was used in the creation of this book.

Edits by ELF

Cover by Jo Clement

# Contents

# Prologue

Rayne

*H*<sup>oly fuck.</sup>

As I zipped up my satin pants, the words kept ricocheting around in my mind.

My ass was sore in all the right ways.

I'd just come like a freight train in some stranger's home office. A dude whose Halloween party I'd infiltrated in order to meet Everett Williams.

Getting fucked by the uptight and by-the-book lawyer had *not* been in my plans. Like, at all.

My body wasn't complaining, but my mind was super pissed. I was supposed to be getting information to him. Not having my ass reamed in all the right ways.

*Holy fuck.*

With trembling fingers, I ensured my harlequin jacket and hat were in place. Thanks to the foresight of donning a condom for tidiness, I hadn't shot my cum anywhere. Everett had taken the condom for disposal, so theoretically, he had my DNA. A risk I'd been willing to take. After all, my DNA had never been recorded by any law enforcement agency or ancestry database, so my jizz would be useless for ID.

I pressed my pants back into place, adjusted the jacket of my costume, and bolted for the door. Just before reaching it, though, I grasped my harlequin mask. A sense of sentimentality overwhelmed me and, on impulse, I left it behind on the desk.

The desk Everett had just fucked me against.

The gold filigree reflected the light from the streetlamps outside the window as I listened for sounds from the upstairs hall.

Hearing nothing, I slipped out, shutting the door behind me. Aside from a light coming from under what I assumed was the bathroom, the hallway was dark. Under the cover of the shadows, I crept to the stairs and took them as quietly as possible, using my utmost stealth and lightness. For a muscular guy, I could be nearly silent.

That helped in my job.

The party was in full swing as I glided down the last few steps.

The host of the party, Quinton, costumed as Asian Ken, stood near his Barbie. I'd heard he was bisexual, like myself, and I didn't know if Barbie was a date or a friend.

I spotted the group of men Everett had been chatting with earlier joking beside the dining room table. A lumberjack, a maharaja, a lion, and Superman. Other guests had arrived, filling the room with music, loud voices, and general merriment. I'd heard these parties were legendary...and I could see why.

The front door was mere feet away, and I was almost out when an attractive brunette in a mermaid's costume put her arm around my neck. "You're very mysterious." She reached for my hat.

Deftly, but hopefully without causing hurt, I slipped from her grasp. "Sorry, love, on my way out. You look stunning, though."

Not all women enjoyed flattery, but this one flipped her hair. "I think so." She offered a broad smile. "Will you be here for New Year's? That party is out of this world."

"We'll have to see." I wouldn't, of course. First, I couldn't risk attending a party without a mask. Being without one now as I made my escape was bad enough. Secondly, I wasn't going to show up anywhere I might run into Everett again. He hadn't seen my face, but he'd looked directly into my eyes. My distinctive eyes. Only as he'd done so, had I remembered I'd neglected to wear colored contacts. By the time I'd realized my mistake, it'd been too late.

Much too fucking late.

"Raina!" A woman in a pink frou-frou princess costume made her way over and grabbed the mermaid's arm.

I slipped out the front door, panicked. *She said Raina, not Rayne.* Because although I'd given Everett my real name—which was all kinds of stupid—answering to the name would be disastrous.

To my horror, I nearly knocked over a woman about to step over the threshold. She was a tall, statuesque stunner with auburn hair and distinctive deep-brown eyes.

Supported from behind by another tall person. A Black man with a bit of a scowl.

I didn't blame him. "Sorry. Just realized I forgot something."

The woman grinned. "Understandable. I'm Loriana. This is my husband, Mitch."

Without any clear comprehension of why Loriana was introducing herself, but again, not wanting to be memorable, I shook her outstretched hand. "Again, apologies. I have to go."

I released her hand, slid around the couple, and hotfooted down the path between the driveway and the house.

Mitch might or might've not said something about rude people.

Loriana's accompanying laughter was the last I heard from them as I turned onto the street.

Running wasn't going to get me far. Undoubtedly, there might be an increased police presence on this night of notorious mischief. The odds of them being on *this* street in *this* little neighborhood were small...but not impossible. Mission City, in southwestern British Columbia, was generally a quiet town.

Except for the criminal element.

As well as stupid teenagers, domestic abusers, drunks, and all the other lovely characters who came from small towns.

I hit the button on my remote to disarm my car alarm. I'd parked more than five blocks away, among many other vehicles, and I was nearly there now.

A giant inflatable pumpkin, along with a dozen beautifully carved real ones, adorned a home with music filtering through the solid-brick walls. Cars lined the driveway, and all the windows shone brightly. Apparently, the party had everyone occupied, and I didn't even spot a surreptitious smoker or vaper. Nope, the entire street was deserted.

Unnoticed, I slid into my car, started the engine, put the car in drive, and slipped into the night.

# Chapter One

M y mind whirled as I headed into my office on New Year's Day. Last night, at Quinton's Out of This World New Year's Eve party, two interesting things had happened.

First, I'd admitted to my new friend Foster about my Halloween debacle two months ago with the mysterious *Rayne*. I'd shared way more information than I should have. Especially to a man I knew so little about.

Except Foster had proposed to a man I knew much better, and been accepted, which spoke well for him.

Arnav was a damn good lawyer and had been my adversary several times. He wouldn't marry someone untrustworthy. And now, damnit, I had to be happy for him. He'd found the man of his dreams.

While I'd now spent two full months obsessing about the man I'd fucked over Quinton's desk. Best lay of my life—hands down. Most infuriating lay ever—without question. A man who'd spent way too long haunting me—absolutely.

As I rounded the corner, footprints in the snowy slush intrigued me. I was a partner in Herrington, Herrington and Sons. Newly minted partner, no less.

Our office, on Third Avenue in downtown Mission City, had a great view of Cedar Valley as well as Mount Baker—the dormant volcano in Washington State. None of the mountain was visible today as the wet snow fell from a heavily overcast sky.

I'd donned my fedora and wool trench coat in deference to the weather.

January had just begun, and the meteorologists were predicting a moisture-laden winter. Both rain and snow. Making the snowy path something I'd no doubt come to expect.

However, this early in the morning, the only footprints I expected to see going up our walk might have been those accompanied by little paw prints. Most of the buildings on the street were homes, and plenty of those homes had pooches.

Pooches who often pooped on our grass.

Fortunately, most owners scooped.

*Most.*

Such cleanup might necessitate trespassing onto our property.

This early, though, on a big holiday, no one else should have a reason to seek us out. But one dogless set of adult-sized footprints led up the path to the front door of our office.

And a figure huddled in the doorway.

The good news? Judging by the freshness of the prints, the person hadn't been there long and so hopefully wasn't too chilled.

The bad news? The person was quite possibly homeless and in need of help, on a holiday when resources would be thin on the ground.

We had too many of those unfortunate people around here. The encampment near the railway tracks spoke to the poverty. The people who lacked housing. Some had chosen to turn down offered shelter beds. Some...but not all. Mission City lacked the proper resources to care for these people.

Hence one landing on my covered entryway.

This wasn't the first time, and it wouldn't be the last.

I considered heading down to Tim Horton's on First Avenue and grabbing a sandwich and a large coffee for them. Maybe even a twelve-pack of timbits. Something to help this poor soul.

Except part of me knew that wouldn't solve this person's problems. One warm meal was a Band-aid on a gaping wound.

I cleared my throat.

The figure stirred.

Given the sheer size, even huddled that way, I figured male. However, if I'd learned one thing in my almost ten years of practicing law, it was not to make assumptions. "Can I help you? I can run down to get some coffee and a sand—"

The words died in my mouth as the figure uncurled and faced me from the compact position they'd taken. With temperatures below freezing, that posture had made all the sense in the world.

Looking into tawny-brown eyes that had haunted my every waking and unconscious moment for the last two months did not.

Neither did the black eye, split lip, and matted hair.

"Jesus Christ." I whispered the words fiercely.

"Uh, no. Just Rayne."

My mind struggled to understand what I was seeing. I couldn't reconcile the healthy, fit, and gorgeous man from two months ago with the poor soul before me. As he rose gingerly and wincing, though,

I noted his body was much the same. Broad chest, muscular arms, slender waist, with strong jeans-encased thighs. Darkly soaked.

"Is that blood, or are you just wet?" I pointed to said jeans. Belatedly, the matching stain on the front of his jean jacket caught my notice. I stood a little taller. "Are you in trouble?"

"It's, uh, blood. But I'm okay." He looked very far from okay, but he was steady, and his voice was strong. I wanted to demand to know what was going on, but I couldn't find the right words.

The snow continued to fall, and a gust of wind blew through the valley.

*Right. Winds picking up in the morning with the possibility of blowing snow.* Since I'd planned to be ensconced in my office, I hadn't really paid attention. "What happened? Were you in an accident? Were you mugged? Why didn't you call the police instead of huddling here in the cold?"

He managed to crack a smile.

Then winced.

"It's a complicated story. I wasn't in an accident. I, uh, wasn't exactly mugged." He shivered. "Can we go inside?"

Manners dictated I should invite him in. Except a small part of me was still hurt that he'd taken off. That he'd seen our tryst as nothing more than a half-a-night-stand while my world had been rocked. *And yet he's here.* "What do you mean you weren't *exactly mugged*?"

"I, uh, might've encountered the wrong people." He eyed me. "Don't worry. I'm pretty sure I wasn't followed."

*Okay, so not an accident. Something's off.* "Encountered? Did someone do that on purpose? Are you in danger? Why are you not down at the RCMP detachment?" Because the Royal Canadian Mounted Police, Mission City's law enforcement agency, sure was better equipped to deal with this than I was. In fact... "And have you been to a hospital? Have you been seen by a doctor?"

"No, to both." He shivered again. "Uh, no. No one knows I'm here."

"Where's your car?" At least I assumed he had a vehicle. Although maybe he'd walked here. If so...from where?

"Where I left it."

"So you walked here. Your footprints—"

"The car's in Abbotsford. I hitched a ride."

"Hitched a ride? From Abbotsford? To here?" I rubbed my forehead. "You came here? To see me? Why, Rayne? Help me understand why I'm not bundling you into my car and driving you to get help."

"I don't need help. Well, not that kind of help."

"What kind of help do you need?"

"I need a place to, uh, lie low for a little while. Like...a day or two. Where no one will notice me."

"You got a ride from Abbotsford, looking like you are, and you think no one noticed? That they might've been concerned? That they might've told the police?"

"That ride was a car of party girls headed to a gathering in Maple Ridge. They were looking for a good time, and I was an afterthought."

"And they didn't question your appearance? You look pretty disreputable."

"I told them I was, uh, attacked."

"They didn't suggest the police?"

Another gust of wind.

Rayne shivered yet again. "No. Well, the driver looked like she might drive me to the Mission detachment of the RCMP. I told them I hadn't known the woman was married, and I didn't want her husband in trouble. In case he went after her."

I arched an eyebrow yet again.

"Totally made-up story. But it got me out of Abbotsford. I'm sure my car's been towed by now."

"Can you pay the impoundment fee?" He didn't appear to have two pennies to rub together.

"They might be watching the lot to see if I show up to get it."

"*They*?" I waited, but he didn't enlighten me. "Okay. And if someone else gets the car, *they*'ll just follow it. Right." I seemed to be saying that a lot. I also wasn't understanding. Clearly he was trying to get away from…whomever had done this to him. But I didn't have enough facts. I worked best with having everything laid out clearly. Rayne was being damned evasive despite clearly being in trouble. I wanted to be an asshole and demand the full story before I helped him. Possibly in justified self-protection. Possibly because he'd walked out on me and I was still hurt.

Well, probably. "I really can't convince you to come down to the RCMP detachment?" I believed they were far better equipped—

He shook his head, and a shudder racked him head to toe. The daylight highlighted the dark-red stains on his clothes.

I sighed. "You might as well come in."

To my relief, he stood back as I unlocked the front door. I keyed in the code to turn off the alarm. Then I swept my arm through the doorway, gesturing for him to enter.

He did. Then whistled. "This place is…"

Yeah, it was. A turn-of-the-century home from one of the city's pioneering families.

Gil's grandfather, the original Herrington, had bought the place back when a Black-owned business was unheard of in town. He'd renovated the stately home to suit an upscale law firm. The living room, just by the entryway, held our receptionist's desk as well as a lovely seating area with that stunning view of the valley. The next room, the former dining room, belonged to our law clerk. Beyond that was the kitchen and break room for our staff.

Abovestairs were three large offices and one small.

Rayne didn't need a law office, though. He needed a hot drink, food, and a cleanup.

He pivoted, looking around with narrowed eyes as if checking for enemies, but what he said was, "This place is amazing. Is that chandelier original?"

I was in no mood to be distracted with architecture. "Take your boots off." I might've snapped that. I closed the front door and removed my shoes.

The office staff swapped outerwear for inside shoes during the muddy and snowy months, so we cut down on the work for the cleaning crew in the private areas.

Truthfully, we never asked clients to remove their footwear. Some would on snowy days as a courtesy, but I wasn't giving Rayne the choice. Maybe I was more pissed at him for vanishing than I realized.

Possibly.

Probably.

I donned my expensive faux-leather shoes.

Rayne removed his boots.

Ignoring the hole in his sock, I beckoned for him to follow me along the corridor leading to the kitchen.

We entered, and he shivered despite his jacket. "How cold do you keep this place?"

"We're closed over the holidays, and so we lowered the temperature." I still wore my trench coat and a thick sweater. I pointed to the sink. "You start cleaning up. I'll see if Gil left a sweater in his office."

He'd kill me for lending his cashmere to a stranger, but things being what they were...

*Is Rayne really a stranger? You know him carnally—*

"It's okay. I don't want to take someone else's clothes."

"Well, you can't stay in a soaking-wet jean jacket and shirt." Plus the blood. "If he doesn't have one, I have a spare." I eyed him. "It'd be a little tight on you."

"I don't mind." His eyes flashed. Begged. "Really. I'd be more comfortable in something of yours."

I took another moment to look over the bedraggled creature before me. I should've been more sympathetic. *Who are you, Rayne? Why did you come here?* I cleared my throat. "It's New Year's Day. You had no way of knowing anyone would be here. How long have you been waiting?" I tried to do the math. He'd said he'd caught a ride with a group of women heading to a party...

"Not that long. I hid in a booth at Fifties and kept ordering food."

"And your server didn't ask any questions?"

He wrinkled his nose. "I made it clear I was okay and I just wanted to be left alone, and she got that. I settled up each time I ordered food so she wouldn't worry about me taking off. I might've left her massive tips every time."

"I'm still surprised she didn't call the cops."

He shrugged. "I gave her the same story. Married woman, with a disgruntled husband I hadn't known about."

"And you came here when?"

"A couple of hours ago. Fifties started to get crowded, so I left. The server said she'd be back later tonight and working the graveyard, and I was welcome to come back." He sniffed. "Implicit in that offer was that I keep buying food."

"And leaving big tips?" That didn't sound like the Fifties crew.

He shook his head. "Nah. After the third tip, she asked me to stop. I didn't—and I think that might've irritated her."

"Could you afford that?"

"I'm not broke." He might've spat the words.

I raised both hands. "Okay, I hear you. Not my business. Get undressed and wash off. I just remembered I have a clean sweatsuit here for when I go to the gym after work." For some reason, I wasn't going to tell him we had a fully decked-out basement gym right here that Nicole, Gil, as well as the rest of the staff used. I couldn't explain the logic, but I felt I should keep some things close to the vest.

He fumbled at the front of his jacket as if his hands were stiff.

In a moment of compassion, I moved closer. "Do you need help? Are you going to be able to get out of those wet clothes?" *What if he can't? Are you going to undress him?* Isn't that a bit personal after two months of fucking radio silence?

*He's hurt. I should be helping.*

*You should be running to the police. Or maybe calling a doctor...*

"I don't need help. But thanks." He yanked off his coat, let it drop to the floor, then pulled his henley over his head.

My breath caught. And not because of the sculpted muscular chest, the ripped abs, or the bulging biceps.

Okay, maybe a bit for those things.

Most, though, for the bruises that mottled the formerly pristine skin of his torso. The light tan wasn't enhanced by the purple-and-green contusions.

"Put your shirt back on. We're going to the hospital." I scooped it up from the floor, where he'd dropped it, and gently shoved it back at him.

"No." He jutted out his chiseled jaw.

*Seriously? You've* got *to stop ogling him and you've* got *to convince him to go to the hospital.*

I stepped closer.

He flinched.

*If he doesn't trust me, why's he here?* But I also hated someone had given Rayne that reflex.

I raised my hand slowly and brushed his hair gently back from the wound on his head. "Wow, your server didn't question this?" He had a goose egg and a bad scrape.

"I told you—I begged her not to. She leant me a toque to wear while I was at the diner. I had to give it back, though, when I left."

"Was that Sarabeth? Long blonde hair? She's very kind."

"Yeah, I think that was her name. Jesus, that hurts."

Yet I continued to palpate the wound. "What caused this? Is this grit? Did you hit your head against a brick wall? Or scrape it on a gravel road?"

Silence.

"You might have a concussion."

He held my gaze with those mesmerizing and unforgettable eyes. "Sidewalk. And no, I don't have a concussion."

I sighed. He was quickly rising in the ranks of the most frustrating men of my acquaintance.

He shrugged. "I had a concussion while playing football in high school. This doesn't feel remotely like that."

"Well, considering your graduation was ten minutes ago—"

"Hey."

"What?" I tried to move more hair, but the strands pulled at the dried blood.

"I graduated from high school more than ten minutes ago."

"Oh, sorry, an hour." I was poking at him, but I also wanted to judge his mental acuity. My fingers itched to grab my phone and call both the ambulance and the police. He needed a doctor and a cop.

I was neither.

"I graduated six fucking years ago."

"And that makes you...?"

He shifted. Finally, he muttered, "twenty-four."

A good ten years younger than me. "Which high school?"

"No way. I'm not telling you any more than that."

"You think a good Google search won't give me your real name?"

"Rayne is my real name."

*Rayne. With a y.* A memory from two months ago surfaced. His breath tickling my chin as he'd shared his name.

"I have my doubts."

"Pfft. That's on you, not me. My name is Rayne. Drove me nuts in school, but I'm kind of over that."

"A distinctive name and a distinctive spelling." I sighed. "Okay, I'm going to get clothes for you. You might as well follow me upstairs. I'm going to need to clean that wound. The first aid kit is down here, but the bathroom's too small for me to work in."

"I get to see your office?"

"No." I met his gaze and gave him my sternest look. "You get to sit on the toilet seat as I take care of this. If you feel woozy, I expect honesty. If you pass out, you're going to the hospital."

"Well, there's an incentive to stay conscious." He snickered. Then winced.

I rolled my eyes.

As he moved, I caught sight of his side, his battered skin scored by a deep, wet, red line. "Is that...?" I pointed.

"A graze." He didn't meet my gaze.

"I'm pretty sure I'm obligated to report bullet wounds."

"A graze." He reiterated the words, this time meeting my stare head-on. "Nothing to see. Nothing to report."

*Jesus fucking Christ, what have I gotten myself into?*

I guessed I was about to find out...

# Chapter Two

Rayne

Somehow, I'd expected more fuss about legal reporting requirements for the bullet wound.

Bullet graze.

How the fuck I'd been shot at from close range and they hadn't managed to hit me properly was sort of beyond me. I should've been killed. I might've been running away, but I wasn't exactly a small guy. No, I made a big target.

Of course, the guy had been running as well...

I followed Everett up the hardwood staircase, irrationally worried I might slip, fall, and hit my head. Again. Would be an ignominious end to a clusterfuck of a night.

Well, morning now. Like that somehow made things better.

It didn't.

But I tried to convince myself it did.

"In here. Sit and don't touch anything." Everett pointed.

"Can I, uh…" Heat flooded my cheeks.

He arched an eyebrow, but I caught a hint of a smile. Then he scowled. "You're practically naked—"

"Oh, I can get all the way naked. Nothing you haven't seen before—"

He stepped right within my space. "Take a piss, Rayne. Just lift the lid, okay? And don't ever—and I mean ever—mention that night to me again. Bad things will happen, I promise."

Then he disappeared into one of the closed offices.

I squinted. *Gil Herrington.*

Okay, so not Everett's.

*Sheesh. Two months and he's still that bitter? Not like I didn't get him off before I split.* But maybe the night had lingered in his memory, as it had in mine. Enough to leave some hurt or anger behind.

That hadn't been my intention. I couldn't have stayed a minute longer. And explaining now would just complicate things. I needed to get my thoughts unjumbled. The fact someone tried to kill me last night should be my top priority. Whether or not Everett decided to help me hide out despite his pissy mood was the real issue. My head ached, and strategizing my way out, in this moment, just wasn't possible.

Given my bladder was about to explode, I really shouldn't have hung around staring at that closed office door.

And yet I did.

For a moment.

This man was a bundle of contradictions. Rightly, he should've shoved me off his front stoop and sent me packing. Hell, he should've called the cops. At the very least, he shouldn't be helping. The fact that I wasn't a fugitive—that I was a victim—only carried so much weight. Especially since he didn't know this. He just knew I'd been injured. To this point, amazingly, he hadn't asked for details. To my embarrassment, I'd barely scratched the other guy, but I wasn't some innocent, naïve to violence.

From now on, I'd have to be careful not to use up all the goodwill I'd attempted to amass over the fifteen minutes with Everett. *I may be swaying him to my side. But that means balancing being honest and keeping certain information to myself. I don't want him to get hurt in all this.*

"I don't think you're pissing." His deep voice resonated through the closed door as if he knew I was standing there.

I hustled into the palatial bathroom. Aside from the clawfoot tub, the bright, modern room was completely at odds with the rest of the house. Well, house turned law firm.

I laid my henley and jean jacket on the side of the tub. I unbuttoned my jeans and, on impulse, yanked them down along with my underwear.

Fuck, fuck, fuck, fuckety fuck.

The fabric stuck to my wounds, and when I pulled the denim, skin stretched. And not in a good way. Still, I managed to yank everything off. The road rash from when I'd been dragged along the sidewalk had left bleeding, raw patches of missing layers of skin. The bruises everywhere—and I meant everywhere—hurt like a sonofabitch. Everything ached. The graze on my side burned. Of all that, though, my head was the worse. A headache unlike any I could remember pounded through my temple. I needed painkillers, but wasn't about to go rooting around for them. I raised the toilet seat lid—as I always did, thank you very much—and pissed.

My bladder thanked me even as I struggled to remember the last time—

Tim Horton's. About ten minutes before being shot at.

*Should've gone to Starbucks.*

Except the odds were just as good—or as bad—that the bad guys might've been hanging around there. All of it was shitty luck on my part. I'd been heading to Wellington Park for a completely unrelated case.

Go figure.

I flushed the toilet, then ran my hands under hot water, repeatedly adding soap and trying to wash the blood off. I also tried not to look in the mirror. Yet I did and regretted it instantly. Not that I was a vain person—or so I told myself—but I'd planned that if I ever saw Everett again, I'd wanted to be at my best. To explain things in a rational and adult manner.

Or, even better, never see him again at all.

Yet the way the man haunted me at every turn, there was an inevitability to this meeting. Nothing I could've done to prevent it.

Well, except getting shot at.

Bad luck, that.

The bathroom door opened. "Okay, so I've got..." Everett met my gaze in the mirror. "You really do look like shit."

I shivered again. "Yeah."

"Do you think you can have a shower?" He put the clothes down on the edge of the tub and then began a thorough examination of all my injuries.

To my surprise, he didn't make a comment about my nudity.

I wasn't certain why, but I expected him to come out with a snide remark. Not about my body or anything like that. No, I anticipated a comment or ten about the number of injuries he was scrutinizing. "A shower sounds heavenly."

He scrunched his nose. "I don't know if it's safe, though. I don't have medical training. I should call—"

"No." I said the word forcefully. "No call. No one, okay? I'm fine."

Another snort escaped his lips. "You are so the opposite of fine."

I tried for mock offense, then winced when I arched an eyebrow.

He scowled. "Your bullet wound seems to have stopped bleeding." He bent to look at it. "Jesus, you were lucky. You probably don't even need stitches. Be careful not to touch it or you might open it up again. Any active bleeding and we're going to the hospital. Am I clear about that?"

I nodded.

"Any soap you use is going to sting."

"So will the antiseptic wipes I see you're anxious to deploy." I gestured to the first aid kit.

That elicited a grin. "Oh, my sadistic side is just itching to come out and play." Then he sobered. "I found a fresh bar of soap—I think plain is best. Nicole uses a softer shampoo, I think. Some floral stuff." He sniffed. "At least you'd smell better."

Instead of being offended, I laughed. "Eau de blood isn't your favorite?"

"No." Sharp and abrupt. "I'm not certain you should be joking about this."

"What choice do I have?"

"You can go to the cops."

"Okay, that's it. Threaten one more time, and I'm out of here. I don't need you haranguing me. I'm not going to the police. No amount of pressure or snide comments are going to change my mind."

He pursed his lips. Then he handed me the bar of soap. "I'm waiting here, just in case."

"You'll be bored."

"Making certain you don't pass out? Not likely. You can tell me your life story." He pointed to the shower. "You're going to get cold."

Funny how the air temperature barely registered when he was this close to me. The last thing I should've been feeling right now was lust...and yet I was.

Everett in just a henley and jeans was sexy as fuck. Pity I was too exhausted to really appreciate the sight.

"You're not seeing clients today?"

"No. Shower. Now." He spun me around and tapped my ass.

And not in the way I wanted.

*Yeah...I've thought of nothing but having sex again with him for the past two months. Now I'm naked and sex isn't even a possibility. I'm in such a mess. And everything fucking hurts.* Still, as I ran the water as hot as I could stand, I admired the man sorting through my blood-soaked clothes. Someone less considerate might've shoved them into the garbage. Not Everett, though. I suspected he'd try to get them laundered. If he could explain the blood, that was.

I stepped under the spray and winced as the near-scalding water hit my chilled, tender skin and burned along the raw line on my side.

"Start talking. Where were you born?"

"None of your business. Why do you care?"

"Because I need to keep you talking and conscious. Plus, we're getting to know each other better. Logical, right? Since we've got *carnal* knowledge of each other." His lips twisted, and something about the way he said *carnal* sounded bitter.

*Shit. I really did hurt him. Still, there are worse topics...like what happened to me tonight.* "Born in Vancouver."

Pause.

"Vancouver's a pretty big city."

"Not as big as, say, Toronto, or New York, or Los Angeles, or Sydney or—"

"You're getting off topic."

"I didn't know we had a topic."

"Rayne."

That warning tone that normally made my cock sit up and take notice. At the moment, though, it was about the only part of me that wasn't battered. No action going on there, despite the knowledge the gorgeous man of my wet dreams stood on the other side of the shower door. "Somewhere in Vancouver. That's all you need to know." *Can we drop this already?*

"Is Rayne your real name?"

"Yes." No need to prevaricate about that one.

"And the spelling is the one you gave me? Rayne with a *y*?"

*Shit, shit, shit*. Oh well, I'd stepped into that one. "Yes."

"So if I googled Rayne and, say, Abbotsford, what would I find?"

"Nothing of interest."

"Right."

Gingerly, I scrubbed my knees. My jeans had taken the brunt of the impact and, thank God, had not torn. The damn things were still a mess.

Knowing he was googling even as I tried to find the courage to wash my sore chest wasn't helping the situation. I still had the pavement scrapings on my face. I really did look awful.

"Interesting."

I grunted. Finally, I wet my face. I didn't enjoy this at the best of time. I wasn't a guy who would stand with my face in the spray and enjoy myself. I envied those guys in the commercials. Alas, that wasn't me.

Slowly, I ran a soapy hand along my scraped cheek.

And hissed.

"You okay?"

"Yes." I might've said that through gritted teeth. "I'm fine."

"Well, you are that."

At least that's what I believed I heard, even as the water cascaded around me and I probed gently at my cheek. No blood appeared on my fingers, so I gently continued to soap the area. "What did you find in Abbotsford?" Because curiosity really *was* going to kill me. Much as it had the cat.

"Lots of interesting things."

*Liar.* I almost said the word out loud, but held myself in check. To the best of my knowledge, I didn't have a footprint in Abbotsford. I neither lived there nor had spent more than a few hours there in my life. Now, there might be other Raynes in Abbotsford...or he might've widened the search and discovered something more interesting about me. Something I didn't happen to want him to know.

The floor creaked as he shifted his weight. "How's it going?"

"I haven't died yet." I might've felt like death warmed over, by my heart still beat strong.

"Oh, well, that's a relief. Hard to explain to my partner why I had to call the police to investigate a dead body in our shower." He snickered. "Have you washed your hair yet?"

"You offering to help?"

Another pause.

*Yeah, that's what I thought.* "Just about to."

"All right. I'm going to put your clothes in the washing machine. Try not to keel over in the five minutes I'm gone."

Part of me was intensely curious about why the law office had a washing machine and the rest of me was grateful for the respite. Honestly, I was surprised he'd given up after essentially one question. And yeah, I'd answered it honestly enough. Vancouver was just big enough to make it a needle in a haystack. Especially because I hadn't specified whether I'd been born in Vancouver proper or the Metro Vancouver

Regional District. Which had almost four times the population and spanned over twenty-one areas—the City of Vancouver being only one of them.

I touched the road rash on my forehead. The shampoo was going to sting like a bitch, but getting clean would be awesome. This shower was a luxury I hadn't dared dream of, huddled against the cold on a law office doorstep—

"When's your birthday?"

My breath caught in my throat. Somehow I'd missed his return. I supposed I expected a change in air pressure or temperature, but I'd felt nothing. "You honestly think I'm going to tell you that?"

"Well, you said *twenty-four*. I'll work off the assumption you were born in—"

"Yeah, you can do that math." Allowing he had the correct year still gave nothing away.

"So did your parents place a birth announcement?"

I laughed. I didn't mean to, but I did. "Uh, no. My parents weren't *those* kinds of parents. And social media wasn't a thing back then." Thank God, or he'd now have a weapon against me.

Another pause.

"Tell me about your parents."

*So much for the interrogation being over.* "Nothing to tell." I wasn't going to tell him how I didn't know them. Because that just sucked donkey balls, and I wasn't looking for sympathy. "How about you? How old are you?"

"Old enough to know better." With just a hint of amusement.

I really wished I could see his face. Likely wearing a smirk.

A sexy fucking smirk.

Instead I asked, "Where were you born?"

A long pause.

"Vancouver."

*So, not forthcoming either.* "And your parents?"

"Alive, well, and happy in their respective employments."

"That sounds...nice."

"Unlike your own, I assume."

"I said there was nothing to tell." Because there wasn't. Or so I'd maintain.

"Why do I think you're lying to me?"

I soaped the shampoo into my hair, mindful of every sore muscle as I raised my aching arms to do it. *Could've used a hand.* Not that I would've asked. As much as I wanted Everett naked again, I didn't want to be indebted to him. "I'm not lying. I literally have nothing to tell about my parents." Right now, though, I mostly wished I didn't have so much hair. Shorn—like Everett's—would've been better.

Interesting that his head had been shaved at Halloween and now the hair had grown in a bit. But it was still short.

"You surviving in there?"

I wanted to snap back, of course, but restrained myself. I was here on his good graces—pissing him off would accomplish nothing. "Yes, thank you." I finished rinsing my hair, then just stood under the spray, letting the heat seep deep into my muscles.

"What are your plans?"

*To not get shot again.*

Probably not the smartest response. "I need to figure out what to do next."

He snickered. "That's a given." Then sobered. "You're certain you weren't followed? By the guy or guys who attacked you? Who shot at you?"

"I've been here for hours."

"But they might find this place, right? They might be waiting for you. Are we even safe here? Did you *think* for one moment before turning up on my doorstep?"

"We're safe." *For now.* With a serious amount of regret, I shut off the water. "Unless you are into something shady that you're not sharing with me."

He sort of choked out his, "Yeah, no."

"Yes, that guy's looking for me. I'm not even sure how I got away. Sheer luck, I guess." *And running faster than I'd ever run before.* "He doesn't know where I am. No one does. I wouldn't have come here if it put you in danger. I don't know why you're judging me so harshly." *And I'm sorry I walked out on you. Is that why you're being so mean? Just assuming the worst about me?* Maybe I deserved that. Maybe I didn't.

I pulled back the shower door and stepped into the room, ensuring I stood on the bathmat. The floor looked cold, and I didn't want to drip water everywhere.

See? I could be respectful.

Or try to be.

He handed me a towel, apparently unconcerned with my nudity. *Nothing he hasn't seen before.* Except Quinton's den had been illuminated only by the lights from outside coming through the slatted blinds. This was the full-on view with bright lights. *And here I am looking like road-kill.*

With gentleness, and trying not to wince, I set about drying myself. *Easier said than done.*

"Here, let me." He all but snatched the towel from me, with clear exasperation in his tone and consternation in the form of a furrowed brow.

I held my tongue.

Where I expected him to be rough, though, he was gentle. Where he could've been cruel, he was kind. Where I expected clinical detachment, he was examining every inch of me intently.

When he appeared finished—and I was much drier than before—he snagged a towel and moved to dry my hair.

Our gazes clashed.

"Thank you."

"I'll bet all that hurt."

"You'll never know."

He cocked his head. "Yeah, but I can guess. Turn around."

"So you can ogle my ass?"

"Been there, done that." He tried for nonchalant.

He didn't fool me. Still, I turned and let him have his wicked way with me.

Or, in this case, dry my hair.

# Chapter Three

Everett

*How can he sleep so soundly?*

As if Rayne didn't have a care in the world, he slept the sleep of the dead on my couch.

If I'd had the shit beat out of me a couple of hours ago, and then had been shot—not shot *at*, however much he tried to minimize it, he'd had a bullet score his flesh—I was quite certain I wouldn't be sleeping soundly on some stranger's couch.

*We're not strangers. Two months ago, your cock was—*

Yep, so not going there. That I'd been balls-deep in him was of no relevance. Well, perhaps a smidgen. He'd shown up here, after all. If we hadn't fucked, I couldn't imagine he'd have picked my stoop to grace.

*He's damn lucky you came to work today.*

Especially after having enjoyed the celebration at Quinton's Out of this World New Year's Eve party last night. By all rights, I should've been home sleeping off a hangover.

Except I didn't drink.

And I didn't know how to not work like a workaholic. I had a big case coming up in a month—the opportunity to put in some serious time while not having to worry about distractions had held appeal.

Gil liked to confer on things, and a day in the office when he wasn't likely to be around would've let me get a head start on my research.

I looked at Rayne again before I continued my on-line search for traces of my mystery man. The one I'd started ill-advisedly two months ago. On another first of the month. The first of November—after the infamous Halloween party.

I'd drawn blanks back then. What little more he'd shared this morning didn't help me narrow the search. Instead, I scoured news and police sites from around Abbotsford and Cedar Valley from the past twenty-four hours.

Nothing. No mention of shots fired. Nothing about suspects being sought. No sign of any crime at all. Which might or might not have been all that unusual. Truthfully, I didn't follow all that went on. If it didn't involve a client, I didn't really care. I might read the local paper to stay abreast of the news that centered around Mission City, but random crime news from elsewhere had never been my thing.

To be safe, I did a search of the Mission City Gazette's website. To see if perhaps Rayne had been lying, and the encounter had occurred right here.

Nothing except a bad crash on the highway with drunk driving suspected. Fire crews, paramedics, and the police had been dispatched.

A black-and-white photograph of a firefighter. Familiar.

I nearly snapped my fingers as I tried to remember the guy's name. Cute. Redhead. Gay. All things that caught my notice in our small town.

Finn.

Finn the firefighter.

Right. Someone I might, in the future, ask out on a date.

*If* I found the courage. *If* I found the time. *If* I could get the mysterious *Rayne* out of my mind. Having him on my couch wasn't helping in that respect.

I refreshed the Abbotsford News website again, and a headline grabbed my attention.

*Shots fired in Wellington Park, steps away from family homes.*

I wasn't familiar enough with Abbotsford enough to know where the park was. I clicked on the map and found it right in the middle of central Abbotsford. The photo from the article showed yellow police tape in focus with a row of blurred townhouses as the background.

Yeah, the residents were lucky no one had been injured.

The article itself was incredibly unhelpful. Shots fired. No suspects or known motives. Neighbors thought they heard firecrackers, but when one of them found a spent shell casing while walking their dog this morning, they called the police. A bullet retrieved from the façade of a wood-siding building nearby had been saved for ballistics. No immediate known danger to the public.

Apparently, a homeless encampment in the park had been dismantled a week ago, and neighbors speculated someone might've been angry about that.

Homelessness might be a big problem in Cedar Valley, but I doubted very much someone was randomly taking potshots at houses. No, city council and the mayor might've been targets, but a blank wall?

According to Google maps, the park had townhouses on two sides, a street on another, and a brick building housing a couple of restaurants next to a hotel on the fourth. Down the street from several fast-food outlets. Half a mile from city hall and the nearest police station. Several hundred feet from the local mall.

*There's got to be something you're missing.*

Was Rayne—if this was Rayne at all—running into the park or away from it? Had he been on a rendezvous, or was this happenstance?

*Who'd you piss off?*

I had little doubt the man was quite capable of that. I'd been ready to throttle him—and I barely knew him.

*You know him in all the ways that count.*

Yeah.

Carnally.

I knew what my cock felt like in his mouth.

How it felt to be intimately connected with him.

The feelings of anguish when he'd run like a thief in the night.

*And now he's back.*

I reread the article, making a few notes on my yellow legal pad. When I'd written out every scrap of information I knew for certain, any conjecture I could conjure, and any potential hypotheses, I shut the browser down, put the paper in my desk drawer, and locked it. He didn't need to know what I'd been up to.

My chest squeezed as I gazed at his bruised face. He'd been lucky. Hell, he might have a concussion right now. Perhaps I should be googling concussion protocols instead of examining his face in repose. Trying to get the measure of the man.

"I can hear you thinking from over here." He stretched his arm.

I startled. "Well, you know."

He cracked an eye open. "No, I don't know."

"I'm trying to figure out what might be safe for you to eat for lunch."

"I don't have any allergies, so I'd say everything is safe."

"Well, you might—" I gestured up and down, "—have a concussion or something."

"Been there. Done that. Know for certain I'm okay this time."

"I doubt that. Have you looked at yourself in the mirror? Black, blue, green, and yellow, not to mention the bump making you look like a rhinoceros."

A brief shadow flashed in his eyes.

*Fucking hell, I didn't need to be so blunt. So cruel.*

Then he grinned. "Every day and twice on Sunday. I like looking at myself in the mirror. I'm a handsome guy." All cocky arrogance.

I tossed my pen against the blotter.

"Jesus, you use a fountain pen?" Slowly, he pushed himself up into a sitting position.

Hard to miss the wince or the press of his fingers to his temples.

"How bad?"

"I'll live."

I arched an eyebrow.

He met my stare.

Finally, I broke eye contact, snagged the pen, and started twirling it in my fingers. "I'm old school."

"Yellow legal pad?"

My gaze shot back to his.

He grinned. "You're so predictable."

"You think so? Boring-and-predictable Everett would've called the cops the moment your head hit the pillow. I'm just going crazy today. Off script and every-thing. My new year's resolution is to be less staid and boring."

"Oh."

"That's all you have to say for yourself?"

"Well." He fingered my sweatshirt. "I suppose I could thank you."

"And then some." I held my chin high.

"I don't suppose...?"

After a moment, when he didn't complete the thought, I rolled my hand to implore him to finish his words.

He cleared his throat. "I don't suppose we could get some food? The waffle at Fifties was nice, but I'm starving."

"Oh." I pointed. "How's your head?"

"I could use another painkiller."

After checking my watch, I shook my head. "Too soon. Unless..."

"Unless?" He perked up a little, despite still being pale.

"We can alternate types of painkillers. None of this is ideal. Are you certain you won't reconsider—"

"I'm not going to the hospital."

"Okay, but I could call a doctor and—"

"No." He nearly shouted the word. "God, you're like a broken record. I'll bet you asked your mom the question *why* about a million times a day."

"Well, since Mom was a high-school principal and my father was a stay-at-home-dad who happened to also be a writer, you missed the mark on that one. And he loved when I queried him on *everything*. He would give me all the facts on some issue and have me debate my mother when she came home." I considered. "Given how tired she must've been, I'm amazed she never declined the challenge."

"Hence you becoming a lawyer."

"Well, yeah, I suppose. I'm not certain, when I was five, that he planned for me to go into law. He feels teaching is the noblest profession. Mom was a teacher for fifteen years before going into administration."

"Were you a later-in-life child?"

I considered. "Well, my parents were in their early thirties. That was considered older back then, I suppose. As much because they were late marriers." I frowned. "I thought we were talking about food."

"We *were* talking about painkillers."

"Well, you need food in your stomach."

"So we can do Boston Pizza?"

I goggled at his hopeful expression. "Someone just tried to kill you and you want pizza?"

"Actually, their ribs are amazing. Oh, or their chicken wings. So good." He licked his lips.

My cock noticed.

*Fucking hell.*

I opened my favorite browser. "I assume they use a delivery service app?"

"Yep." He named one.

Dutifully, I entered it into my browser. And discovered the service was connected to just about every food establishment in Mission City.

Huh.

*Things I would never have known if I hadn't met you.*

Like what it felt like to be dumped before the relationship had even begun. Okay, maybe the relationship had been in my head, but we'd had *something*, a special moment, a connection, before he cut and ran.

And on that note… "Do you want ribs? They look…" I moved closer to the screen.

"Do you need reading glasses or something? You should, like, see an eye doctor."

"They're called optometrists, and I see mine every year." I scowled. Probably because said optometrist wanted me to wear progressive lenses. Not only would they improve my vision, but they'd reduce strain. Too vain for that, I wore contacts that often hurt my eyes, and squinted when necessary. "The ribs look good—but these photos are always doctored."

"Well, they're as good as they look. Do you mind ordering and paying?" He bit his lower lip. "I've only got five bucks cash, and obviously my credit card could be traced, and—"

I held up my hand to stall his words. "They can track your credit card? How sophisticated are these guys?"

"Do you want to take the risk?" He batted his absurdly long lashes over those tawny-brown eyes that, fortunately, appeared clearer than they had earlier.

I opened my desk drawer and tossed a bottle of painkillers to him. "Better taken with food, but something tells me you'll survive. Ribs, veggies, and side salad?" Remembering his six-pack—eight pack—I didn't figure he ate fries often.

"Can I have fries?"

"You may have whatever you wish." I started clicking on various keys to organize the order. I did *not* have a six-pack. I considered myself attractive, but I focused on endurance rather than strength. Swimming topped my list, along with hiking the nearby mountains. Still, as I perused the offerings, the salads didn't appeal. I'd mainly eaten appetizers last night and had skipped breakfast this morning—having planned to wander down to Timmies on my break.

"Are you always so indecisive?"

I glared. Then caught myself—I seemed to be doing that a lot. Understandable, but still too much. *Keep frowning and when the wind changes, the scowl will become permanent.*

Or something like that. My mother's expressions didn't always come back to me the way they should. But the sentiment echoed through the years.

"Just selecting my sides." To go along with the steak I fully intended to enjoy. In the end, I chose steamed vegetables.

And fries.

*When in Rome...*

Or some shit like that.

I pulled my wallet from my back pocket, then yanked my credit card out. Ensuring he couldn't see, I entered all my personal information. I loathed doing this—what with all the data breaches—but I didn't have any other options, and leaving him alone to go to the restaurant and waiting while they prepared the food felt too precarious. So did leaving him waiting in the car. Mission City might not be Abbotsford, but what if the young women heard about the shooting and decided to contact the police? How close to my building had they dropped him off? He'd wound up at Fifties, but what about before that? What if someone had noticed him this morning, but hadn't approached out of fear? Why couldn't I trust him? What—

The computer binged.

I startled.

"That's just confirming your order has been placed." Rayne's amused expression caught me off guard.

Almost as much as my computer talking to me. Usually I had it muted, but— "Yeah, okay." A memory of listening to my favorite soundtrack while I'd tidied my desk last night flooded back.

My year-end purge. A ritual I enjoyed.

The shredder was full.

My desk was clear.

The recycling needed to be emptied.

But everything was in its proper place.

I squinted. "It says thirty minutes."

"Sounds about right. Are you far from the restaurant?"

A reminder he wasn't from Mission City.

"No, not at all. Will they knock on the door?"

"Yes. But you'll get a text when they leave the restaurant so you can be ready at the door. Did you give the driver a big tip?"

"Uh...yes. Of course." Anyone willing to make my life easier was always rewarded. I was debt-free except for my mortgage. Years of lean living meant I could be generous to those who were less fortunate than myself. "Look." I took a deep breath and let it out slowly. "You can't stay here. I've put your clothes in the dryer, but they're still torn. Are you certain I can't—"

"No."

"You don't even know—"

"Cops. You're a broken record—same thing over and over again. I can leave..."

"Before you've eaten the ribs I just paid a shit ton of money for? Don't be ridiculous."

He pursed his lips. "I'll pay you back."

"With your five-dollar bill?"

"Uh…" This time, he blew out a breath. "I'm a little short."

"Like, totally broke short? Otherwise I'd suggest you hole up at the Grand Hotel until things blow over. I know the manager, Aaron. He'd let you stay for cash if I gave you a reference."

"That's a big offer. What money I have is in my bank account, and obviously, I might be tracked."

"We could drive to Vancouver, and you could use a random ATM."

"Actually, I don't have the money."

"Again, what did that admission cost you?"

His eyes turned flinty. "You're enjoying this."

"I have to find some amusement in this clusterfuck of a situation. You can't stay here. I could put you up at the Grand myself, but something tells me you'd just get into mischief."

"Not necessarily."

"But not guaranteed. I'm not risking my relationship with Aaron to—"

"You have a *relationship* with him?"

I sighed. "He and his husband Noel are friends. End of story. Jesus, you'd think you were jealous or something." Because, if I didn't miss my mark, there'd been an element of jealousy.

And I rarely missed my mark.

That said, this guy was frustratingly difficult to read.

"I'm not jealous." Said with an edge that left room for him lying.

My phone buzzed with an incoming text. "The driver left and is on their way. Isn't that fast?"

"If there aren't other orders, it's possible. The restaurant is barely open at this hour. And it's New Year's Day. I suspect they're not overrun yet."

I closed my laptop. "You need water to take the pills."

He snapped open the vial lid, shoved two into his mouth, and dry swallowed them.

I nearly gagged.

He grinned and tossed the bottle back.

I barely caught it. Frustrated, I shoved it back into my drawer along with my migraine medication which I was certainly not giving to him. "Let's go." I rose.

"I'm comfortable here."

"I don't give a shit. You're not staying in my office alone. You can stay out of sight in the kitchen when the food arrives. We can also eat in there."

"Not in here?" He swept his arm in an arc around the pristine room.

"No one eats in here." *Except Gil and me.*

So what if I'd just lied to Rayne? I was positive it wouldn't be the last time.

# Chapter Four

Rayne

**B**ourbon barbecue baby back ribs had never tasted so good.

And the crispy fries were pretty sweet as well.

Sitting across from a damn handsome man in this nice kitchen was pretty sweet as well.

Having people trying to kill me should've put a damper on the mood—but it didn't.

I used the wet napkin to wipe my fingers. I would've licked them, but even I understood the difference between chowing down at the bar with buddies and eating with someone who consumed his French fries with a knife and fork.

Not that I had many buddies. No, I'd lost touch with my high school football-player friends, and my profession didn't exactly lend itself to making lifelong friendships. Or even relationships that might end after a night at a bar.

Now, a night in bed? No problem finding a willing partner for that. I knew where to look for that kind of companionship.

"What are you thinking?" Everett placed his knife and fork at the five o'clock position and eyed me.

Because of course he did.

"That I'm lonely." I popped the last French fry into my mouth.

He chuckled. "That doesn't say much about my company."

"Oh shit. I didn't mean—"

He held up his hand, effectively halting me. He regarded me, but I couldn't get a read on what he was thinking. "I think that's the most revealing thing you've said today—and God knows I've asked plenty of questions."

"Yeah." I pushed my plate away.

"You don't want the cheesecake?"

My eyebrows shot to my hairline. "Cheesecake?"

"Yes, with either blueberries or strawberries. I figured I'd let you pick, but if you're not—"

"Oh, I'm hungry enough." I rubbed my belly. "I can always make room for cheesecake."

"How you eat all that and maintain your, uh, physique...is impressive."

I grinned. "You noticed, eh?" I flexed my arms in the strongman pose. Then winced. "Hard work, my friend. Hours of hard work each week. Completely worth it, though."

He eyed me. "Are we?"

"Are we what?" I glanced at the smaller bag I hadn't noticed that obviously held the cheesecake. "You have a preference between blueberries and strawberries? Because I really don't—"

"Are we friends?"

His question stopped my thoughts as if he'd just slammed on the brakes.

*Well, shit.* "I, uh, thought so. Like, I'm here now."

"Which you still haven't explained."

"Bad guys. Guns. Shooting. We've been over this."

"True. But you haven't—to my satisfaction—explained why you're *here.*" He said the word with emphasis. "On my doorstep."

"Because we're friends...?"

"Is that a question or a statement?"

"Both...?"

He huffed. "I honestly don't care about berries. If you don't either, then flip a coin." He rose, grabbed our dishes, and headed to the sink.

"I can help." I didn't move, though.

"How about you start explaining why you thought an upstanding citizen, and current member of the bar in British Columbia, would be the right person to help someone who, for all I know, might be fleeing law enforcement?" He scraped the bones into the compost container and put our dishes in the dishwasher.

"You checked the websites." This was easy.

"Naturally."

"And you didn't find anything."

"Shots fired near Wellington Park. One hit a building. There could have been people. A stray bullet might've gone through a window and hit a child."

*A bit extreme...but yeah, possible.* "But none of that happened, and I wasn't the one shooting. I think it's important to keep that in mind."

"Always with the half-assed unhelpful answer." He placed the cheesecake slices on separate plates. He brought them over. He was just about to put one before me, but he pulled it away at the last minute. "Can you be honest with me? Truly?"

I closed my eyes. *How badly do you want him to keep you safe? How much will telling him the truth cost you? Hell, what are you willing to do for cheesecake?* I snapped my eyes open. "I prefer blueberry, and I *might* know why they're after me."

His eyes flashed triumph as he placed the plate before me. He stalked away and returned moments later with two forks and the containers of compote. He sat.

And stared expectantly.

I opened the plastic container and dumped the blueberry mixture onto my plate. I preferred fresh, but anything in the stores this time of year came from down south, and that meant trucks to bring it up here, and that was just bad for the environment.

*You're thinking of the environment while he's staring at you.*

*What do you expect? That I tell him the truth?*

*If you don't want to get turfed, that might be a necessity.*

Fuck. Sometimes I really hated my conscience.

"Thank you for dinner and now dessert. I don't know how you knew I liked cheesecake."

"Well, unless you were lactose intolerant and had a peculiar dislike of graham cracker crust, I figured you'd enjoy it. Or at least not be picky."

"Because I'm not really in a position to be picky."

"And yet you requested ribs."

I held my fork over the cheesecake. I met his gaze. "How much is this going to cost me?"

"The truth would be nice."

*Ugh.*

"It's about a case I worked. Am working," I clarified. I sliced a small piece off with my fork, dunked it in the blueberries, then took a bite.

After what felt like forever—but was probably only thirty seconds—Everett replicated my actions.

We ate in silence.

I could admit this was some of the best cheesecake I'd ever eaten. That might've been assisted by how freaking hungry I was. Like, sated from the ribs and fries, but still hungry. Like the need in my belly. The sexual need as well as the overwhelming urge to blurt everything out. "So, am I staying here tonight?"

He stopped eating, his fork halfway to his mouth, and he gaped.

I gestured for him to continue eating.

He put his fork back on his plate. "Uh, no. You're not staying here. No offense, but I don't trust you."

"No offense taken. Hell, I don't think I'd trust myself." I winked. "Now—eat up. You're going to need your strength."

"Oh no. Oh hell, no. We are *not* having sex."

I grinned. "I didn't mean that. But I'm glad you've got sex on the brain. I have plans."

"Those plans better just include your right hand—because no way am I fucking you again." He held up his hand. "Or letting you fuck me. Just so we're super clear about what will and will not happen."

*There's always blow jobs.*

I kept that thought to myself. "Got it. So..." I twirled my fork in the air. "We're going back to your place?"

"I...guess."

"You could always put me up in the Grand Hotel." But he wouldn't. Not with the possibility of me mucking up his friendship. Or, heaven forbid, getting shot while there. That would ruin the place's reputation. As well, I had a feeling the guy didn't like spending money. I almost felt guilty asking him to buy me lunch.

*Almost.*

"I have a three-bedroom townhouse up in the Glencairn estates."

"Sounds fancy."

"It's not." He grabbed my plate.

I grasped his wrist.

His gaze flew to mine.

"Thank you."

"Don't thank me yet. If I could lock you in the spare bedroom, I totally would."

Slowly, I released my grasp. When he didn't pull away, I caressed the inside of his wrist. As I ran my fingers across his pulse point, said pulse jumped.

His breathing shallowed. His pupils dilated. His throat worked as he swallowed.

Abruptly, he yanked his hand back. "It's not going to work." He grabbed our plates, rose, and headed to the dishwasher.

*Yeah, we'll see about that.*

A couple hours later, as I sat in his spare bedroom, I could admit things hadn't gone as I'd hoped.

I remained in his sweatsuit while he'd shoved my clothes into two cloth shopping bags. He'd given me a baseball hat with the Vancouver Canucks logo, and we'd scurried to his SUV after he'd armed the alarm and locked the front door of the office. He had his messenger bag, but he hadn't put any paperwork in it. Which likely meant he still didn't trust me.

Hell, I didn't trust me.

But I didn't have the computer skills to crack his password, so I wasn't likely to be able to see what was on his computer.

Much to my frustration.

I needed access to his files.

Sitting here, tapping my fingers on the pretty soft-gray comforter wasn't getting me closer to my goal.

I eyed my phone, lying on the bed next to me. Shattered screen, out of juice, and probably unfixable. As much as I wanted to ask Everett for help with that, I wouldn't.

*Yet.*

Eventually, though, I'd need a burner phone. I had a couple of numbers memorized.

*Not enough.* None of anything I had was enough.

Somehow, Everett had managed to get the blood out of my jeans and shirt. What he couldn't excise was the memory of the bullet whizzing by me. Or, now, the image of a child being accidentally shot. He'd been right—way too many bad things could've happened. He was wrong in his thinking, though—I couldn't have done anything to stop the bad guys. Such a stupid way to think of them. But if I used their names, I might say them out loud. Even their nicknames might be enough for Everett to do a successful search.

All not good.

A knock sounded at the door.

"Yeah."

The door swung open.

Everett poked his head inside. "You okay? Have you even moved?"

I shrugged. "I don't have anywhere to go."

He pointed to the television on the wall. "Even my parents take advantage when they come to stay."

"Your parents live thirty miles away." He'd told me a little as we ate.

"Sure. But they claim coming out here is a mini-vacation." He chuckled. "Yeah, I know how that sounds. But I'm always so busy...they know if they don't come here, that I'll never see them."

"Okay, that's pathetic. Nothing is more important than seeing your parents."

His gaze narrowed.

I blinked. "Okay, maybe I don't know that from experience. But if I could spend time with my family, I totally would." *Bald-faced lie.*

"Well, I went to their place for Christmas. I spent Boxing Day with my friend August and his husband Julian. I've been pretty busy."

"Two days is busy?"

"Plus New Year's Eve."

"Quinton's party." I was familiar with that one.

"Yes, Quinton's party."

"You thought I might be there."

He swallowed. After what felt like forever, he finally admitted, "I looked for you."

*Ouch.* "I'm sorry."

"I'm not. I enjoyed myself last night. If you'd been there, I probably wouldn't have."

*Double ouch.* Still... "Why?"

"Because I wanted to confront you about Halloween. Wanted some kind of logical explanation as to why you took off after we—" He waved his hand in the air.

"Fucked."

"Yes, that. Met, fucked, connected."

"I can offer apologies."

"But they wouldn't be sincere." He straightened. "I've made a green salad with grilled chicken. It's been a few hours since lunch."

I glanced at my watch. Then gazed over at the windows. Only to remember the blinds were closed.

The first thing Everett had done when we arrived, was to order me to stay in the car while he closed all the blinds.

I attempted to point out that his neighbors might be just as suspicious about having all the blinds closed as they would be to spot a stranger.

He'd glared and pointed out how little privacy townhouse complexes offered—and how people often had their blinds drawn.

I asked whether he was one of those people.

He admitted that, since he rarely had gentleman callers, that he didn't close them often—that he enjoyed natural light.

To my credit, I hadn't commented on his lack of sex partners. For all I knew, he went to other guys' houses. The idea of which made me uncomfortable for reasons I couldn't fathom. "Five-fifteen?"

"As your watch says." He glanced at my phone. "Ouch."

"Yeah." I drew in a breath. "I need to get another one."

"Well, we're not running down to the electronics store. Would they even be able to port your data?"

I shrugged. "No idea. But I can't take the risk anyway. I meant a burner phone."

He pursed his lips. "This is getting out of hand."

"You said something about grilled chicken salad? Do you have ranch dressing?"

After a long moment, he nodded.

"Great." I popped off the bed with way more enthusiasm than I felt.

Only to have my body scream in protest.

Everett rolled his eyes.

*Yeah, this is going to be fun.*

Not.

# Chapter Five

Everett

"It's not what you think." I drummed my fingers in rapid succession lightly on my desk.

"Stop tapping your fingers." Gil's voice rang through my phone.

I pulled it back to ensure I hadn't accidentally put the call on speaker.

Nope.

And I certainly wasn't making enough noise to carry through even those most sensitive of phones. I glanced from my desk to the inky darkness outside. My home office, on the ground floor of my three-story townhouse, faced my pretty front yard, gate to the communal walkway, and through to my neighbor's ground-floor room. Only, the people directly across from me used it as their child's bedroom. The eldest of five. In a three-bedroom townhouse with a den.

Personally, I didn't know how they managed.

Well, they sent the kids out to the front yard during all kinds of weather, except downpours, and the kids often howled.

A problem I knew I might encounter when I'd chosen a townhouse. But I couldn't afford a single-family home—even the rundown and derelict ones—and I wasn't old enough for the fifty-five-plus townhouses in town. Something I'd consider—twenty years from now. If I still had neighbors with kids who drove me nuts.

"Everett!" Gil nearly shouted.

"What?" I snapped back.

"Are you tapping your fingers?"

"Yes." Another snap.

"Well, I think that tells you everything you need to know. You're clearly indecisive."

"Wow, it took a law degree for you to figure that out?"

He chuckled. "Putting me in my place. You know, my husband is quite capable of that."

Said in jest. Cullen adored Gil...and Gil was devoted to Cullen and their children.

"What's your point?"

"That you're clearly not telling me the entire story."

"I did." *Yeah. So not.*

"You found a guy on our stoop, and you brought him home? But you can't leave him at home, so you might wind up bringing him into the office, and I shouldn't ask about the bruising. Do I have that right?"

I winced.

"Okay." He didn't wait for me to answer.

Because we both knew I was lying through my teeth.

"I'm fine with you bringing someone to the office, but maybe bring him through the back so clients don't see his face? We'll have to tell the others."

The others being Paxton, our receptionist, Georgie, our paralegal, and of course, Nicole—the third lawyer.

"Sure. That's fine."

"I don't like this."

*Neither do I.*

"What if I say he's a client?"

"To me or to the others? Lying's not your strength, Everett. You can bluff like nobody's business…but you're shit at lying."

"Uh…" I didn't have a snappy comeback. Unless a client's life was in the balance, I wasn't going to lie. Prevaricate and evade? Certainly. Outright falsehood? No.

And Gil knew that.

"You could find him somewhere else to stay, you know."

"No."

"Because you don't want to bring danger to someone else's doorstep."

I winced. "I didn't say that."

"You didn't have to. I still recommend the police. Why you're not down at the detachment right now is beyond me."

"I told you—"

"You've told me jack shit. You've told me what you think will placate me. News alert—it won't. But you've never asked me to trust you on something that's clearly important. And not related to the law," he quickly added. Because yeah, a few times in cases I'd asked him to trust that I'd known best. And I always had.

Until now.

"I have to go out to Healing Horses ranch tomorrow for a few hours to spend time with Farrah."

He drew in a sharp breath. "I didn't know you were seeing her at the ranch."

"Well, her therapist is up there. But her living situation became untenable, so Kennedy invited her to live in a prefab house on the property. Kennedy had Simeon build the home for her parents to use when they visited, but Farrah's situation is precarious, and she needed out. Rather than figuring out the logistics and expense of a hotel, Kennedy offered the space."

"That's good of her."

"Kennedy is a good person and an exceptional therapist. Also, the ranch is isolated. No one knows Farrah's up there—so that should help keep her safe." Aside from Dr. Kennedy Dixon, and her sister Rainbow, the ranch manager, only the other counselors would know Farrah was on the property north of town. The ranch's therapy dog Tiffany, although not a protector, would alert Kennedy or Rainbow if anyone stepped on the property. The situation wasn't perfect, but Farrah couldn't afford a hotel. My budget didn't stretch to that either.

"Send me an email or text after you've seen her tomorrow. Call or drop by if you need to debrief."

"I'll have Rayne with me."

"Oh."

I could hear Gil's mind whirling.

"Maybe not. Cullen wouldn't mind, but I don't want to explain bruises to the kids. And the temperature's dropping tonight and not bouncing back tomorrow. You can't exactly leave him in your car."

Well, with the engine running I could. But I wouldn't. "I'll call and let you know how things go. I might have to make a couple of visits before we go to court next Monday."

"Three days."

"Three days." Just in case I didn't remember how delicate the matter was.

"What are you going to do with...Rayne...while you're up at the ranch?"

No missing how he couldn't quite say Rayne without hesitation. Clearly he didn't think that was the guy's real name either. Yet, somehow, I was coming to believe he hadn't lied to me about that. About everything else? Entirely possible. The lies rolled off his tongue easily. "I'll figure that out. As far as I'm concerned, he can sit in the stable. Oh, better yet, he can shovel horseshit for Rainbow." Except he'd likely be sore, and maybe I was being just a little too mean.

*Nope.*

"As you say, you'll figure it out. Call me tomorrow night."

"Yeah."

"Night." Gil disconnected.

I stared at the screen until it went dark.

*There has to be a way out of this clusterfuck of a disaster.*

Except I couldn't see it.

After another hesitation, I scrolled through my contacts and hit send.

The phone didn't even ring on my end, but the call was answered.

"Healing Horses Ranch, this is Rainbow. How may I help you?"

I rolled my eyes. "You realize it's New Year's Day."

"Hello, Everett. I suppose this is a social call, and you're not working either?"

"Uh..."

"Hung by your own petard?" She laughed. Her voice wasn't as husky as her psychologist sister's. "How can I help?"

"Two things." I rolled my eyes, even though she couldn't see. "And I honestly thought I'd be leaving a voicemail message."

"I was checking messages when your call came through. Kennedy and I are just sitting watching *When Harry Met Sally*."

I wracked my brains. "That's got some epic New Year's Eve scene, right?"

"Yep. We're a day late, but, as you know, I was at Quinton's party last night."

*Jesus fucking Christ...that was* last *night? Like, twenty-four hours ago?* God, how much my life had changed in such a short span of time.

"Yes, of course. Quinton's epic party."

"With the epic proposal. Everett, I have to say I didn't see that coming. Foster asking Arnav? I would've thought it would be the other way around."

"Foster's a dark horse sometimes." *In more ways than one.* But that wasn't my story to tell. "Okay, so I won't keep you—"

"Kennedy's stepped away to write a quick email."

"Rainbow, it's seven o'clock on New Year's Day."

She chuckled. "What's your point? The ranch never sleeps. I mean, the horses are down for the night, and our guest is tucked away safely, but Kennedy and I are always on the move."

"And you wouldn't have it any other way." Healing Horses ranch was, for the women, a vocation. A calling. To help patients heal psychological trauma through therapy dogs and horses.

"Nope."

"Okay, well I won't keep you. You've answered my first question, I think."

"About Farrah?"

"Yes."

"She's in the house with the alarm set."

"Great. That's a relief."

A moment's pause. "She's worried, Everett. But she trusts Kennedy. She trusts you. You'll take care of her. Make certain everything works out."

"I'm a lawyer, Rainbow, not a miracle worker. I can only guide her through this—I can't guarantee an outcome."

"Which she knows." Rainbow and I couldn't talk specifics—she wasn't authorized—but she knew what was going on. She had to. "Now, what's the second thing?"

"This is...more delicate..."

"More delicate than Farrah's situation? Now, I'm curious."

In my mind, she sat up straighter, and her light-blue eyes flashed interest.

"Well, not to be too dramatic—" I winced since that was exactly what I was about to be. "—I have a friend with me. He, uh, needs to come up to the ranch with me tomorrow. I need to see Farrah—"

"Of course." She chuckled. "Sorry to cut you off. Of course to both. Yes, you need to see Farrah, so of course you need to come up. And your friend needs to come with you, so of course it's fine. That's, like, how many times I said *of course*?"

"I've lost count." My mind whirled. Not just at her words, but at the absolute surety with which she said them. I needed something, and she'd accommodate. Really, to her, things were just that simple.

"He won't get in the way. In fact, I might just leave him in the car." *Because then he can't get into mischief.*

"No way. It's going to be below freezing tomorrow." She paused. "Look, I can either put him to work in the barn, or he can hang out in the great room."

The great room which doubled as a waiting room.

"Or I can put him in Denise's office. I mean, if he doesn't mind playing with toy trains."

Denise Lang was the child psychologist in the practice.

"I…" I winced. "That's very generous…"

She chuckled. "With me in the barn, it is. Or I'll sit with him in the great room."

"How did you know?"

"Everett, even through the phone, you're transparent. If you completely trusted the guy, then you'd leave him at your house or your office. That's okay. I'm assuming he's not dangerous."

*Only to my sanity, my well-being, and my lonely cock.* "No, he's not dangerous. He probably won't even get into trouble but, you know how some people just sort of attract trouble?"

"You mean like my sister Spring? Oh, hell yes, I know."

"Well, he's kind of like that. If he were in better shape, I'd offer him up to shovel shit."

"Horseshit is the best. He's out of shape?"

*Oh God, he's in such perfect shape…* "Injured. That's the other reason for my call. I'd prefer Farrah not see him. And I wanted to give you and Kennedy warning."

"Farrah's pretty much sticking to the other house. I think Kennedy planned to have you speak to her there. It's…her safe space."

"I'm glad she has somewhere."

"Well, you know how hard Kennedy works to make the ranch a safe place for everyone."

*And here I am, bringing trouble to its doorstep.* "You do as well, Rainbow." I'd witnessed her try to deflect praise back onto the counselors—who all did amazing work. But Rainbow was the glue that kept the place together.

"You're very kind, sir." She laughed. "Oh, Kennedy's back. Did you want to speak to her?"

"I won't disturb her. You'll fill her in?"

"Of course." She snickered. "Oh God, I'll have fun explaining this to Kennedy. We'll see you at eleven. Plan for you and your friend to join us for lunch. Bye." She cut the line.

Because she knew I'd have refused the invitation. The ranch normally had a full counseling schedule on Saturdays, accommodating people who couldn't make appointments during the week—but they were supposed to be closed until Monday.

*Damn woman.*

I had the choice of calling back, texting, or accepting her offer, thankful for the generosity with which it had been extended.

No-brainer.

*If Rayne behaves.*

Huge if.

# Chapter Six

Rayne

"Okay. Eight sisters." I scratched my cheek and winced as the stubble tugged against a bruise.

"Yes." Everett sighed. "But we're only meeting two." He signaled to turn into the driveway of Healing Horses.

No driver was behind us. Probably not for miles. But I *knew* Everett was a rule follower and probably always signaled before turning. Not that signaling was a bad thing, just one more difference between him and a lot of the people I hung out with.

"The eldest's a psychologist." I scratched my nose. My skin felt itchy and too tight. I'd used Everett's very boring body wash this morning. I missed my extra-moisturizing formula. I'd have to write to the company and let them know how effective their product really was.

"Yes." Everett smacked my hand. "You need to stop doing that."

"Wow, you are *such* a control freak." Probably right in this case, but control freakery gone wild. "And Rainbow is...?"

"A younger sister and the manager of the therapy ranch."

As he drove up the driveway, I glanced out the window and up. The trees soared, blocking out much of the daylight. Not a huge loss today as the clouds obscured the sun entirely. Snow in the forecast for later in the day. "Okay, this sounds simple."

"You're going to stay with Rainbow. You're going to do everything she tells you to do, and you'll do it without complaint."

"Yes, Mr. Boss Man. Jesus, you're a hoot. I can stay in the car—"

"You can't and you won't. It's going to be cold, and I'm not leaving you the keys to run the heater."

"You're afraid I'm going to drive away."

"I'd been more concerned about the wear and tear on the engine and using gas but yes, now you mention it, I'd prefer you not drive away with my car." He pulled into a parking spot, put the car into park, and cut the engine. He unbuckled his seatbelt, then he sighed. "Just try to be good, okay?"

"I'm always good." I puffed out my chest.

"Good people don't generally get shot at. Good people don't steal away like a thief in the night."

Before I could respond, he was out of the car and slamming the door shut.

*Sheesh. Walk out on a half-a-night stand without saying goodbye and he never lets you live it down.*

*You were a shit.*

*I had my reasons.*

*Tell him that.*

*No, thanks, anyway.*

I undid my seatbelt and slipped out of the car. As I closed the door, I caught sight of a blur of yellow fur barreling toward Everett.

He crouched.

The furball stopped short and plopped onto its butt. Then it extended a paw.

Everett grasped the fuzzy foot. "Hello, Tiffany. Nice to see you again."

Tiffany launched herself up at him, and he caught her easily.

"Hey, Tiff!" A woman wearing jeans, boots, and a winter jacket rounded the corner of the ranch house and waved. Her black hair was in a ponytail, and it swung as she jogged over.

"All good, Rainbow." Everett laughed. "She knows she's got my permission."

The dog continued to give him doggie kisses.

My first thought was *gross*, but she was just so adorable, and she was making Everett laugh, so that had to be a good thing.

The attractive woman petted the dog on the head, then approached me. "Rainbow Dixon."

I grasped her hand and followed her lead with a strong, but not overpowering, handshake. "Rayne."

"Cool. You're my helper for the morning?"

If she wondered about my omitting my last name, she showed no sign of it. If she was curious about the bruises, she also kept that well-hidden.

"Uh, yes, ma'am."

She burst out laughing. "Even my mother doesn't go by ma'am. And I don't figure I'm half-a-dozen years older than you."

I offered a shy smile. "A gentleman never asks a lady her age."

Everett snorted as he set the dog down and rose, wiping the dog fur off his jeans.

I pivoted my attention away from the sexy man and directed it back toward the lovely woman. "I understand you're in charge?"

She shot a glance at Everett.

Who shrugged.

"My sister Kennedy founded the ranch and owns it. I run the day-to-day operations with the horses and so on."

"Don't let her fool you. She claims to *just* be a hand. She's the reason this place runs so smoothly."

"That she is." Another feminine voice came from just beyond my line of sight.

A stunning brunette stepped into view. Her long, chestnut-brown hair flowed around a beautiful face, and her dark-brown eyes sparked interest as her gaze met mine.

"The older sister, I presume?" I held out my hand. "Rayne."

"Kennedy." She grasped my hand. "That's quite a shiner."

I winced as she released my hand. "Apologies." I almost said *ma'am*, but figured if one sister didn't like it, the other might not either. "Long story."

She glanced over at Everett. "I'm certain it is." She gazed back at me, her eyes laser-focused. "You're going to behave, right?"

"Kennedy—" Everett began.

I held up my hand to halt him. "I'm not normally a brawler. I got into a dispute with someone. Absolutely won't happen again."

"Today." She murmured the word.

The response *ever* was on the tip of my tongue. Except she was right—in my line of work, *ever* was a big word with little meaning. "Today," I repeated.

"Good to know." She pivoted back to Everett. "Your client's in the small house, waiting for you. Rainbow baked some cookies for us to take over. You don't mind if I join you?"

"I'm assuming my client requested your presence?"

She nodded.

"Then I have no objections. We won't be talking about privileged information. Merely strategy." He cut his gaze to me. "Try to stay out of trouble?"

I saluted him. And winced inwardly at the unseen bruises that screamed in protest.

Everett and Kennedy took off around the side of the house.

"Woof?" Tiffany gazed up at Rainbow.

A whistle came from where Kennedy had just disappeared to.

"Go on." Rainbow made a shooing motion.

Tiffany took off.

Rainbow laughed. "She hates to miss out."

"And she doesn't think she'll miss out if she stays with you?"

"Uh, no. She's a therapy dog. Her happy place is helping others. She knows very well I don't need her help. Not in *that* way."

"But Everett's client does?"

One delicate eyebrow arched.

I waved off my question. "Sorry. Too nosy for my own good."

"That's all right. In some ways, Healing Horses holds many secrets. Although clearly, his client is seeing a psychologist and a lawyer."

"Which means things aren't okay." Because as messed up as I could be at times, I'd never needed either. Probably should've gone for counseling—but I never had. "So...shoveling horseshit?"

She pressed a hand to my arm. Then quickly withdrew it. "Sorry, I don't have your consent."

I nearly shot out a pithy response, but her distress was genuine. "You've got it. I...like touch." I almost added *from a beautiful woman*—because, hello, *bi* all the way—but that felt inappropriate. I wasn't here to flirt.

Much as I might've wanted to.

No, with Everett just down the way, I needed to watch myself. And as much as I hated to admit it, the guy was sort of getting to me. In all the wrong ways.

After a moment, she pressed her arm back to mine. "You look way too sore to shovel shit. But you can sit on the bench and keep me company. Or you can pet the horses. They never get enough attention." She winked.

In other words, the horses got plenty of attention, but would always accept more.

Fifteen minutes later, I'd met Sugar, Sienna, Briar, and Fallon. All were retired show horses chosen for their incredibly placid natures. As Rainbow extolled the virtues of animal therapy, I understood not only how integral Tiffany and the horses were to the counseling process, but how the gentle nature of all the animals was so critical.

"Rainbow?" Another voice came from just outside the stables. Somewhere between Kennedy's husky timbre and Rainbow's lighter tone.

Immediately, I stepped into an empty stall. The fewer people who saw me, the safer.

"In here, Torah." Rainbow finished sweeping the dust and hay away from the main area. She hadn't let me do a damn thing except pet the horses.

"Hey, I brought a new dog, but he's very spooky. I'm going to walk him in slowly. Don't look at him, don't make sudden movements, okay? Come, Sarge."

Rainbow's brow furrowed. "Sarge?"

A woman stepped into the stables. I peered through the slats of the stall, and I did a double-take. She could've been Rainbow's twin. Same blue/black hair. Same stunning pale-blue eyes. Except this woman's was cut short. She halted just inside the door.

A big, thick-coated German shepherd slunk through the doorway behind her.

She murmured, "Sarge, sit," and held down a treat without making eye contact.

The dog did not sit. Didn't take the treat. He stared my way as if he could see through the partition, the tip of his tail beginning to wave slightly. His flattened ears rose, and then he barked. And barked.

"Who's there?" the woman asked, frowning at where I was hiding.

"Um, just me." I stepped into view before the dog lost his mind.

The dog whined, looked at me, at the woman, and then backed up to the limit of his leash and cowered low.

The woman on the other end of the leash blew out a long breath. She turned to her sister. "You didn't say you had company."

Rainbow arched that eyebrow she was so proficient at. "There is a car in the driveway."

"Isn't that Janice's?"

"No, Everett's. Does Janice have the same car? I really should pay more attention—"

A loud whine from the dog interrupted them.

Then a volley of barks made me flinch back. I was having a hard time reading his body language.

"Apologies." The newcomer continued to grip the leash. "I'm Torah. This is Sarge."

"Okay..." Still not really an explanation.

Rainbow said, "Torah's my sister."

*No kidding.* I managed to hold in the snicker.

Barely.

"She's also a dog trainer. Best in Mission City."

"The whole Cedar Valley," the trainer quipped.

Rainbow grinned. "Yeah, okay, that's true."

I gestured to the dog with my chin.

"Newcomer." Torah frowned. "His owners bought him for Christmas. Something about needing a guard dog."

Rainbow groaned.

"Right? They didn't really question the previous owner, and the dog doesn't have a microchip. Basically untraceable."

"How did you wind up with him?" Rainbow clasped her hands together. "Is he dangerous?"

"Well, here's the thing. To the husband and the kids? Not seriously. With the wife—for whom the dog was a surprise gift? Maybe. He was terrified of her, and yes, a scared dog can be dangerous. Mostly he cowered and whined, and peed on the floor if she approached. But he did growl too. The husband brought him down to Zephyra and told our lovely sister, the vet, to *fix* the dog."

She appeared to offer some of that explanation for my benefit. Appreciated, because I hadn't realized one of the eight sisters was a vet.

Rainbow frowned. "Fix. Right. Like we have instant solutions for fear."

"The wife thought Zephyra could give the dog some magic pill and it wouldn't react negatively to women."

Rainbow sighed. "Yeah, talk about clueless."

"Right? So Zephyra explained there isn't a pill that will erase anxiety or fear-aggression and the dog would need a full workup, meds, and, without an iota of doubt, months, maybe years, of training. Even then, she couldn't guarantee the dog would ever be *fixed*."

I winced. I hadn't spent time around a dog in a lot of years, but I understood most *bad* dogs were that way because of owners who didn't understand them or give them what they needed.

"What happened at the vet's?" I had to ask because I was so intensely curious.

Torah's gaze shot to me as her eyes widened. Almost as if she'd forgotten I was here. "The man walked right out the door. Didn't pay for the exam. Didn't make arrangements for the dog. Just let go of the leash, strode out, and drove away. No name, no contacts, just left the dog cowering in a corner of the waiting room."

"Oh God." Rainbow placed a hand to her chest. "The poor baby."

"More like poor Zephyra. The dog was the last appointment of the day, and no one could take him, and he was terrified of her."

"She called you."

"She called me. I was able to coax him into my SUV. He saw the blanket-covered crate as a hiding spot." Torah eyed the dog. "I've kept him separate from King and Bishop. My two other dogs," she clarified, likely for my benefit. "But that's not sustainable. And until I've done a ton of work with him, I can't just let him go with some stranger who isn't prepared for the challenge. Plus, Zephyra will publish notice of abandonment as soon as possible, but the owners have ten days when they can still take him back. So I can't give him to anyone permanently yet."

I gazed at the dog.

Those dark-brown eyes, that I expected to be frantic and angry, appeared sad. Forlorn. Almost like he knew he was completely unwanted.

"That's it? What happens now?" I cocked my head.

The dog did the same.

I straightened.

Sarge did as well.

"I try to find him a home or at least, a foster. I have a lead. A guy up in the hills. Bit of a loner." Her nose twitched. "Okay, very much a loner. Sarge needs someone who can handle his strength and energy, certainly, and a peaceful environment as we treat his fear, but he also needs to be socialized. Complete isolation isn't ideal. But being a woman, I'm not ideal for him either, and I'm busy. I've got a training class of new dogs starting Monday."

"Oh, is Chia in the class?" Rainbow cocked her head.

Torah shot me a glance. "Chia is the new dog of two friends of ours—Simeon and Ryan." She pivoted back to Rainbow. "Yep. Looking forward to it. I think she's got the making of a good therapy dog."

"Oh, that would be so great for Simeon and Ryan." Rainbow's eyes brightened, and her smile grew wider.

"Would you put Sarge in the training class?"

Torah shook her head. "I can't. He's too unpredictable. At least for the first few lessons. He needs a safe space and continuous work for weeks just to get to the point where I can consider that. He'll be a lifelong project, even if I can find the right person."

I held Sarge's gaze.

Finally, I broke the gaze to glance at Torah. "What would that person have to do?"

# Chapter Seven

Everett

S pending time with Farrah was always an exercise in patience.

Fortunately, I had that in spades.

Well, except when dealing with an exasperating sexy man with a penchant for finding trouble wherever he went.

Still, I pushed thoughts of Rayne aside as Kennedy and I sat with Farrah. "Do you understand?"

Slowly, she nodded. She continued to stroke Tiffany, whose snout was in her lap. Her black hair veiled her face, so I couldn't see her dark-brown eyes.

This shyness was completely new, according to her friend Olivia. The two women attended the university over in Abbotsford.

I corrected myself. *Had* attended.

Olivia was still a student, but Farrah had dropped out in October. Her brother, the titular head of the family, had decided she needed to marry. To secure some kind of alliance. With a man nearly three times her age.

I tried to understand how parents would make that choice for their child. Different cultures approached things differently. Maybe they had wanted her security. Or so I told myself.

Witnessing Farrah's misery, it was clear that this hadn't been what she wanted.

In the end, she'd essentially been blackmailed into the marriage—coerced into signing a document in a language she didn't speak—that bound her to the man. The next day she'd been dragged before a clerk and forced to marry.

My anger simmered to a near boil as I thought of the clerk, who could've stopped this.

Farrah had begged the man for help, and he'd ignored her, choosing to believe she'd agreed to the marriage and was being *compensated*.

For her trouble, once her new husband got her home, she'd received a beating by her husband and her male relatives and nearly died.

A female relative of the old guy had called an ambulance.

Thus had begun the nightmare.

An annulment and charges against the men who beat her should've been easy.

Except life never was. Now she was testifying against the perpetrators while trying to get the contract undone and her marriage annulled.

Olivia, upon learning all that had happened to her friend, had gone to her aunt Marnie and her uncle Jake for assistance.

Jake McGrath, a reporter for the Vancouver office of CNC, had covered a trial a year ago that I'd argued successfully. Since we all lived in Mission City, he decided to reach out to me.

With little hesitation, I took the case. I had Gil's support to do some pro bono work. Helping Farrah meant I'd have to work doubly fast for my paying clients, but nothing mattered except getting justice for this young woman.

As a step toward dealing with the trauma, Olivia suggested Farrah see Kennedy as a therapist.

Olivia and Marnie were former clients of the ranch, and persuading Kennedy to take Farrah as a client was easy. Her safety was tougher. She'd been staying with the McGraths until the family received death threats.

Marnie and Jake had a toddler. As much as they wanted to support Farrah, the risk was too great.

Kennedy had offered up this small house. The security system was top-notch, and Kennedy and Rainbow were always on the property with Tiffany as sentinel.

Thus far, everything was working.

"I understand." Farrah gripped her hands so tightly in her lap that her knuckles were nearly white.

"You only have to be in the courtroom for your testimony. I'll escort you in and see you out. Constable Seth Jacobs is going to testify just before you. You remember the RCMP officer, right?"

The Royal Canadian Mounted Police officer had responded with paramedics to the call and had been first on scene.

In confidence, he'd told me he'd wanted to beat the living shit out of the men who'd done this. Slapping on cuffs had been satisfying—but only to a point.

Generally, courts didn't take kindly to batterers. But the lottery for judge had undesirable results. The guy had a habit of giving the minimum sentence to perpetrators. He contended rehabilitation was possible.

In some circumstances, I agreed.

In others, I wholeheartedly thought the judge was delusional.

So I was more worried than if we'd drawn a judge who would be harsher.

And all that assumed a guilty verdict. All it took was one sympathetic jury member, and the entire case could go up in smoke.

Kennedy caught my eye.

I read her message.

Farrah had taken about as much as she could handle.

"So, Constable Jacobs is going to stick around. He'll be right outside the courtroom. He'll escort us back to my office, where Kennedy's sister Spring will swap places with you. We'll get you out the back and into Ryan's car, and he'll bring you back here. After a couple of hours, I'll come to see you."

I hadn't wanted so many people involved, but if something was going to happen, the time after Farrah's court appearance was the most likely. Spring, with similar hair color, would hang out in my office for a few hours until Farrah was safe.

Ryan volunteering to help was unexpected. I'd mentioned worrying about a client, and my new friend had said he'd help in any way he could. As a former soldier, he had some knowledge of evasion tactics. Moreover, no one would think anything of seeing his car around, as he lived near my office in downtown Mission City. Connecting him to Farrah was nearly impossible and, as a client of the ranch, his heading here was perfectly logical.

Still, a million little things could go wrong, and that disturbed me more than I was willing to admit.

"I need to lie down." Farrah finally met my gaze. "Thank you. I'll never be able to thank you. Still, I have to go." She rose and made her way to the bedroom.

Tiffany glanced at Kennedy, clearly asking permission.

Kennedy nodded and pointed.

The dog entered the bedroom.

Farrah closed the door.

Kennedy let out a long breath. "That went okay."

*Okay.*

Not well. Not perfectly. Not even helpfully. Just...okay.

We both knew what was at stake.

Kennedy wanted to attend Farrah's testimony, but that put this pseudo-safe house at risk.

She met my gaze. "This wasn't why we had Simeon build this house, but I'm so glad we did."

I looked around. "He's a talented guy." And also Ryan's partner. The relationship was very new.

Personally, I was thrilled. I'd sort of been set up with Simeon by some of our friends. The gentle and shy handyman was a wonderful person—and truly not my type. Now, I wouldn't have pegged Ryan as *his* type, but clearly I would've been wrong. They made a great couple.

"We've invited Ryan and Simeon to dinner on Monday night. I don't know if Farrah will join us, but hopefully she'll feel safer having them on the property. If they need to, they can stay in our spare room."

"Hopefully it won't come to that."

Kennedy rose. "We'll leave her be. Let's go see what Rainbow has made for lunch."

"You don't know?" I stood as well. I slipped into my coat and grabbed my messenger bag.

"Uh...no. She wanted to *surprise* me." Kennedy used air quotes and gave me a huge smile.

A little forced, but I'd take what I could get.

Just before we headed outside, she set the perimeter alarm. Then, once we were in the fresh air, she shut the door and locked the door with a key.

"Farrah has one as well." She pocketed the key.

"You're putting yourself in danger."

"Nah." She grinned. "Living an adventure." She started walking toward the ranch house. "Doing what's right." She sighed. "It's killing Olivia. Not being able to spend time with Farrah. They talk a lot, though."

"Olivia would testify, if she could."

"She's done it before."

Olivia had been kidnapped by her mother's boyfriend when she was a young girl and held in a basement for four years, then left in a field to die. She'd survived, testified, and somehow put her life back together. All this had been reported by the news back in Toronto. She now lived quietly in a threesome with two people who understood her past trauma and loved her, but they understandably avoided the press. If Olivia's friendship with Farrah became known, it would complicate everything.

"Bravely." I reflected on all I'd read about Olivia. "When the men are found guilty, and when things die down, I don't see why they can't resume their friendship."

"The friendship is still strong," Kennedy corrected. "But yes, I hope they can spend time together. Farrah's not even fully healed physically."

"True. But Remy Stevens, the crown prosecutor, pushed hard for this trial to move at lightning speed." Nearly unprecedented just how fast.

"And the men wanted out of jail, so they didn't fight it. No doubt their lawyer wants Farrah fragile, too." Anger threatened to overwhelm me.

Kennedy opened the door to the ranch house.

I stepped in.

She took my coat as I removed my shoes.

I sniffed. "Garlic?"

"Spaghetti, I suspect. Unless Simeon dropped off a lasagna from Nanny."

My saliva glands kicked into overdrive. "That might be Nanny's lasagna? Oh God, Kennedy. Don't tease me." Simeon's grandmother made the best lasagna in all of Cedar Valley. Even better than the diner Fifties. That said something.

"Come on in, you two." Rainbow appeared in the door to the kitchen. "I have a treat for you."

"Cookies?" Kennedy's nose twitched.

"Better." She disappeared.

"What's better than her cookies?" I set my messenger bag down by the door.

"Well, Nanny's lasagna." Kennedy hung her coat as well. "But I'll take anything I didn't have to make myself."

"You've had a rough couple of days."

"No more than usual." She offered up a genuine smile. "It's never boring around here."

"You missed Quinton's New Year's party."

She glanced back from where we'd come. "Some things are more important."

We made our way to the kitchen.

My eyes settled on Rayne immediately.

And the tan-and-black German Shepherd on a leash by his side.

Torah stood on the other side of the dog. "Everyone just ignore Sarge. Don't look at him, no sudden movements, especially from the women. Rayne, you take a seat at this end of the table, and let's see what he wants to do. Move slow, keep the leash short."

"Okay." Rayne pulled out the nearest chair carefully, then lowered himself into it. The dog ducked under the table and leaned up against Rayne's leg.

"Good boy," Torah crooned. "Give him a treat, Rayne."

Rayne held down a bite of something.

The dog sniffed his fingers, but didn't take it.

"Okay, see that?" Torah said. "A dog who won't take a treat is too nervous. Talk to him gently. He seems to like your voice."

"Good boy, sweet boy."

That soft murmur in Rayne's deep voice did something odd to my insides, but I ignored the sensation, watching the dog.

Rayne hummed. "Yummies, baby, tasty treat."

This time, the dog lipped the morsel out of his fingers.

"Well done," Torah breathed. "He's settling. Everett, we'll have you sit next to Rayne. Sarge trusts men a lot more than women. The rest of us can squeeze down toward the other end. Move slow. And if anyone drops food, don't exclaim or reach down, okay?"

"My turn?" Because I spotted a pan of lasagna cooling on the stove.

"Yes." Torah eyed me. "He's scared, go easy."

I pulled the chair back an inch at a time, then perched on the seat and eased it back in.

Sarge glanced up at me. Then turned his attention to Rayne.

"Yes, very good boy." Rayne smiled down at Sarge. "Such a brave boy. He seems to like you."

He said the words without looking at me, but instinctively I understood he meant me.

"Let's eat." Rainbow gestured to the empty chairs at the other end of the huge kitchen table.

Torah took the seat to Rayne's left where she could keep an eye on Sarge.

Kennedy sat next to me, leaving the foot of the table for Rainbow.

As Rainbow served the food, a whine came from beneath the table, followed by a low growl as she moved closer to Rayne.

"Just set things on your end of the table, Rainbow, and we'll pass them," Torah told her. "Let Sarge hang out between the two men where he feels less threatened, and keep your distance." She told Rayne, "Reassure him with a happy tone. More treats. Tell him everything's fine."

I hoped that Sarge felt *less threatened* by me, although as I glanced down sideways at him, his flattened ears and wide eyes made that hard to believe. But I knew Torah was the best. Again, in all of Cedar Valley.

"Isn't this fun?" Rayne told the dog in a cheerful voice. "Look, Sarge. Treats. Happy lunchtime treats. Such a brave boy."

The dog sniffed his fingers and eventually took a bite. Then another.

Rainbow placed the lasagna on her end of the table, using oven mitts.

She then brought fresh baked rolls over while Kennedy served lasagna on plates and slid them carefully our way.

Despite wanting to feel helpful, I held myself still, barely reaching for a plate when it came my way.

Rayne murmured to the dog and fed him more treats, then let him lick a bit of tomato sauce off his fingers.

Gradually, the dog's ears came up and he nosed Rayne's fingers more eagerly.

"So, what's Sarge's story?" Kennedy gestured for us all to start eating.

Torah said in a cheerful voice that belied her words, "Such a good boy, but afraid of women, poorly socialized, dumped on Zephyra at the clinic. She passed him to me. He seems to like Rayne."

Rayne tried to cut his lasagna with his fork, fumbling with the food and sloshing a bit of sauce on the table. "Fuck. Sorry,"

I cocked my head.

"He's got a grip on the leash." Torah sliced of a piece of gooey pasta goodness. "Mm. Nanny's truly is the best." She raised her fork. "Rayne, slide your plate to Everett and let him cut it up for you. And give Sarge more dog treats, less tomato sauce. Don't feed the dog human food at the table."

A huff came from under the table.

I frowned. "He understood that?"

"Recognized his name." Torah put the cheese-dripping bite in her mouth and hummed with pleasure.

I pivoted my attention to Rayne.

"He's really smart, Ev. Seriously."

Pointing out my name was *Everett* not *Ev* felt childish—so I didn't. At the moment. But we'd have words later. Didn't help that *Rayne* couldn't be shortened.

Well, that wasn't true. I could shorten it to *Ray* but I'd had a guy in my business law class with that name, and he'd been a jackass.

Although maybe that was appropriate for Rayne.

"I'm glad he's smart. That's good news." I reached for Rayne's plate. Carefully, with an eye on Sarge. "Let me cut that for you."

"I'll keep him in my room when we're not there. Torah says he's not destructive—"

My fork clattered to the plate, and Sarge whined. I blinked. "I'm sorry, can you repeat that?"

Torah eyed him with her icy-blue stare.

He shrugged and turned to her. "Well, you can't keep him, and he can't go to a shelter—"

"The dog can absolutely go to a shelter." I gestured. "That's why shelters are around."

"It will be terrible for him. He's scared now, and he'll get worse."

"We'll make a donation to the shelter, pay them to work with him." I met Torah's gaze. "Which one?"

She held my gaze for far longer than I was comfortable with. Usually, I was able to maintain the upper hand.

Not with the Dixon sisters, though.

"I might be able to find one in Vancouver. A foster home would be better. He needs round-the-clock training and guidance. He needs a detailed behavior-modification program. A foster home with no females in residence would be best."

"Like us," Rayne said.

"Well, that's not going to happen. Obviously, I can't take him to work with me—"

"But I can work with him while you're gone." Rayne caught my eye. He tried pouting.

I glared.

He backed down.

A quarter of an inch. "He needs a good place to land. Until he can be taught that the world isn't so scary, and he can trust people."

"Rayne." I tried to moderate my tone. "The townhouse association isn't going to allow it. German Shepherds are on the dangerous breeds—"

"Tell me your townhome association." Torah had her phone out. "Most only ban the pit-bull-type breeds."

I told her Glencairn Estates, and she scrolled quickly. "Nope. Pitties, Staffies, Bull Terriers. Not that any of those breeds deserve it, but nothing about Shepherds." Torah tore her roll in half, then started buttering it.

I still hadn't taken a bite. Not with my stomach in knots. "Oh, really." I eyed Rayne. Likely he'd been the one to give away my location. "Look—"

Rayne's words came out in a rush. "I can drop you off at work and then either drive up to the ranch or Torah's property to train Sarge. Torah figures after a month, he may be ready for a new home. Lifelong training, of course, Prozac, but—"

"You expect me to let you drive my SUV? With that dog in it?" My jaw dropped. Gobsmacked, I whispered sharply, "Are you out of your mind?"

Sarge whined.

Rayne cleared his throat. "You practically didn't let me out of your sight today. I thought you wanted me close."

I actually laughed out loud. "You're out of your freaking mind. What I want is for you to—" I cut off the sentence as I found three very keen Dixon sisters staring at me with open curiosity. "I'm hungry." I dug into my food.

Somehow, with Sarge in a big crate installed into the back of my SUV, we headed back into Mission City about an hour later.

Rayne rode in the back seat, twisted around in his seatbelt, crooning to the dog and passing him treats through the bars, instead of sitting next to me.

I didn't mind that one bit, of course. Less distracting than having his knee inches from mine. Better all the way around.

# Chapter Eight

Rayne

I *knew* I'd pissed Everett off.

Calling him *Ev* had been a mistake. I'd recognized it the moment the word left my mouth. His wince and then glare had been epic.

Well, not as epic as the, uh, anger. He'd been pissed.

Not that I could totally blame him. I had sort of implied back in the barn, both to Torah and Rainbow, that Everett would be fine with a canine guest.

Truth was, I didn't even know how he felt about dogs. Or animals, for that matter. He owned neither dog not cat. Nor hamster nor goldfish.

Much like me, growing up. All my experience with dogs had been with my friend Jace's Border Collie.

Smartest dog on the planet, but also into trouble of every kind.

Jace's dad was great with her, and he taught me some things, but it wasn't the same as a dog of my own. My grandparents made fun of me for even asking, though. No pets for me.

Evertt had muttered something about never having a dog, too, apparently. Something about a sister being allergic. He had *three* younger sisters.

As I had no siblings, I couldn't even fathom this. Or the Dixons, because seriously?

Everett pulled into a driveway. A long, winding driveway.

"This isn't your place."

"Really? And here I thought I'd moved."

A lovely house came into view—made of dark wood with light-blue trim. "This place is charming."

"Make sure you say that to August." He got out and walked a couple of steps toward the house before yelling, "Hey, there!"

"That's rather rude," I murmured to Sarge. I rolled down my window so I could hear Everett.

Sarge poked his nose up against the end of the crate—obviously to get a better look.

The front door opened, and a man stepped out. Reddish hair, medium height, wearing jeans and a plaid shirt. "Oh my God, it's a lumberjack," I said.

I thought I was too quiet for Everett to notice, but nope. He laughed. "Maddox is the lumberjack. Julian is...Well, he's an arborist. His husband is my best friend, August. And you're going to be nice."

My heart sped up at the thought of more strangers, more risk of my hiding place getting back to the wrong people. "Sure. Okay. Wasn't planning to be rude." I grinned, faking calmness. "Wasn't planning to make you look bad."

"And yet you manage at every turn."

As he said the words, a handsome Black man stepped out of the house and placed an arm around the redhead. Assumedly the man's husband. August.

Everett headed up the walk toward the men.

August waved. He and Julian descended the staircase and offered hugs.

Everett leaned into their embraces in a way that spoke of true friendship.

Something I was completely unfamiliar with since I was what? Ten years old? The year Jace moved away.

All three men turned and look at me.

Feebly, I waved.

Everett beckoned. "Come on. Meet the guys."

"I think that'll be too much excitement for Sarge. I can stay here. You talk about whatever. Leave the car running. We'll be fine." So far, these guys hadn't seen my face. Better for all of us.

Everett's brows drew down. "Can't your dog stay in his crate? I want you to meet my friends. It's important."

I was such a fucking sucker. My life on the line, and I couldn't say no to Everett.

I looked at the dog. Not *my* dog, *the* dog. I needed to remember that.

Sarge had been standing and panting most of the drive so far, but now his breathing eased.

He turned in a circle and then lay down, seeming more relaxed than I'd seen him. "You like your crate, boy?"

Sarge lowered his chin to one big paw and eyed me. His ears were up for a change, his eyes less strained. Maybe it would be good for him to take a break in the drive.

I opened the door, then eased out of my seat.

Sarge turned his head to watch me, but didn't seem worried.

When I slowly closed the door, he set his chin back on his foot. "Okay," I told Everett. "But we leave the heat on, and I want to keep an eye on the truck."

The Black man said, "We can sit in the front room. It looks out this way."

I took a few steps his direction. Looked back at the SUV. All I could see were Sarge's shoulders and the tip of his ears.

He was still lying down.

I whispered to myself, *"Please be good, okay, Sarge? If you lose your shit, then you'll be at the animal control center in Abbotsford before the day is over. Last chance central."* I hadn't wanted to know that option existed, but Everett had pushed Torah into providing the information.

She'd suggested bringing the dog back to her, but admitted she had no room and no good alternatives.

Sarge needed peace, quiet, training, and socializing—things Torah couldn't give him. At least not the full-time he needed.

And since I needed to hide out until things cooled down, this felt like the perfect solution to me. I could work with Sarge. I could feel like I was contributing. I could feel useful. That I was rescuing someone.

Much as Everett was rescuing me.

Even if he didn't want to admit it.

"Why don't you come inside?" August gazed upward. "It's supposed to snow again." He grinned. "But don't plan to stay long—don't want you snowed in."

"We appreciate this." Everett followed the two men toward the door.

"I think..." I eyed Sarge. "I want to watch him for a couple more minutes. Just in case he starts freaking out about being alone," I rushed to add.

"No worries." Julian moved to my side. "I like a guy who cares about animals." He turned to Everett and August. "You head inside. Maybe some hot chocolate?"

August gently shoved him. "Any excuse."

"Hey, you love it has much as I do."

"That is true." August saluted me, then he and Everett disappeared.

I backed away from the SUV, step by step.

Sarge raised his head to look my way.

I stopped and lifted my hand, palm up, like Torah had shown me for the "Down" command.

To my surprise, Sarge resettled himself down in the crate.

Julian chuckled. "Well-behaved dog."

"He is." I kept my eye on Sarge. "When he's not freaking out and apparently peeing on the floor."

Julian said, "Poor guy. Is that why you're not bringing him in? He'd be welcome. Floors clean up."

"Yeah, I mean, no. It's for his sake. I don't want to over-stress him."

Or maybe that was me projecting onto the dog. I was panicked I'd do something wrong, and we'd end up at animal control. "I'm not sure why Everett brought us here."

Julian grinned. "A test. For you. Maybe also the dog. By the way, I'm guessing your name is Rayne...?"

I blinked.

He laughed. "Oh, Everett tells August everything—with the understanding much of that information will be passed on to me unless it's intensely personal."

I cocked my head.

"A half-a-night-stand doesn't constitute protected information."

"August's a lawyer?"

Julian burst out laughing. "He's an arborist. He's actually my boss, although he's making noises about me buying into the business. I'm like, whatever. He's given me access to a good pension plan, we've got fantastic benefits, and I get vacation. Why would I want to lose some or all of that for half the profits when I didn't do half the work?" He swept his hand to encompass the house. "We went halvsies on the house. Well, he came into an inheritance and bought it, and I'm paying back for my share—much to his eternal consternation."

"If he's Everett's friend, I can totally see that."

Again, Julian grinned. "Ah, so I see you're getting the lay of the land. I adore my husband, but his desire to give me more than I think I've earned drives me nuts. We have a good life—why fuck that up with money shit? I pay him what I would've paid on my mortgage for my old place. We split expenses. If he's got spare cash, he can reinvest with his very successful business."

"Sounds ideal. Idyllic, even."

He tilted his head. "I think I like you. You'll keep Everett on his toes."

"You don't know me."

"Ah, but there you're wrong. You came back. Might've taken you two months..." He gestured to me.

I nodded.

"Right. So you came back. You're going to do right by him."

"Uh...I don't even know what that looks like. He's stuck with me out of a sense of honor today—not because he wants me around."

Julian started walking toward the house, gazing back and gesturing with his chin for me to join him.

I glanced back at Sarge one more time before I followed.

"He's not *stuck* with you," Julian continued. "Everett's one of the most independent people I know. At least as stubborn as August. He'd beat Gil and Cullen as well. His boss and the boss's husband."

"Are there a lot of gay men in Mission City?"

He squinted humorously. "Depends where you look. Well, I've met a bunch. Some homegrown, some who've made their way here. Cedar Valley's quite religious—all kinds of religions. Some that are queer-friendly and some that are vehemently opposed." He scratched his bearded cheek. "We've found a way to make things work. We have a rainbow on our truck, and I often wear my unicorn shirt. We've only been run off by one person. People queue for August's service. Most aren't stupid enough to lose their spot because they might be homophobic. A few have changed their tune. Whatever. Live and let live."

We walked up the steps.

Julian grabbed the door handle, then paused. "August is the best man I've ever known. Well, except maybe my dad and grandpas."

"That's a given."

He grinned. "You understand. Family's everything." He appeared to consider. "Everett is basically family to us. So know if you hurt him again, I will put your nuts in a vise and torque them really hard. Let's go."

On that note, I followed him inside.

# Chapter Nine

Everett

I still wasn't one hundred percent certain why I'd brought Rayne to meet my best friend and his super awesome husband. Fear? Assurance? Resentment? Some weird combination of the three?

August and Julian sat on their super comfy faux leather couch, their shoulders, hips, and thighs touching. Julian had his arm around August's shoulder while my friend leaned in.

Adorable.

Rayne perched on an arm of the recliner.

I sat in the rocking chair, slowly rocking as I observed everyone sipping their hot chocolate.

Every couple of minutes, Rayne peered out the window toward my SUV.

Julian gestured between the two of us, nearly sloshing his hot chocolate. "So you're *not* together?"

Rayne cut me a glance.

I shook my head.

Slowly, he acknowledged me with a nod. "Uh...no?"

August chuckled. "You don't seem certain about that."

"I mean, you are both sitting here." Julian offered a shit-eating grin.

I remained as impassive as I was capable of—not moving a single muscle except the light press of my foot against the floor to keep the antique wood rocking chair in motion.

"Yeah." Rayne cut me yet another glance.

I gestured for him to speak. To say whatever was on his mind. All the while, I was slowly dying of curiosity.

"Like, some guys hit me yesterday."

August burst out laughing. Then he pressed a hand to his mouth. "Apologies. I just...well, that's obvious. It didn't look like you walked into a wall or fell down stairs. You're stiff as well, so no doorknob. I thought maybe a car accident, but that shiner is just too much punched-in-the-face..." He shrugged. "And as annoyed as Everett is with you, I didn't figure he beat you up and then brought you here for our inspection."

"Is that why I'm here?" Rayne met my gaze. "For inspection?"

"No." Julian said the word with certainty. "But we know who you are, as I said. Everett wants us to either tell him he's nuts to consider having you around or to confirm that clearly you need his help. Unless you happen to know who beat you?"

"He knows." My gut churned. "He just won't tell me."

"Oh, hey, Rayne, will you tell me?" Julian perked. "Of course, then I'll have to keep it a secret."

"Which you're incapable of." August stroked his husband's beard. "I love you, but you couldn't keep a secret if your life depended on it."

"Ah, but I could keep a secret if *your* life depended on it. Or Everett's. Or Rayne's."

His words gave me pause. Truth was buried somewhere in there. Julian *was* terrible at keeping things to himself—unless someone else's well-being was on the line. I trusted him with mine. Rayne didn't know him, though.

"What are you suggesting?" Rayne glanced around in true confusion.

"That you tell me, tell one of us if you won't tell Everett, so that if anything happens to you, someone actually knows what's going on." For once, Julian's entire face took on a serious air—no smile to be found.

The contrast startled me. Aside from when August's beloved sister had died, I'd never seen Julian serious. About anything.

And although this hadn't been my thinking when I'd arrived, his plan was sound. Rayne had made it clear he wasn't going to share anything with me. If something happened to him, the bad guys would get away with it. If he vanished, I wouldn't know where to look.

That didn't sit right with me.

But, with our history, he still didn't trust me.

Even though he'd been the fucking one to walk out.

"We were thinking burgers on the grill." August extracted himself from Julian. He met my gaze. "Everett and I can grab our coats and fire up the grill." He turned to Rayne. "Thirty minutes?"

"You seriously want me to spill my secrets to a stranger?"

Julian fixed that uncharacteristically intent gaze on Rayne. "I seriously think you need some kind of backup. You won't go to the cops. You won't talk to Everett. You seem to be all alone. What other options do you have?"

Rayne got up and paced to the window, staring out at the SUV.

I clenched my hands to keep from reaching out, pressed my lips together, and let him think.

August and Julian exchanged looks and were silent as well.

After a couple of minutes, Rayne turned. "Okay, you're right. I'll tell you a little. As long as you know that this isn't safe stuff. You could be putting yourself in the line of fire."

August cleared his throat. "Julian? Maybe—"

"Nope." Julian patted his husband's arm. "Go play with fire. I'll be fine."

August sighed, but I bet he didn't win many arguments with Julian, then eyed Rayne. "Okay. Twenty minutes?"

"Uh, yeah. Won't likely even need that much."

*Give me strength.* I wanted to demand why he just wouldn't tell me what was going on. Still, we weren't at a place in our relationship where I could do that. Him staying in my spare bedroom wasn't really situation critical. As long as no one knew where he was, my life wasn't in danger. All I had was *Rayne* and shots fired in Wellington Park.

*I need more.* Even as I had the thought, I rose, then followed August into the kitchen. I strained to hear the conversation, but this older house didn't have the open floor plan mine did. The living room was separated by a door from the dining room and the kitchen was beyond that. I sighed.

August nudged me with his shoulder. "You *will* survive."

"Will I? I'm not convinced."

"He's safe with Julian." He grabbed the handmade patties from the fridge and put them on the counter. Then he pulled out a bowl of salad and dressing. "Add this."

"It'll get soggy."

"Not in the twenty minutes it's going to take to grill these. We should've grabbed our coats to use the outside grill. That was my plan."

"We're good, hearty Canadian lads."

He laughed. "You'd never survive in the Yukon."

"Neither would you." I dumped way too much salad dressing on the lettuce and smiled. I didn't have a New Year's resolution to eat healthy. I didn't believe in that shit. I'd swim, hike, and generally take care of myself. A few extra calories for salad dressing wasn't going to kill me. August and Julian both had physically demanding jobs, and Rayne...

*Those abs...*

*Sigh.*

August retrieved a bag of pre-cut French fries from the freezer and turned on the oven. "The burgers are going to be done before these."

"We didn't eat that long ago."

He cut me a glance.

"Oh, I can totally eat more. Even after Nanny's lasagna, I can always make room for a Julian burger."

"Not as good as Fifties'." August spread a layer of fries on the tray.

"True. I love Julian."

He laughed.

"But even he can't match Fifties. Best burgers in Mission City." I quipped that as I grabbed the ketchup and barbecue sauce from the fridge.

August and I had done this often during the years after I'd moved to Mission City from law school in Vancouver. Adding Julian to the mix had been natural. Easy. The guy was a gem and had made it clear to me from the beginning that he didn't see me as the third wheel. He might be August's partner—and eventually his husband—but he understood the depth of my relationship with my friend.

From day one he'd become my friend as well.

I'd brought a few guys around to make a fourth—mostly friends like Simeon.

*I need to have him over with Ryan. Introduce Ryan to everyone.* I would do it with Simeon's guidance, though. Ryan had been through a lot with the war over in Ukraine. Even I didn't know the extent of his injuries. I'd let my friend guide me as to how much his new boyfriend could take in the socializing department. And Julian, for all his railroading personality, could also be incredibly gentle, intuitive, and kind. He'd wrap Ryan up in a proverbial hug and welcome him to the fold.

Because that was just the kind of guy he was. Jovial and unserious until the moment he was called up to step up—and then the most loyal and stalwart friend a person could ask for.

*What are you thinking? Introducing Rayne to new people? You're acting like he's a guest and not some guy hiding out from dangerous people. You need your head examined.*

August opened the back door, and a gust of cold air swept through the room.

"Jesus, give a guy some warning."

He shoved the plate into my hands. "I'll grab our coats. You go get the grill going."

I pursed my lips as I stepped onto the raised deck.

My friends kept the house slightly chilled, so they encouraged guests to keep their shoes on—as long as they weren't dirty.

Despite me having been out on the ranch, I'd stuck to paths and my shoes were clean.

Rayne's were not, and he'd shed them.

*At least he's wearing a pair of my thick wool socks that don't have a hole.*

*Right, because* that's *the important part of this.*

"Get your head out of your ass."

August grabbed the plate, then shoved my jacket at me.

In the time he'd been gone, I'd accomplished nothing.

The oven dinged.

"I'll put the fries in and set the timer."

"Then you're coming out here to help. I'm not freezing my gorgeous ass off out here alone."

I snickered as I put the tray in the oven.

Moments later, I joined him on the protected deck. "August."

"Yeah?" He hit the starter, and the flame flickered to life.

"It's snowing."

"What's your point?"

"I dunno...that we're barbecuing and it's snowing...?"

He laughed. "The grill inside isn't as good. We don't do this often. Only when friends visit."

I cocked my head. "You didn't know we were coming. Were you expecting someone else?"

"Uh...no..."

"So why were the burgers ready?"

"Might've been a special occasion."

"And that is?" I wracked my brains.

"Nya's birthday."

My heart seized. "Shit, August. I totally forgot."

His adored sister. Who had died so far ahead of what should have been her time.

He put the burgers on the grill. "I don't expect you to remember. You remembered the anniversary of her death. You and Julian came to the cemetery with me. That was the tough part."

"Because you still feel guilty you weren't there even though you couldn't have done anything." She'd died in her sleep. With no symptoms. If she hadn't known, how could he possibly have? Yet he still harbored the belief if he'd seen her that day, he might've noticed…something. The medical examiner had told him repeatedly that brain aneurisms rarely gave symptoms. That he wasn't at fault.

His sister's death still lay heavy on him, though. Fortunately, he had Julian there to counter the pain. To coax a smile. Or, if that failed, Julian would call me, and I'd come over. Such was our friendship.

"I'm sorry I didn't remember." I even had a note in my calendar. The calendar I hadn't consulted. I'd known I was seeing Farrah, and every other scrap of my mind was absorbed by the man inside.

Once August had finished laying the patties on the grill, he slapped me on the back. "She'd be tickled pink to find you here. All verklempt." He laughed. "I think she'd find Rayne a hoot."

"Yeah, she probably would."

The siblings grew up with alcoholic parents, always relying on each other. They'd known each other through and through.

"Did you—" I drew in a breath. "—hear anything Rayne might've said to Julian."

August's dark-brown eyes lit. "Oh, you bet. You wouldn't believe the shit that guy's up to."

"Yeah—"

He smacked me on the chest. "No. Even if I heard, I wouldn't tell you. And they were busy talking about Sarge. You and a dog." He snorted. "That's a hoot."

"August." I tried for seriousness.

But he just kept laughing. "The look on your face."

"This is important."

"Of course it is. But if you were truly worried about our safety, you wouldn't have come here. I'm assuming no one's following you."

"Yeah, impossible to follow someone around here and not be spotted." I leaned my hip against the railing. "I kept a close eye on that. I am worried."

"When are you not worried? If it's not about your clients, then it's a friend, or your boss or—"

"That's not what this is. Back in university—"

"We were young and carefree." He opened the lid, and a waft of hot air hit us. "And then we grew up. At least you're not in charge of a billion-dollar foundation."

"No, I'm not that." I tried to be serious, but I had to laugh. Nya had created an app and sold it for a couple billion dollars. About a month before she passed. She'd been in the process, with my help, of setting up a foundation to disperse the funds to various charitable and worthy endeavors. Especially underrepresented communities in the sciences. Laudable stuff.

Then, she died, and everything had fallen to August. I'd set him up with E.J. Ward, a woman with tons of experience in such things. She ran the day-to-day operations of the foundation and made the recommendations. August signed off on everything. Still, he often sought my counsel. He was completely capable of doing this himself—he did run his own million-dollar business—but he sometimes felt uncertain what Nya would've wanted. I didn't blame him for the hesitation—a couple billion dollars was a lot of money.

"Hey, are you guys cooking or yakking?" Julian stepped out, wrapped in a blanket.

Rayne followed, wearing the winter coat I'd loaned him.

As Julian insinuated himself between August and me, Rayne headed around to the corner of the house, clearly spying on Sarge again.

"Is he doing okay?" I called.

"Looks like. I don't want to leave him too long." Rayne didn't turn my way.

Julian clapped me on the back. "Welcome to the joys of parenthood."

I swayed. "At least a dog poops outside, and Rayne will do all the scooping."

"Or so you tell yourself." August kissed Julian's cheek. "Grab the buns? I'll toast them and then we can eat."

"Perfect." Julian bounded into the house.

"Luckiest man alive," I whispered.

"You know it." August grinned.

Yeah, despite it being his sister's birthday, he was going to be okay. Rayne's situation still loomed ominously, but I decided I wasn't going to let it shadow this day for August. I forced my mind out of worry mode and grinned back.

# Chapter Ten

Rayne

Sarge was down for the count in my room.

He lay on an old blanket Everett had dug up, tucked inside the dog crate he clearly felt was home.

I tried to make the blanket into a little bed.

The dog had turned three times, flopped down, closed his eyes, and was out.

I'd borrowed Everett's phone to text Torah to let her know we'd survived. She sent back six texts of advice for the night and next day, mostly stuff she already told me before we left. Was she more worried than she wanted to let me know?

Leaving Sarge alone, I closed the door securely and crept into Everett's room while he was in the bathroom. I'd shed my shirt and socks. Now I lay on the middle of his bed with just my jeans—undone and hanging low on my hips, of course.

My torso left much to be desired. Oh, my abs were awesome. Sculpted. Rock hard. Pure perfection.

The yellowing greenish purple bruises, however, marred my beautiful skin.

I tried to tell myself I wasn't vain.

I tried to tell myself Everett would look beyond the injuries to what I was obviously offering.

I tried to tell myself we could have sex, and I'd be fine.

*Delusional.*

Still...if he did all the fucking and went gentle with me—

"What the hell are you doing?" Everett exited the ensuite bathroom wearing just an itty-bitty towel.

"Do you sleep in the buff?" My cock, vaguely interested before, perked right up. I hadn't gotten a good look when we were in Quinton's dark room, but now I could look my fill—all dark skin, sparse chest hair, dark nipples, and, oh God, he was an outie. I wanted to run my tongue the length of his sternum, swirl that belly button, and then head down his happy trail to the beautiful cock I just *knew* that towel hid.

"None of your business." He scowled. "Don't you have a dog to look after?"

"Down for the count."

"How can you be certain?"

"We had a heart-to-heart. I told him I was about to get lucky and asked him to behave while that was happening."

"And you think a one-year-old dog has the capacity to understand what you said to him?"

"Uh...probably not. But he's fast asleep in his crate and Torah said he slept through the night last night. I've closed my door and I've closed your door, so as long as you don't make me scream—"

"No screaming." He shook his head. "There will be no screaming. There will be no sex at all."

"I hadn't thought of sex." A total lie, but he couldn't call me on it. I did beguiling really well.

"Right, you're half naked in my bed so we can talk?" He stalked over to his dresser, yanked it open, then he rifled through everything until he finally located pajama pants. He pivoted and headed to the bathroom.

"You can get changed in here." I batted my eyelashes.

The hand not holding the pants wagged a finger at me. "You're incorrigible."

"Uh." I watched him go into the bathroom. Where I expected him to slam the door, though, he closed it quietly. *Ah, so he's thinking of Sarge as well.*

Moments later, he reemerged.

And oh, my cock perked right up. The green-and-blue plaid pants rode low on his hips. I arched an eyebrow. "Are you sure sex isn't on the table?"

"You just said you hadn't *thought* of sex." No masking the exasperation.

I shrugged. "I see you mostly naked and I think sex."

"Whereas I see you and think *how the fuck do I get him to leave*?"

"Well…" Lazily, I ran my hand down my belly, lower still, and rested it on my perky shaft. "I could give you a blow job."

He blinked. "You're not in any shape to do that."

"Oh, I most certainly am. Nothing wrong with my mouth or my hands. Or my cock, for that matter."

"Jesus Fucking Christ. You're going to be the death of me."

"So we can fuck? Because I think if I lie on my good side—"

He gestured up and down my body. "There is no *good* side. You're a disaster area. Purple, green, yellow...you look like a freaking monster. Don't even get me started on that." He waved at the bandage I'd taped over the graze in my side.

"Hey." I frowned. "You don't have to be so mean about it. You took me out in public."

"A miscalculation on my part. I thought if I left you here, you might get into mischief. I take you out and you bewitch my friends and bring home a fucking dog."

"Hey." I repeated the word. "Don't talk about Sarge like that. You might hurt his feelings."

"He's a dog."

"A very sensitive dog. Who doesn't have any balls." Inwardly, I winced as I remembered Julian's threats of what he'd do with mine if I hurt Everett. I didn't intend to—but the added incentive of not having my family jewels in a vise was a strong motivation.

"What do balls have to do with anything?"

"Well, mine are fine, so let's do something."

He sputtered. "Have you heard a word I've said? You're bad for my sanity."

"You know you love me."

"I most certainly do not."

"Are you saying I have a face only a mother could love?"

He rolled his eyes. "When you're healthy, you're also just fine looking."

"How do you know? I wore that mask."

"You should've worn contact lenses. Your eyes are so damn distinctive. There's no way you can hide from anyone. One look into your eyes, and the game is up."

"I didn't know we were playing a game. What do you suggest? I'm very good at strip poker."

"You're incorrigible."

"You said that before."

"I'm saying it again to remind myself why I'm *not* getting involved with you. You are going to tell me who wants to kill you, we're going to tell the police, and then you can go back to wherever you came from *with* your dog, and I can move on with my life." He scratched his stubbled jaw. "Are we clear?"

"So if you lie on the bed and I give you a blow job, that would be okay?" I cupped my thus far neglected cock.

"Do you ever listen to anyone? Sometimes I think you're just an airhead."

Words my grandmother used to speak bore down on me. Fun suddenly became something much more bitter. I blinked. "I'd like to think I'm more than that. I do good work. I help people. Maybe not like you..." I swallowed. "I'll go." Even as I tried to rise, though, my body protested.

"You're going to be the death of me." He moved toward the bed. "I'm going to regret this."

"How could you possibly regret me?" Yet I knew the answer to that question. Plenty of people regretted me. Very few wanted me. Why I'd thought Everett would be different, I wasn't certain.

He placed one knee on the bed, then the other. Next thing I knew, he was crawling toward me.

I shifted uncomfortably. But this time the pain wasn't because of my injuries. Something inside me stirred, then shifted. He hadn't wanted this—but I'd taunted him until he gave in. This wasn't real.

*He can make his own decisions. If he demanded I leave, I would. I swear.*

He lay beside me.

I slid my hand up his thigh to grasp his cock.

He moaned.

"Let me." I whispered the word.

"You're injured. It would be wrong."

I could think of many things that would be wrong. Me bringing him pleasure wasn't one of them. I wasn't going to get aroused anytime soon, but I could do this for him. As a way of making up for walking out in October? As a way for thanking him for not booting me to the curb at his office? As a way to show gratitude without having to come up with difficult words?

Yeah, all those things.

I might be hurting, but bringing him to climax would be worth any discomfort I had to endure. So I ran my thumb along his slit. Then I brought said digit to my mouth and sucked.

His breath hitched.

Our gazes clashed. In the low light of the bedside lamp, his pupils nearly obliterated the dark-brown irises I found so damn compelling.

"A hand job." His expression hardened. "And if you're in pain, we stop."

*I'm always in pain when it comes to you—physical...emotional...it's always there.*

Yet I couldn't say the words out loud. Too soon. Too raw.

Too true.

I grasped his cock. "Lube."

"I'm too close."

An echo of my thoughts just a moment ago.

So I held on and pumped his shaft.

The angle was shit, and my shoulder hurt, but none of that mattered. Because, soon enough, his breathing hitched. He surged in my hand. He arched his neck so his head went back as he moaned his release. *Have to be quiet here because of the dog. Like at Quinton's...*

Guilt about that night swamped me, and heat raced to my cheeks. I'd been wrong to leave—but I'd also had my reasons.

He softened in my hand as I coaxed him through his release. His cum coated my hand, his thighs, and some even hit my belly. He wrapped his hand around mine, effectively stilling me. "Sensitive."

"Yeah, I'd say. You went off like a rocket." I injected amusement in my voice to mask the anguish. My words came out a little hoarse, though.

"You okay?" He squeezed my hand—now it no longer gripped his cock.

"Fine. Why wouldn't I be?"

Our gazes clashed.

He cleared his throat. "Just we...you know..."

I extricated my hand, rubbed it on my belly, and rolled off the bed.

Thank Christ he didn't see the involuntary wince or, hopefully hear my intake of breath. "I need to take care of Sarge. I, uh, think I'm going to change his name to Champ. He's been passed around like a hot potato several times. I think he needs a name that reflects his mindset—not something that connotes strength or even..."

"Force?"

"Yeah, like that."

"Isn't it going to be hard on him? Hasn't he been through enough?"

I bit my lower lip. "Yeah. Maybe. But he needs a fresh start. I can give him that."

"I know you can." His gaze softened. "Are you sure you're okay? I don't just mean physically—"

Having regained my equilibrium, I strode to the door. "I'm fine. Just going to take care of my dog." I was careful to ensure he knew

Champ was mine. That I'd take responsibility for him. That Everett didn't need to worry.

I entered the bathroom and shut the door. I wanted to crawl into bed, but I didn't want to smell like cum, especially having no idea how the dog would react, so I figured a shower was in order. I dropped my jeans to the floor and ran the water as hot as I could stand on my raw spots. As I stood under the spray, my muscles thanked me for having taken this moment. The ends of my hair caught a little spray, but I didn't want to sleep with it wet so I skipped the shampoo. Eventually, Everett's hot water ran out, ending the blessed massage.

As I toweled myself dry, I eyed my jeans. Fuck it. I'd wear a towel around my waist. I'd change into Everett's sweatsuit, which I still had. Eventually, I'd need to launder it and return it.

Like Everett, I slept in the buff. However, having a dog no doubt meant unpredictability, so I opted to put on the sweats.

I cast one longing look at Everett's closed door before pivoting and entering the room that was, for the moment, mine.

Champ glanced up from where he now lay, offered what I considered a grin, then put his head back down.

"You know you have a perfectly good bed on the floor."

He snuffed. But didn't move off *my* bed.

I pulled on the sweatsuit. "Do you need to go out?"

He didn't stir.

"Right. You're shedding all over Everett's duvet."

Not a whisker.

"Oh, and I'm renaming you Champ. I think that suits you better. Everett agrees." He hadn't technically, but if I just kept calling the dog by his new name, he'd come around—both Champ and Everett.

I made a note to text Torah before we went for our lesson tomorrow.

*Damn. Did I tell Everett about the training? He'll need to either drive me or let me drive. Or maybe Torah will come here...?*

Too many thoughts to deal with.

I eyed the snoozing dog, whose half-closed eye showed he was watching me, and texted Torah.

*—Is Sarge sleeping on my bed a problem? —*

*—Better not—*

*Does the woman ever sleep?*

*— If you have a nightmare and make noise or lash out, or even just kick him in your sleep, he might bite you in reaction. If he won't stay on the floor, put him in the crate and lock it. —*

*Fuck.* But I could see the wisdom of that.

I lured him down to the crate and convinced him to go in for some treats. Once he was in, I latched the door. But when he pushed a paw up against the wire, his eyes fixed on mine, I couldn't just leave him. Tugging the blankets off the bed, I made myself a nest beside him, curled up and put my fingers through the crate to stroke his fur.

*My body is really going to hate me in the morning.*

In this moment, though, I didn't care. I needed comfort only he could offer. I needed to forget how I'd just walked out on Everett again.

Most of all, I needed to convince myself my heart wasn't involved.

*Easier said than done.*

# Chapter Eleven

Everett

*I* *shouldn't be doing this. I shouldn't be doing this. I shouldn't—*

Oh fuck it.

After the mind-blowing orgasm, delivered by one of the most frustrating men on the planet—

Well, at least of my acquaintance.

—I was scouring the 7-Eleven for burner phones. Yes, I'd gotten out of my cum-smelling bed, changed the sheets, had a shower and, after lying in bed for an hour with zero sign of sleep, I changed into jeans and a long-sleeved thermal shirt, had bundled myself up, and headed to the store. Crazy because the snow was coming down pretty heavily.

The selection seemed pretty slim, but Rayne didn't need the communication device for anything other than that—communication. Function over style.

With the help of the clerk, I'd found the model that was the most logical. I rolled my eyes at the fact the damn thing was also the most expensive. I bought a SIM card, 10 hot wings, an icy sugary concoction, and then I left.

Inexplicably hungry, I devoured all ten wings in one sitting. A bit unusual for me, but whatever. I slurped the drink, giving myself an ice cream headache, even though I hadn't enjoyed any ice cream. The blue-colored drink tasted good, though, so that made the brain freeze worth it.

After wiping my hands on a napkin, I put the SUV in reverse and backed out of the parking space. With my seatbelt secure, and winter gear in my trunk, I ventured back up the hill toward home.

Mission City had plenty of hills, and I lived on a high one. On a good day, I had a clear view of Mount Baker—the inactive volcano in Washington State. Although my bedroom faced north toward the rest of the townhouse complex, my two back bedrooms faced the mountains. I'd set up one as a spare bedroom—where my wayward guest and his even more wayward dog slept soundly—and the second was my den. I'd pushed the desk right against the window and, on sunny days, I could see for miles. A breathtaking view worth every penny I'd paid for it.

As I crested the first hill, flashing lights appeared in my rearview mirror.

*What the fuck?*

I couldn't see another car for the entire length of the street.

Quickly, I pulled over, waiting for the police car to pass me.

He didn't. He pulled in behind me.

He? She? They?

I had no idea.

Quickly, I reviewed all my actions.

We didn't have tags in British Columbia anymore, and my insurance was up to date, so that wasn't the reason. The road had been clear when I'd pulled out, so I hadn't cut anyone off. I'd been driving up the hill, so I hadn't come anywhere near speeding. If I had a taillight out, I certainly didn't know. I'd be happy to get that fixed. Would prefer not to get a ticket—and did they even give tickets out for that these days?

I put the SUV into park, rolled down the window, and cut off the engine.

Snow blew into the cab, but I didn't care. I wanted this resolved as quickly as possible. I kept my hands at the top of the steering wheel and waited patiently.

In the side mirror, I caught sight of an officer leaving his car. I would work with the assumption he was a constable as corporals and staff sergeants didn't generally ride around in marked cars.

"Keep your hands where I can see them."

"Okay." I tried to glance over at him, but the bright streetlight behind him obscured my view. "Can you tell me what I did wrong? I apologize if it's a taillight. I can't see them—"

"This is a nice SUV you're driving."

"It is. My salary as a lawyer affords me the ability to buy a nice SUV. I drive the hills of Mission City and so need—"

"Shut up."

A cold chill ran up and down my spine. *Oh shit*. I took a deep breath. "If you contact Constable Seth Jacobs, he can verify—"

"I said, shut up."

"Right. Sorry." I took another breath. "Let me get my license and insurance. You'll see—"

"Step out of the vehicle. Reach your hand out to the handle. Keep the other one where I can see it."

Again, I tried to see him.

This time, the light glinted off his gun. Which was pointed right at me.

Indignation rose, hot and furious. Heat shot to my cheeks.

*He's got the gun. You can sort this out later. Just...stay alive.*

"Do what you're told."

"Of course." I didn't like the fear in his voice.

"I've called for backup."

*Thank God.* I didn't just know Seth—my interactions with various members of the Mission City community, including criminals, had brought me into contact with a number of cops. Hopefully one with more sense would arrive, and this could all be resolved.

"Now!"

I eased my left hand out of the window and slowly grasped the outer handle—all the while keeping my right hand clearly visible. I hadn't worn gloves, so the cold metal bit into my hand.

That chill helped keep me grounded.

Once I'd grasped the handle, the mechanism gave easily. I met the constable's gaze.

He nodded.

The gun wobbled.

*Jesus, I'm going to die on the side of the road. Rayne won't understand. He's the one in trouble, and I'm the one who's going to die.*

*Regrets...I had a few. I should've pushed him to tell me the truth. I should've done more to help him. I should've called Julian and demanded to know what was going on. I should have—*

"Step out of the vehicle."

I followed his instructions, keeping my hands visible at all times. "I'm no threat to you, okay?"

"Just shut the fuck up. I need to think."

I heard a vehicle's engine revving as it made its way up the hill.

Snow continued to fall, heavy and wet. I hadn't worn a hat, so it melted as it hit my shorn head. That water fell in rivulets down my neck, ears, and forehead.

I blinked several times.

The cop glanced at the newcomer.

*Jesus, I could totally grab his gun.*

I wouldn't of course. The damn thing might go off. But the constable's inexperience was showing in every moment of this interaction.

Someone put the second car into park—a regular car and not a cruiser—cut the engine, and then emerged.

"Janic, what the hell are you doing?"

Oh, thank God. Corporal Dorrie Duhamel. She worked sex crimes—which begged the question of why she was out at two on a Sunday morning—but that didn't *really* matter. What mattered is she'd recognize me.

"This guy's driving an SUV. We had a report of a stolen vehicle—"

"Of a gray SUV. This one is burgundy. Put the gun away. Now." No-nonsense Dorrie was on full display. This woman didn't take shit. From anyone. And had put more perpetrators of violence away than just about anyone—despite her relatively young age. Partner to Corporal Colton Pritchard, she was usually the *bad* cop of the pair. Tonight, thank God, she was taking the same tough-ass position she took with perps.

"I—"

"Gun. Away. Now. That's a direct order."

"Right." Slowly, while keeping his gaze on mine, Janic put his gun away. He continued to stare at me. "But he's—"

"Janic, I don't care. If he broke traffic rules, then you either give a warning or you issue a ticket. You do not pull someone over and get them out of the car for..." She sighed. "Please tell me this isn't because he's Black."

The constable rubbed his face.

"All right. You're going to apologize to Mr. Williams. You're coming back to the station with me where we're going to talk to Greg."

Their Staff Seargent.

"And then, whether you still have a job or not, you're going to issue a full written apology. Mr. Williams is a member in good standing with the Bar Association of British Columbia. Sometimes he works as a defense attorney. Sometimes he works as a victim's advocate. What he is *not* is a car thief."

An RCMP officer couldn't just be summarily fired. But he could have his life turned upside down in an investigation. These days, much of the brass was aware of appearances of prejudice. One too many encounters with racialized Canadians—Indigenous populations in particular—had a lot of Canadians looking askance at the nation's police force. Didn't mean the cops didn't still cover for a lot of racist behavior, but with Dorrie on my side, this guy might get an actual consequence.

"I just—"

"Jerry, I don't give a shit."

Dorrie spoke so forcefully that Jerry took an actual step back.

*Jerry Janic? Poor guy. What a crappy name.*

*Oh God, are you feeling sorry for him?*

*Just for the name. The rest of him can go to hell.*

"Get out of here. Go back to the detachment. Go into interrogation room one. I'm radioing Colton to ensure you don't speak to anyone till I get there. Got it?"

He blew out a breath.

Just before he moved away, I caught the look of pure hatred in his eyes.

It nearly stole my breath.

He got into his car, did a U-turn, and headed back down the hill.

As soon as the taillights were out of sight, Dorrie placed a call.

She was still far enough that I couldn't make out all the words. The snow also had a weird deadening effect. Everything had a peculiar serene quality to it. That something so pure could've covered up something so heinous.

After a moment, she cut the call and headed my way. "You want to get into your SUV? I..." She swallowed hard as she stepped toward me, well out of my personal space. "I don't even have words. Honest-to-God, I don't know what to say. *I'm sorry* feels wholly inadequate."

"It's a start." Finally, I wiped my face and tried to push most of the moisture to the back of my head. The water ran down my neck, under my coat, and down my spine.

"You must be freezing. Look, I need to get your statement. You know that."

I sighed. I did *know* that. And the sooner I offered my details, the sooner I could get home. Back to Rayne. Back to bed.

Dorrie's phone rang.

I waved for her to answer it, choosing to step back toward my vehicle.

Snow had begun to accumulate on the driver's seat. I trudged to the trunk, popped it, and grabbed both the snow brush and a towel. My fingers were ice as I tried to mitigate some of the damage. My leather seats would be okay. My ass was bound to get damp, and I was thoroughly soaked and frozen at this point. The idea of sitting at the detachment held less-than-zero appeal.

"Everett?"

"Yeah." I worked hard to keep the weariness from my voice. I owed Dorrie everything. If not for her. I might've been shot. I might've...

*Don't go there. It didn't happen. It's amazing you've gone thirty-four years without being pulled over for* driving while Black.

"So Colton called Greg, and he's on his way down. He's going to lead the investigation of Janic. I need to be there to give my side of the story. We still need yours, but Colton's offered to escort you home first. If you don't mind him coming into your home, you can put on dry clothes and maybe have a chat?"

Her words were gentle, and her demeanor sincere.

I could always offer to come down to the station in the morning, but my potential statement would weigh on me tonight. Better to get this over with. I offered a weak smile. "That's a very generous offer. If Colton wants to come to my place, of course he's welcome. I can even put on a pot of coffee. Unless he was headed home to bed?"

Dorrie shook her head. "Well, maybe if he's with you long enough. We just wrapped up a big case—we helped Vancouver with a human sex trafficking ring. You'll hear about it on the news. Three of the victims were here, in Mission City. We took their statements and have arranged for social services to take care of them until they can be reunited with their families."

Despite my scalp freezing and my back aching, I found myself asking, "Are they from around here?"

She shook her head. "Two are foreign nationals—that's all I can say. The third girl is Indigenous. From a reserve in Northern Alberta. Her family reported her missing a year ago."

*A girl.*

*A year ago.*

Jesus. I didn't want to think what she'd endured during that time. "Anything I can do to help?"

Dorrie smiled.

"You're a good man, Everett. Let Colton know you're willing to help the victims. He'll see if there's anything. Now, just give me a minute, and—"

Even as she said the words, another car crested the hill.

She waved.

The person behind the wheel, whom I assumed to be Colton, flashed his high beams.

"You okay to drive home?" She met my gaze with her blue eyes shining.

"Yeah. And thank you. You—" I swallowed. "—saved my life."

To my nauseated discomfort, she didn't disagree. *See, not my imagination. It was that close.* She merely nodded and walked back toward her car. I appreciated she didn't try to minimize what had just happened.

With shaking hands, I laid the towel on the seat and got in. I put the keys in the engine ignition and started the SUV. Then I waved, rolled up the window, and slowly pulled out onto the deserted street.

The snow now covered the ground entirely, no longer dissipating when it hit the wet asphalt. The plow trucks would eventually come through. I might be facing a snow day tomorrow if the plows didn't make it up my way.

*It's Sunday. You're not going in to work.*

Well, I'd planned on it. But I had my laptop, and—

Shit.

I'd left the laptop at home.

With Rayne.

He didn't know the password, but what if he was some cyber sleuth? Or a cybercriminal?

Too tired to really give a shit, I drove home slowly.

Colton followed.

# Chapter Twelve

Rayne

H earing the garage door lessened my panic.

I'd heard Everett leave. Part of me figured he was going out to get lucky, and part of me worried he might be leaving to get away from me.

Neither idea sat well.

*You seriously think he's going out to hook up with someone else? That's so pathetic.* And so unlike everything I knew about Everett, that it bordered on absurd. Still, my mind wouldn't settle.

After about an hour, I'd come downstairs. Sarge—I mean Champ—picked his head up when I rose, and he whined, butting at the door of his crate, so I brought him down with me. I'd grabbed a throw blanket, stretched out on the couch, and tried to read a paperback book I'd found.

Champ sniffed around the room, tail low, ears at half mast, but when nothing spooked him, he'd lain down on the floor near my feet.

About two pages in, I'd realized this book was some kind of literary thing. I recognized most of the words, but had never seen them put together in this way before. After thirteen pages, when I hadn't seen a single line of dialogue, I'd given up. I'd gone to the bookshelf and found more literary stuff, law journals, and a collection of Blu-rays that included documentaries and foreign language films along with a few classics. No *Blade Runner* or *Die Hard* or *Barbie* to be found. Something called *American Fiction* looked interesting, but by that point I couldn't focus.

Champ tried to jump on the couch.

I took one look at the faux leather and gently guided the guy down. I ran upstairs, grabbed his blanket, brought it back down, and made a bed for him at my feet.

He eyed me on the couch, clearly considered trying to jump up again, calculated the odds of success, and settled back onto the blanket.

I murmured, "Down. Good boy." *Should have brought his treats down.*

Torah had emphasized rewarding every calm behavior.

I reached down slowly and was thrilled when he rubbed his cheek on my hand, soliciting pets. Having my touch be a reward for this nervous guy elicited a warmth inside me. I spent some time massaging his neck and ears before settling in to doze on the couch.

Almost an hour went by before I heard the garage door opening below us.

Champ did as well, as he raised his head and whined.

I said in my warmest voice, "Hey, we're fine, Sarge-Champ." The sooner he got used to his new name, the better. "Good boy, Sarge-Champ, let's happy chill." But I couldn't help tensing as a car pulled in. *Everett, right? Has to be.*

As if sensing my trepidation, he sat up—obviously on high alert.

"It's just Everett. You know Everett. You like Everett."

The dog cocked his head. "Your name is Champ." I said the word slowly. "That's my boy, Sarge-Champ. Sweet boy, Champ. My name's Rayne." I pointed to myself. "His name is Everett." *Like I expect the dog to know our names.* But the byplay helped me keep a lid on my own worries.

The door to the garage slammed.

Champ leaped to his feet and started to head that way.

"Sit."

He did.

"Bingo." I used the reward keyword Torah had been teaching him, wishing I had treats. His flattened ears and raised ruff showed his worries. "Good boy. Stay."

He did. Although he didn't look happy about it.

"Stay, stay. Good boy. Stay." I eased off the couch to where could I kneel by him and could hold his collar, making no sudden moves.

Champ flicked a look at me, but his raised hackles flattened as I reached for him and he leaned his shoulder into my side.

Torah had said my presence seemed to calm him, one of the main reasons she let me foster him.

He did look less worried.

I told him, "Bingo. Good job, stay." and rubbed his chest with my free hand.

"So let me make you some coffee. Unless you'd prefer tea or coffee?" Everett's voice carried as he walked up the stairs.

"I know this is going to sound off, but do you have some kind of cola? I need the caffeine, but I've drunk more than, I think, a pot of coffee in the last twelve hours."

"Dorrie told me..." Everett's voice trailed off. "Rayne?" His gaze met mine as he stood in the kitchen and looked past the dining room and to me on the couch. The open plan spanned the length of the townhouse. "You're up?"

"Uh...yeah."

The man behind him stepped my way, extending his hand.

Champ bristled and whined, ears going flat again.

The guy stopped. "Corporal Colton Pritchard, RCMP. Mission City detachment."

My chest tightened. I didn't want to shake the guy's hand. Didn't want him to see me, know who I was.

*I can't believe Everett betrayed me.*

Still, nothing more suspicious than balking.

Right.

"Rayne." I pushed to my feet, keeping hold of Champ, and kept my tone soft for the dog's sake. "Hey, there."

He eyed me up and down with typical cop suspicion.

"Rayne...?"

"Just Rayne."

"Ah." His nearly black eyes assessed me, lingering on my face. "That's quite a shiner. Skinned yourself too."

"I walked into a wall." Thank God I was wearing the sweatsuit and he couldn't see any of the injuries.

"And your jaw?"

*Shit.*

"The wall hit back."

The corporal glanced over his shoulder at Everett. "Really?"

"Oh shit. Not him, okay? It's not like that..." *Jesus fuck. Jesus fuck. Oh shit.* The last thing I needed was a cop getting up in our business.

Pritchard held Everett's gaze for a moment before returning his attention to me. "I would be surprised it Everett were responsible. But I've misjudged people in the past."

"He didn't—"

"So just tell me who did. We can clear this confusion right up."

"A wall—"

"Look, uh, Rayne." He said the word as if he doubted even that part of my story was true.

"It *is* Rayne."

"Rayne." He repeated the word softly. "I've been a police officer for more than ten years. Four years in sex crimes. I've seen what a fist can do to a face. To a body. You probably don't realize you're holding your side. Or that you keep shifting your weight. Now, a guy like yourself is in good shape. So why wouldn't you be able to stand properly?"

"Because I like slouching?"

We continued to hold glares.

*Don't back down. Don't let him see you sweat. Don't—*

"Rayne." Everett's quiet voice pierced the silence. "He's not here because of you. He's here because of me."

"What? You can't possibly have done anything wrong." He was the most upstanding guy I knew. Which made my leaving him—twice—all the more guilt-inducing.

"Mr. Williams was involved in an unfortunate incident this evening. I'm here to get his statement."

That had me easing right around the cop, keeping myself between Champ and Pritchard, and heading over to Everett.

Champ whined but stuck close to me.

I cupped Everett's face with my free hand. "Are you okay? Why'd you go out? What happened?"

He pressed a full paper bag into my hands. "I went out to get you a phone. To replace the one that got—" He glanced toward Pritchard. "—broken in the...incident."

"Accident," I prompted.

"God, you're both in on this?" He pointed to me. "I want the truth."

"The wall hit back." I jutted my chin in absolute defiance.

"A strong wall." Everett placed his hand at my lower back. "Bad accident."

The cop pursed his lips. "I will figure this out."

Everett gripped my hip. "Colton, as a friend, I'm asking you not to. I think you and I have enough to deal with tonight—given what happened. I don't want to make a formal complaint—"

Pritchard's eyes widened a fraction.

I tensed.

Champ leaned against me, and I felt his muscles tense. A little grumble echoed from his throat.

"Hush, Champ. Good boy," I crooned. I told Prichard, "The dog's a new rescue, jumpy, nervous about strangers. Keep your voice soft so we don't have a different problem."

Everett said to Prichard, "If you could just let things go. I'll give you my statement. Then you can leave. I trust that you'll see that Janic gets...some education."

*What the fuck happened? Who's Janic?*

The cop's jaw ticked. Finally, he said to Everett, "I didn't know you had a dog."

"This is Champ. He's my dog. My foster, anyhow." I petted the dog on his neck while not letting go of his collar—using just the right amount of fingernails that he loved. See? I was already getting to know him.

"Champ?" Everett met my gaze while still standing close, rubbing circles on my back. "I thought his name was Sarge."

"I don't want people to be intimidated by him. Sarge is so…military. Police. That kind of shit." I smirked at the cop in the room. "Oh, sorry, no offense meant."

Pritchard gave us an amused smile. "None taken."

"But Champ? He's a champion, don't you see? Not in the blue-ribbon kind of way…but he's survived to this point. Torah thinks he can be rehabilitated. I mean, look at the progress. He hasn't growled at …" I gestured to the cop. *That little grumble didn't count.*

"Torah Dixon?" The cop shifted from foot to foot.

"Yeah."

Everett sucked in a quick breath.

"She's my ex-sister-in-law." Colton pursed his lips. "She was worried about this dog? Is he safe here?"

"Sheesh. First you think I'm not safe and now you're worried about the dog? Something happened to Everett—and no one is telling me what." I didn't stamp my foot—but came damn close. Might've, except no sudden movements, right?

Champ whined anyway.

I scratched his neck harder.

"Why don't you and Champ head upstairs?" Everett leaned my way, slow as molasses, and when the dog didn't react, he pressed a kiss to my temple.

"No." I pulled back to meet his gaze. "I know you're pretending not to be upset, but even I can tell you are. And I'm not the most perceptive guy in the world." I met the cop's stare. "I'm staying." In my mind, I added, *unless there's some legal reason. Please let there not be a reason—*

Pritchard gestured to Everett with his chin. "His call. He's the victim."

"Don't say that." Everett whispered the words. "I'm uninjured."

"Thanks to Dorrie's quick thinking." The cop continued to regard us both.

"Yes, I might owe Dorrie my life." Everett let out a long breath. "You said you wanted a soda. Regular or diet? I have both."

"Diet would be great." He moved to the dining room table and pulled a notepad and pen out of his pocket.

Everett continued, "Rayne—"

"I'm staying."

"I was just going to ask you what you wanted to drink. You seemed to really enjoy the hot chocolate earlier. Or maybe something without caffeine?"

"As if I could go back to sleep." I held his hand. "Diet cola is fine, or I can make a hot chocolate. More importantly, what would you like? I'll get it." Wouldn't hurt Champ to have a bit of distance from the stranger.

"Early Grey with vanilla tea. We need to boil the kettle."

"Uh, and I'll have my hot chocolate. I'm not a huge tea fan." I smiled. "Let's do this quickly so we can send the asshole on his way."

"I heard that." Pritchard's voice was low as requested, but it carried.

"You were meant to." I pressed a kiss to Everett's cheek before heading to the fridge. I grabbed a diet cola as well as the milk. No way was I having powder and water for my hot chocolate.

Fifteen minutes later, with a leash on Champ, tea brewed, and my hot chocolate hot, we joined the cop.

He was on his second cola—requested sheepishly.

I'd smiled secretly as I'd delivered it with a flourish.

He'd arched an eyebrow.

I'd winked.

He'd arched an eyebrow again.

His reactions didn't allow me enough to get a read on him—obviously by design. Cops, like lawyers, couldn't let their every emotion be seen. And ex-wife didn't guarantee hetero, but I sure wasn't getting a single gay vibe from him. No latent homophobia either. He'd been comfortable with both Everett and the PDA he'd initiated between the two of us.

Or had I started it? I'd cupped his cheek out of concern.

He'd put his hand at the small of my back and then kissed my temple.

*So comforting. So confusing.*

Still, we sat next to each other with Champ on a short leash by my chair, chewing a bone treat.

To my shock, Everett took my hand.

He drew in a deep breath and let it out. "So, I went to the 7-Eleven to buy Rayne a phone—"

"A burner phone?"

Everett arched an eyebrow. "This is my story to tell."

Pritchard eyed me. "Right. True. Apologies. You tell me what happened."

And Everett did. In one very long monologue, punctuated by sips of tea.

The retelling took, I was quite certain, more time than the actual events.

As Everett recounted every word, my anger grew and grew. I might've grown up in a very exclusive enclave in West Vancouver—and my neighbors might've been more uniformly white than other parts of Greater Vancouver—but I'd still never witnessed such outright bigotry. Blatant unashamed racism. I wasn't naïve. I knew this shit was out there. I just never thought it would happen to Everett. He was a lawyer, for Christ's sake. And although his SUV was top-of-the-line, the thing wasn't ridiculously luxurious.

And even if it was, no one had the right to question his ownership. Any Black man's ownership.

Just...gross. Disgusting. Horrifying. *Fucking scary.*

If something had happened to him—

"Not so tight, sweetheart." He cut me a look.

I loosened my grip on his hand.

He turned back to Pritchard. "That's it. Truly."

"Our staff sergeant will take care of things." He clicked his pen shut. "There's going to be hell to pay."

Everett wiped the hand not gripping me on his thigh. "I'm not going to raise a fuss. Obviously, I'd like to see him fired, but I don't know if that will happen. Are we finished? I'm cold—"

"What?" I reached for his shirt and found his collar damp, the fabric soaked all down his back. "You should've gotten changed."

His gaze shifted between Pritchard and me. "You think the two of you were going to behave if I left you alone together?"

"Probably not." Admittedly, Pritchard had earned my respect—grudging as it was. Although I was intensely curious about his ex-wife. I wondered which Dixon sister she was.

Pritchard rose. "Have a hot shower and try to get some sleep. We'll be in touch. Likely Greg, as he'll want to handle this himself. He's a hands-on guy."

After a moment, Everett rose as well. "I know. I don't blame Greg—or the force. I get the bad apple thing. That's why the law society has a disciplinary board. People with bad intentions are everywhere."

Heat flooded my cheeks. *Yeah, he* probably *doesn't mean you, but you still haven't given him any reason to trust you.*

Sometimes I hated when my inner voice was right.

I remained still as Everett walked Pritchard downstairs. The garage door opened, and about a minute later, it closed again. *Right, two-car garage. Everett's only got one, cop probably used the spare with this snow.*

So if I managed to get a hold of my car, then I could bring it here and hide it.

Wasn't likely to happen. I'd be shocked if the thing hadn't been towed and, even if it hadn't, it might be under surveillance.

Still...

"You okay? You look deep in thought."

I met Everett's gaze. "Just thinking."

"Oh, watch out, that can be dangerous." He snagged our empty mugs.

I unleashed Champ and petted him. "Such a good boy, Sarge-Champ. You did great. Look at you being all calm."

He looked up at me from his chew toy and actually thumped his tail before going back to it.

I couldn't help grinning down at him. *Progress.*

I rose, grabbed Pritchard's three empty cola cans, and followed Everett into the kitchen. I put the cans in the recycling container as he put the mugs in the dishwasher.

When he closed the dishwasher door, however, he didn't move. He just stood there, staring blankly at the cabinets.

I held myself still.

"I thought I was going to die. I thought, *he's going to shoot me, and my blood is going to mar this beautiful, white snow.* I thought no one would know to tell you."

"Everett—"

He held up his hand. "But somehow, I'm here. Dorrie rode in to the rescue—a heroine in a gray police-issue sedan. And she defused the situation. She talked Janic down from his incredibly precarious perch."

"He should face charges."

"He'll have people to answer for. He drew his weapon. He clearly used racial profiling on me. There...I'd like to think there will be consequences."

"Well, if there aren't, you should go to the media. Tell them what happened."

Slowly he turned to face me. "To what end? I've spent most of my life trying to get people to see beyond the color of my skin. Why would I want to draw attention to it?"

His words slayed me.

*God, I've lived in a bubble my entire life. Whatever rejection I faced from my family, it's nothing compared to the racism he's had to live with his entire life.*

That fact hurt my heart.

Everett shivered.

There, at least, was something I could do for him. "Truly, you need a shower. You should've gone right up. I would've behaved, for your sake, while you got warm."

"I'm numb. I mean physically and emotionally numb. I didn't even feel the cold, you know? The discomfort pales in comparison to the fact I might've died tonight and you wouldn't have known."

This was the second time he'd referred to me this way.

The police would've shown up here eventually.

I would've been out of my mind with worry, but they would've shown up here to see if anyone needed to be notified. And I'd have faced the same scrutiny from Pritchard—or whoever might've shown up. Worse, with Everett dead, me in his home, and no one to vouch for me. I would've had to explain myself. I would've been turfed on my ass at best, arrested at worst. Champ might've bitten them, been shot too.

I moved toward Everett, wanting to hold him, needing to help. "Let me take care of you, okay? Do you want a bath or a shower? If you choose a bath, I can read to you from that weird lit book you're making your way through."

He chuckled. Forced...but a laugh nonetheless. "Marnie, the librarian, suggested it to me. She knows I like speculative fiction. I think...that one is beyond salvation."

"It's wretched. And I don't even know what speculative fiction is."

"I'll explain it to you."

"While you take a bath?"

"I'll take a shower."

"But I can sit on the toilet seat while you talk to me?"

He sighed. "Yeah, I can do that."

"And then you'll let me hold you in bed? You're not going to send me back to my room alone, are you? I'd only have Champ as a bed companion."

Everett shot me a *what the fuck, dude* look.

*Oops.* "Not like that, you dork. Anyhow, Torah says no dogs on the bed. But...you will let me?"

He shook his head.

Then he nodded. "Yeah, you can hold me. As long as it doesn't hurt your injuries."

*It hurts. Physically, it hurts. But it'll hurt more to be in the guest room while you suffer alone.* "I'm a big boy. If that wall ever comes after me again, he better watch out."

Another hesitant smile. "Yeah, okay."

"Do you mind if I put Champ's bed on the floor by yours?"

He sighed. "Something tells me I don't have a choice."

I grinned. "No, not really."

Forty minutes later, Champ had settled on the floor, and Everett lay in my arms under his comforter.

Surprisingly, he fell asleep before I did.

*He must be exhausted.*

And I hadn't even thanked him for the phone. Or for making it through that mess alive. *Thank you.* Aches and pains or not, I pulled him closer.

# Chapter Thirteen

Everett

"I think this is the biggest fake tree I've ever seen." I examined the thing looming in the ranch's front room.

"I'm certain you've seen bigger." Rainbow nudged her shoulder against mine.

"Well, sure. Like at the mall or something. But in someone's home? No." I gazed up at the white tree. Easily twelve feet. Good thing the great room was two stories. Of course, Kennedy and Rainbow would've bought a shorter tree for a smaller space.

"I have to go out to help Torah and Rayne." She checked her watch. "My sister said twenty minutes, and it's been twenty-two." She pointed to the tree. "Do you think we can ease it down? That should make removing the lights easier."

The tree was now bare of ornaments, but the lights still had to be removed before the sections could be dismantled.

"You know, you have a barn and stables. You'd think you could store it somewhere intact and then you wouldn't have to do this each year."

"But where's the fun in that?" She bumped me again. "I suppose we could wrap it in garbage bags. Otherwise the dust would do it in."

At the sound of clacking on the hardwood, we turned in unison.

Kennedy slowed her approach. "Shouldn't have put my boots on."

I glanced down at what she called her indoor cowboy boots. Way too pristine to be worn out in the snow, mud, and crud. The ranch had received even more snow than I had. My first task upon arrival had been to help Rainbow with the shoveling, her feet in ugly, practical Sorels.

Rayne groused about not being able to help, and Rainbow had basically told him off.

Something about liability insurance—which I was quite certain was a lie. Since I didn't want Rayne exerting himself, I just shrugged as if saying *nothing to be done about it* as opposed to *I don't know what the fuck she's talking about*.

My father taught me to never contradict a lady.

Rainbow exaggerating potential liability to keep Rayne from injuring himself did *not* require me to interfere.

"Help us tip the tree over?" Rainbow asked Kennedy. She shrugged at me. "Sorry, I don't want to store it intact. You don't have to help—"

"Of course I have to help." I eyed the tree. "The three of us should be able to manage." If Rayne wasn't injured, I'd have asked him to come in and help as well.

Within moments, the three of us had the tree on its side on the hardwood floor.

"Okay, gotta run."

Rainbow offered Kennedy the least-contrite smile I'd ever seen.

She thrust her feet into her boots, grabbed her scarf and coat, and was out the door in no more than a couple of heartbeats.

Kennedy laughed. The rich sound filled the cavernous space. "She's all about the decorating and putting up. Taking down makes her sad. I think she'd leave it up year-round if she thought she could get away with it."

"But you won't let her?" I snagged the end of the lights and followed it to the tree. Then I began the painstaking process of unhooking each light.

"Maybe if we'd selected a green tree? We could've claimed it was part of the décor. But she talked me into the white tree the year we opened the ranch—after the extensive renovations required. I agreed, believing putting it up every year would be fun. I was right—the decorating party is legendary. We just hadn't factored in the take-down process."

"You should have a party for that as well."

She stilled. "You know, that's not a bad idea. Make it fun for the kids and put the adults to work. Stanley and Justin, with Ravi and Maddox's help, would have the thing down in no time."

"Yes, but what chaos would Victor and Violet wreak upon you in the process?"

"Oh, fair enough."

Maddox and Ravi's two-year-old twins were hell on wheels. Stanley and Justin's son, Angus, was old enough to be responsible. Even he had trouble wrangling the twins, especially if we added in his four-year-old sister, Opal.

"I'm pretty sure Dean and Adam would come."

Kennedy met my gaze. "He's a different man."

I knew she was referring to Adam. Before Aussie Dean had come into his life, he'd been a total recluse. Hell, I'd lived in Mission City for almost ten years and had never met him. An odd friendship with Maddox had led to his accepting Dean as a roommate and...magic. Now, married, the men where due to return from their honeymoon soon. "Yeah, he's so changed. In a good way. I don't know if it's the ranch or Dean."

Adam was open about having come here for therapy. If others knew he'd reached out for help when he'd needed it, maybe they would as well.

"We've had a few successes over the years." She grinned. "I think the newest couple can attest to that."

I laughed. "Simeon and Ryan literally met on the ranch. You know you're going to have to host their wedding too."

Her eyes widened. "I was referring to Foster and Arnav. Rainbow offered the ranch to them after Foster's bold proposal."

"In the middle of Quinton's New Year's party. Yeah, I was there. Out of this world." I smiled.

She grinned. "I'm sorry I missed it. But yes, Simeon and Ryan as well, if they want. I think it's a little early in their relationship to discuss marriage. Although one never knows." She sighed. "We're going to become known as a wedding venue."

"Would that be so bad? Crap." I sucked my finger into my mouth.

"You okay?"

"Caught my finger. I'm fine." I angled my arm to pull the string a little farther. "You didn't see this place as a wedding venue?"

"My old business manager got married here. She and her husband, both wound up here for Sunshine's wedding to Colton. Mere months later they were married while Sunshine and Colton were headed to divorce court."

"Ouch." I pulled another string, mindful of a particularly dangerous-looking branch. "They didn't last long?"

"Fuck."

"You okay?" I nearly dropped the string of lights as I tried to make my way over to her.

"Sorry. I'm fine. And that vulgarity was very unlike me."

"You can say that again." No one here had a potty mouth within the ranch—too easy to slip up around clients. "What happened?"

"I scraped my hand. I've been doing this nearly ten years—you'd think I would know how."

"You only do it once a year. Seriously, are you okay?"

"Yep. The scratch isn't all that impressive, and it certainly didn't draw blood." She resumed her work. "Sunshine...well, you've met her."

"I have. I love visiting The Owl's Nest." The local bookstore where Sunshine worked. "She's a great salesperson, and she keeps her boss on his toes."

"Well, yeah. That's her nature. She just...she's so sunny. But she has terrible taste in men. Damn."

"You okay?" I was beginning to sound like a broken record.

"Fine. Just fiddly fu—fudge."

I laughed. "Yeah, okay."

"I love her first ex-husband. He's a good man. He also came back from his deployment overseas a different man."

"He served?" I didn't know him.

"Yeah. Only he was with the Canadian Forces."

"Okay, so he came back changed."

"I'll say things went south very rapidly, and Sunshine had to leave him. Well, they left each other. Complete disaster." She stood, stretched, then stooped again. "Ill-advisedly, but with typical Sunshine abandon, she married Colton."

"Okay." *Am I making progress? Well, more lights are unhooked, so surely the answer's yes...*

"Colton's..."

I glanced up.

She met my gaze. "Intense."

"Yes, he is that."

"Things were okay for a while. I think. But then he got promoted to sex crimes, and..." She sighed. "I'm really saying too much. Although not anything that isn't generally known around town. They had one particularly epic row down in The Junction. Three people called me to let me know my sister was acting unhinged and Colton wasn't doing much better. That was pretty much the end of that marriage, although he remained intense and...yeah. No restraining orders were necessary, but things aren't great."

"Oh."

"You know him in a professional capacity, right?" She straightened again. "Please tell me you're not bosom buddies and I didn't way overstep." She sighed. "I'm tired."

"You hosted a wedding at Christmas, continued to see patients over the holidays, and now have Farrah under your roof with all the stress that comes with that. You're entitled to be tired. You're entitled to overshare with someone who will keep your confidence. Besides, who would I tell?"

She closed her left eye as if thinking really hard.

"Rayne and I don't have *that* kind of relationship."

She held up her hands. "You don't have to tell me anything. I'm curious as hell. I mean, I love that you're helping me, but surely he could've come here with Sarge—sorry, Champ—by himself. Brilliant name change, by the way. Torah grudgingly approved. She did say take it gradually, use both names together until the dog answers to Champ.

But she's a big believer in fresh starts. And she loves how Rayne is helping that dog."

"I…" I sighed. "Rayne's trouble. As well as *in* trouble. I'm afraid to let him out of my sight. If I didn't trust Torah implicitly, I'd be out watching him right now."

"Okay…should I be worried about my sisters?"

"Their virtue is safe." I hesitated. "You know, I haven't ascertained if he's gay or bi. So maybe I spoke too quickly. Although nothing suggests he would hurt them, either way."

"Oh, Torah will take him down if he tries to get fresh with either of them. That wasn't what I meant."

"Well, no one knows we're here. I'd kind of prefer to keep it that way."

"My sisters know that what happens on the ranch, stays on the ranch. Even wild-child Spring will always follow that edict."

The sister who wrote articles for the Mission City Gazette.

Right.

See? I could keep track.

Most of the time.

"So, about Colton…" I drew in a breath. "I saw him last night. Well, this morning…"

Kennedy arched an eyebrow. "Do we need a drink? I don't have whisky, but I make a mean cappuccino."

"Sounds perfect."

We abandoned the Christmas lights and headed to the kitchen.

"What happened?" Kennedy grabbed milk from the fridge and headed to her fancy coffee maker.

"Driving while Black."

She pivoted abruptly. "Not Colton."

"Oh Jesus, no. Sorry." I held up my hands. "Another police officer. A guy I didn't know. A guy who saw a Black man driving a nice SUV and thought *that guy must be a thief*. I don't know when he spotted me, but I don't know many car thieves who stop for wings and an icy drink at 7-Eleven."

"No." She turned on the machine. "I just..." She drew in a deep breath as she met my gaze. "I know it happens. Not just from the news, although that's bad enough. I had a client who had something similar happen to him. It scarred him, Everett. Like down-to-his-soul affected him. Changed his life. Obliterated his trust. Not just in law enforcement, but with friends. He tried to talk about it, and they tried to downplay what he'd been through."

"At least..." I sighed. "Rayne didn't do any of those things. He..." I swallowed hard. "He let me hold his hand when I gave my statement to Colton. He even held me when we finally crawled into bed. I've never felt so...treasured. Safe."

Kennedy handed me a mug. "That's incredibly powerful, Everett. And I think it's great. Just watch out. He's been in your life for mere days. It's easy for feelings to accelerate after trauma."

"That wasn't trauma, Kennedy. That was just bad luck."

She eased her hip against the counter. "You're friends with August."

"Yeah."

She waved her hand around. "He's done some work on the property for me."

"He's constantly in demand."

"Right. And we both now know Foster."

Who'd come here and been in counseling with Justin. Something my new friend spoke openly about. "Yes."

"So if either man came to you and recounted what happened to you as having happened to them, would you not believe they'd been traumatized?"

I frowned.

"I'm not telling you how you feel or even how to cope. I'm thrilled Rayne was there for you. I hope, if it's what you want, that he'll always be here for you. But I'm just saying you had a profound and disturbing thing happen to you. I'm mad as hell about it. You have every right to feel how you do. Just don't dismiss it. That's all I'm saying." She turned back to make a drink for herself.

Leaving me with my thoughts. How did I feel? What were the long-term effects? If this had happened to Foster, August, or any of my three sisters, how would I deal with the anger?

I just didn't know.

Kennedy turned to me, her mug in hand. "Rayne sounds like a good man." She offered a smile over the rim of her cup. "I still don't have his story—and you don't have to share—but guys like him..." She glanced out toward the riding ring where the three adults were working with both Champ and Tiffany. "They always have a story."

"Someone's trying to kill him."

She straightened.

"Or, well, tried to kill." I winced.

"You don't have to talk about it, but I kind of get the feeling you need to. I'm a good sounding board, and you know I won't speak to the authorities unless a child is in danger or I'm worried someone might harm themselves. I take it neither of those issues are at play?"

I shook my head.

She settled back. "So, talk."

# Chapter Fourteen

Rayne

"Thank you so much for bringing me." I petted Champ's snout as he rested it on my knee. He'd done so well in the car before, we'd decided a harness and seatbelt would work, and we didn't have to wrestle his crate out of the bedroom. As long as I was beside him, he'd handled the drive all right, just a little anxiety about one loud truck that pulled up beside us. I rubbed his ears.

He snuffed.

"How did it go?" Everett signaled to turn right out of the ranch's driveway.

Even though no one was behind us and I didn't see a single car.

*He's a good man. Law abiding.*

*For all the good that did him last night.*

I still didn't like to think about how close he'd come to a stupid death.

My own risks didn't bother me nearly as much. I didn't have people counting on me. No one would mourn me. No hole would be left in the world without me. "It went well. He's had some training at some point. He's good with the basic commands, even a couple of hand signals. When he feels threatened, though, he reacts, either in fear or with aggression if cornered. Now he's becoming protective of me instead of cowering from women. Torah says it's a sign of more confidence, but we need to nip it in the bud."

"He's bonding to you? Already?"

"That's what Torah said. She wasn't thrilled about me having him out of his crate at night—"

"He did well last night—"

"—but she said it's my judgement call, so we need to get him a comfy bed of his own."

"Oh, we do, do we?" Everett stopped at the sign. Turned on his signal. Checked both ways a couple of times. Finally, he pulled onto the road.

"Sheesh. You drive like a granny."

"Look, I was almost clipped by a guy doing about sixty. Miles per hour. Not kilometers—miles. Which is just insane on these back roads. So, if I want to check repeatedly, then that's what I'm going to do." He pulled over to the side of the road so he could look back over the seat at me. "We need to go to a pet store."

"Well…" I pulled my lower lip through my teeth. "He has food."

"What else does she think he needs?" He drummed the steering wheel.

"Food toys. Chew toys. Regular toys. Balls. A bed…and a basket muzzle."

"Really?"

"Yeah. Torah says." She'd tried one out on Champ and he hadn't liked it one bit, but she told me to go to some site called the Muzzle Up Project and learn how to teach him to wear one. After all, he might have to be around women, like Zephyra, his vet, as well as most vet techs, and safety had to come first. I couldn't argue. "And treats. *Lots* of training treats. Squeeze cheese."

"I don't think you've got the funds to pay for all that." Everett sighed and pulled back onto the road. "We'll go to the pet store near the KFC."

"Oh, then can we get KFC?" I drew in a breath. "I swear I'll pay you back."

He barked out a laugh. "I can afford KFC, and I guess we'll just see how expensive all this other stuff is." He glanced quickly at me. "You're thinking of making this a permanent arrangement? Will he be able to stay in your apartment?"

"I'm not going back there. Even if...people stop wanting to kill me...I'm still not going back."

"Finding a rental is brutal enough in Cedar Valley. With a big dog? Good luck."

My heart sank.

He wasn't saying anything I didn't already know.

"Yeah, I get it. I'll just have to find a way to make it work, you know?"

He chuckled. "You're a smooth talker. Knowing you, you'll figure something out."

I took little comfort in his words.

We rode in silence until he pulled up across from the pet store.

He eyed me. "I suppose you both need to come in. I have no idea what I'm doing."

"You think I do?" I might've snickered that—partly out of nerves and partly out of the joy of seeing him uncomfortable. Despite the recent stresses, he had command of most things. When he and Kennedy had joined us at the riding ring, he'd exuded confidence. Authority.

That sort of turned me on.

We exited the SUV. I attached Champ's leash, unhooked his harness, and then opened the back door.

He leapt out of the vehicle, but when I followed him, he immediately sat at my side. We'd worked a good three hours today with lots of play breaks.

Torah said normally she worked in much smaller chunks, but that she wanted to get as much knowledge into my head as she could.

That Champ seemed eager, and absorbed everything, was a bonus. He even seemed to be starting to recognize his new name.

I said, "Champ was great with Tiffany." That introduction had gone super smoothly. If anything, he was more confident with the therapy dog around. "But I don't know if that will be true for all dogs. If not, or if he gets upset with the strangers, I'm going to leave right away, and you'll have to muddle through." I shortened Champ's leash in my hand.

"Let's hope that's not necessary." Everett held the door for Wags and Love open for us.

Upon entering, we immediately ran into a couple with two little dogs. I dug in my pocket for treats and held one in front of Champ's nose. "Champ, heel. Good boy. Touch." He had his ears half-lowered and rolled his eyes at the strangers, but bopped my hand with his nose. "Good boy." I gave him the treat. "Touch."

"Everett, how great to see you." The younger Black man grinned. "And what a lovely dog. I didn't know you had one. Is he your boyfriend's? Is he friendly?" He'd pivoted his attention to me.

Interesting he assumed Everett and I were a couple. Although I supposed standing there with a dog by our sides in a pet store might make us look coupleish.

I smiled at the man "Uh, he's new, and scared. I've only just got him. I'm figuring out how he'll react around little dogs. Give him space, okay?"

Although the older man appeared uncertain—with his pale face going a little paler, the young man offered a big smile. "I'm Carter, and this is my boyfriend, Byron."

Byron gave me a little wave.

I had the impression he also knew Everett.

"These are our rescue dogs, Sheffield and Rosebud." Carter gestured at the two cute dogs in turn.

Sheffield appeared to be a Jack Russell, while Rosebud appeared to be a mutt. Or at least not a breed I recognized.

"I'm Rayne. This is my dog Champ." I had him do another *Touch* and fed him another treat. He took it, although he had to be pretty stuffed by now. He seemed calmer now the strangers were standing still. "You seem to know Everett." I resisted the urge to call him my *boyfriend*. Wouldn't do to poke the bear since he was smiling at the moment—a rare thing, it felt, when he was around me.

The dogs were eyeing Champ.

He'd cocked his head back, ears coming up as if trying to figure out what was going on.

Carter gestured. "May I hold out my hand?"

"Uh, slowly. I just..."

Torah's words came back to me. *He's been fine with other people. If you stay calm, he stays calm. He takes his cues from you.*

"Of course." I said it with confidence. "But watch his cues."

Carter gave me what I considered a knowing glance. Still, he held his hand out toward Champ.

Who took a step back, ears twitching, body language stiff.

*Let him decide who gets to interact with him.* "Maybe just tell him he's a good boy. No touching."

"Such a good dog, Champ," Carter crooned. "Such a handsome boy." He gazed over at Everett. "Lovely to see you again. Byron sleeps much better at night, knowing our legal documents are all in order." He nudged the man. "Now if I can just convince him to marry me."

Byron appeared...older to me. Like, a significant age gap between the two men. And their demeanors appeared completely opposite. Carter was open while Byron seemed...more buttoned up. Of course, having a huge dog looming over his little ones might scare the shit out of anyone.

Rosebud lunged toward Champ, front end down, tail wagging.

Champ stepped back a bit, then his tail waved slowly.

I had a good grip on his leash, keeping him safely away from her.

Carter grinned. "Oh, they want to play."

In fact, Champ's stance was that of *play*. Torah had given me a refresher on how to read dog body language. Champ's softening lips and forward-pricked ears looked happier than a minute ago. He looked up at me and wagged his tail harder. When I pulled out the ball and gave Champ a bit of space to run, he'd wait to be given permission—much like this.

"We should do play dates." Carter's enthusiasm was very clear. He gazed down to Champ. "Rosebud and Sheffield love to play. And, as responsible daddies, we encourage it." His gaze shot between Everett and me before refocusing on Champ. "Would your daddies let you come and play, Champie? You'd have to be gentle. Otherwise, Byron will panic."

Byron cleared his throat.

Everett nearly choked.

Carter winked at me.

"Everyone have everything they need?" A young woman wearing a crisp black shirt with the store's logo embroidered on it offered a wide smile. "I'm Gallia. I don't believe we've met." She gestured toward Champ.

His demeanor immediately changed, sinking back against my leg with his whole body tense.

I said, "This is Champ. I've only had him a day. He prefers men to women, if you have a male salesperson?" Turning to Champ, I said, "Sit." After a second, he obeyed. "Bingo." I gave him a treat. "Touch." He eyed the woman past my palm before complying for his reward. "Good boy. Touch. Bingo. Touch. Bingo." With each "Bingo" and treat, Champ's demeanor softened. His gaze finally shifted from the woman to my face. "Good boy. Paw." He raised a front foot obediently, something Torah said was a sign he was settling down. He didn't like his feet touched when he was stressed. "Bingo. Clever boy." I gave him three treats.

"Oh, he's well-behaved." She stepped back, clearly familiar with dogs and their body language too.

"I'm Rayne, and this guy is..." I let that hang in the air just a second too long, flicking a quick teasing look at Everett.

Everett cleared his throat.

"Everett. My friend." Huge emphasis on the *friend*. I grinned. For the first time in three days, I was truly enjoying myself.

And almost forgetting there were men out there wanting to kill me.

*Almost.*

Well, maybe not the first time, but excluding the making out part last night because thinking of that in mixed company would just be rude.

"Champ, you are a sweetheart." Gallia caught my gaze. "Can I toss him a T-R-E-A-T?"

"Oh, yes, he's allowed. Land it beside him so he doesn't have to move toward you."

Sheffield suddenly started vibrating.

Carter laughed. "I suppose our little ones can have one more."

I wasn't certain how Sheffield—and now Rosebud—knew what they were getting, but they appeared very pleased.

Gallia opened a jar. She had each dog, in turn, do a simple trick or obey a command.

Champ's was *sit*—which he did brilliantly.

I was like a proud papa.

Carter's *daddies* comment returned to me. Had they rescued the dogs together? Byron still wasn't one-hundred percent comfortable, but he was slowly warming to Champ. He even asked for a treat to toss him.

My boy appeared calmer as he responded.

I was sad he'd come from such...bad homes. Places where he hadn't been appreciated.

Carter nudged Byron. "Uh, sweetheart, we need to get going. Tansy's waiting." Carter gave us an apologetic look. "My sister adores the dogs. Well, Rosebud in particular. She's waiting, and she doesn't wait patiently."

*How old is his sister? Of course, if I knew two friendly dogs were on their way over, I might be impatient as well.*

"We should..." Byron gestured between the dogs.

"Yes, we should, once I know a bit more about Champ. He seems really good with your two." He was eyeing Rosebud and tail-wagging again. I straightened my shoulders. Why I was setting up a doggie date when I had no idea what tomorrow might bring—let alone an hour from now—I wasn't certain. Except I wanted to see more of Byron and Carter. I wanted Champ to have more opportunities to play.

Carter and Byron headed out. Well, after another round of treats from Gallia.

She pivoted to us. Champ tensed again, his ears down, head low. She murmured, "I'll send over Rupert to help you. Let him know what you're looking at today."

I liked how she didn't assume we'd be spending money. That maybe we were just looking around.

By the end of the visit, though, we'd stuffed several hundred dollars' worth of dog stuff into the trunk of Everett's SUV. Rupert had been *very* helpful.

I'd taken Champ to a quiet corner of the store, away from women staff and customers, and Rupert kept bringing us things to look at. Useful things. Indulgent things.

Honestly, I'd tried to keep the spending to a minimum. Everett was the one unable to say no—but I'd have to find a way to pay him back.

He'd said, as Champ's *daddy*, he was allowed to spoil his *child*.

A reckoning was coming.

I only hoped it happened between the sheets.

# Chapter Fifteen

Everett

*I* *must be losing my mind.*

Dog bed, dog toys, dog...I'd lost track.

Every time Champ had gotten excited, his fear and reticence turning to a wagging tail, I'd grabbed the item and put it in the cart. Whatever had come before in his life, he deserved pampering now. He'd get that, with Rayne—and the training and socializing he'd need to be a well-behaved dog. Like he'd been with Sheffield and Rosebud.

Only one day, and Rayne's devotion to Champ was clear.

If my spending some money helped build that relationship, I couldn't say no. I'd have to find a way to let Rayne know these were gifts from me—and that I didn't expect him to pay me back.

We were headed north, toward the townhouse complex, when my phone rang.

*Shit.*

I could pull over to take the call, let it go to voicemail and check later, or—

"I promise I won't listen."

Yeah, like I could believe that. Still, Gil's name on my console had me worried, so I hit the button. "I'm not alone."

"Well...that's awkward."

"He claims he's not listening."

Gil didn't laugh. "You need to come to the office, Everett. Right now."

His tone had my chest tightening and my gut clenching. He didn't use this voice with me often. His—*there's shit going down, and it's serious*—tone.

"I need to drive Rayne back to the—"

"Now, Everett. Corporal Pritchard says he wants to see both of you." He sniffed. "How he knows you've got company is beyond me. Just...now."

"Okay. We have Rayne's rescue dog in the car."

"If he won't kill me, he can come too."

I'd already hung a right turn to take us back.

"Do I need to bring anything?"

After a long pause, Gil responded, "Two venti coffees—Colton says black for him and you know how I like mine."

I did.

"And two large drinks for yourselves. I think it's going to be a long afternoon."

"Might be a line at the Starbucks."

He sighed. "Never mind. Just hustle." He cut the line.

I had trouble reconciling *now* with *stop for coffee*, but his assertion we'd be there for a while concerned me.

"I, like, could take a cab back to your place. If they let Champ ride with me." Rayne attempted being conciliatory.

His effort fell flat.

"If Colton has requested you, then there's a damn good reason. Hell, you might be the reason the police are talking to Gil in the first place." *It doesn't have to be about last night. Much more likely it's Rayne's mess.* "God knows, you're not a choir boy."

"Altar boy."

"What?"

"Isn't the expression *altar boy*?"

"That's what you think is important at the moment?"

"Well—"

"The police are at my office. My mind is going a million miles a minute about all the things that might've happened. Do I wish Gil had been more specific? Of course. Was he circumspect because of you, Colton, or both? Who the fuck knows?" I didn't love swearing, but now was so not the time for manners. "What kind of drink do you want?"

"You don't—"

"Yeah, I do. Gil said to bring four drinks. I don't give a shit what you want—I'm doing what my boss ordered."

"A hot chocolate would be perfect. Uh...white."

"Okay." I pulled into the drive-thru at Starbucks and placed my order. Two minutes later, I handed my card to Tristan for him to swipe.

"Everett! How's it going?" The young man offered a broad smile.

"He's stressed." Rayne leaned up between the seats. "But seeing you makes him happy."

*Jesus Christ...like that can't be taken the wrong way. And how does he know I know Tristan?*

"Well, we love to see him—he makes everyone here smile." Tristan handed the card back. "Still have money on it, so you're good. I assumed you wanted the drinks on a tray?"

I nodded.

"Great, they're all labeled. Blake made them with love."

Blake was possibly one of the sweetest people I knew who'd also—very publicly—faced a difficult time with their transition. Small towns could be horrible for some things—including not accepting when someone needed to change. "You thank them for me."

"Will do." He handed me the tray. "Take care, now."

He always said that.

I always did my best.

Next, I pulled into the drive-thru at Tim Horton's.

"More coffee?" Rayne stared at the tray on the passenger seat, as if counting them in his head.

"Donuts."

"Gil didn't say—"

"Gil implied it."

"Uh—"

"He didn't say not to make any other stops. We always do Starbucks coffee and Tim Horton's donuts." I gave my order for twelve assorted donuts to the woman at Timmie's. I didn't recognize her voice. "I mean, if I'm in a hurry, I do Timmie's coffee. Perfectly good. But Gil prefers his Americano, and I like to give my money to several different businesses." *And why am I explaining this to you anyway? None of this really matters.* "And if you want to stay under the radar, flirting with the barista would not be the way to do it."

"Hey." Rayne effectuated annoyance. "I was not flirting."

"He's dating Olivia." Farrah's friend.

I wasn't a gossip, but I did try to keep up whenever possible with current goings-on. And I wanted to point out I wasn't interested in whatever scheme Rayne had going. Trying to palm me off. Whatever.

"I wasn't trying to imply you should date a guy barely out of his teens."

"He's about your age."

"Oh."

*How do I interpret that one word? So many different meanings...*

Moments later, the Timmie's cashier swiped my card, and I had a dozen donuts. If any were left, we could put them in a sealed container and the staff would enjoy them tomorrow. Donuts never got wasted in our office.

A few minutes after that, I pulled up in the parking lot at the back of the law office. "Do you have a hat?"

"Huh?" Rayne frowned.

"Give me a second." I exited the SUV and went around to the trunk. I didn't keep much there—not wanting to be broken into—but I did have some spare clothes and, score, a baseball hat.

I made my way to Rayne's side.

I opened the passenger door, passed back the hat, and got out the donut box , setting the drink tray on top, while he donned the cap. At least that way, his hair, bruise, and distinctive eyes were mostly covered. He retrieved Champ while I ensured the doors were locked. Together, we descended the stairs and rounded the building.

Gil and Colton stood out front. Conferring.

The cold hit me, and I winced. Maybe I shouldn't have stopped for donuts. I might not have—if I'd known they were standing outside.

Then the doorway came into view.

"Son of a bitch." My breath caught.

"Yeah, pretty much." Gil winced.

"The forensics team has done what they need to do." Colton eyed the drink tray. "They were in town for another incident and could spare someone."

I checked each cup until I found his. I handed it to him.

"Thank you. I really appreciate this."

"Have you slept?"

"I got a couple of hours. Seth Jacobs was on duty and called me."

"Oh?" I handed Gil his cup.

"Apparently Jacobs wondered aloud if this—" Gil pointed to the red paint all over our formerly pristine white front door. "—had anything to do with the *trouble* last night." He arched an eyebrow at me.

"Why don't we go inside?" Colton pointed to the door.

"But the mess—" I still couldn't fathom the rage involved in slashing swaths of red-brown across the firm's entire entry, like blood spray from some wild slaughter.

"I've hired Simeon and Giovanni to come and clean it right now. They'll bring drapes and a heater. I'm paying triple time." Gil eyed the door. "With a hefty bonus if it's all taken care of before the end of the day."

"That's good of them."

"The money didn't sway them, to be clear. Simeon was horrified when he heard what had been done. He believes we're the good guys." He eyed me. "We are the good guys, right?"

"You guys are the best." Rayne smiled.

"We haven't met." Gil eyed my...companion? "But since you have donuts and might keep this guy honest—" He gestured to me. "—you might as well stay." He cocked his head. "And a dog...?"

"This is Champ." Rayne puffed his chest. "He's a rescue."

Champ, who had been sitting quietly, sat a little straighter but seemed calm enough.

"Right. Why not?" Gil turned his attention back to Colton. "You were saying?"

"And this might be related to him." Colton arched an eyebrow. "There are so many possibilities here." He gestured to Rayne before then pointing to the door.

I offered him the drink I'd ordered for him.

He donned a latex glove before opening the door.

"I thought you said forensics had already been by." Surely he wasn't worried about contaminating the scene.

"That red stuff is blood." Gil winced. "And yeah, I didn't realize either. The lab will analyze it and confirm what kind."

"God, I hope it isn't human." Because no way could a human being survive losing that much blood.

"Maybe a victim of a vampire?"

Colton, Gil, and I all turned to stare at Rayne.

Who merely shrugged.

"God save me from your imagination." I whispered the words under my breath.

Rayne chuckled.

So apparently I hadn't been quiet enough.

After locking the front door, Gil gestured for us to follow him upstairs.

I gazed down at my boots.

He waved off my concern. Clearly we weren't going to ask Colton to remove his shoes, so what was a bit more muck tromped through the place?

En masse, we tromped upstairs to Gil's office.

Of course, we could've gone to mine. We could've gone to the informal kitchen with seating for six. Really, we probably should've gone to the conference room with seating for ten.

Nope. Gil wanted the upper hand here.

As Colton and I sat in chairs across from him—with him behind his desk—I could appreciate the power dynamic. He was the boss.

Rayne tugged a chair into the far corner of the office and sat, Champ on a short leash at his side. That was probably for the dog's benefit, but it messed up Gil's powerplay to a degree. Typical Rayne.

I brought him his hot chocolate, setting it on the bookcase beside him, and he gave me a grateful smile.

Seeing as Gil's name was on the door, I had no issues with him wanting to be in charge. And if anyone else did, that was their fucking issue—not mine. Certainly not Gil's.

I set the box of donuts on the big polished desk and offered it to Gil first.

He took a chocolate glaze and saluted me.

I hadn't had anything to do with the selection, but I'd happily take credit.

Colton took a kruller, I took a honey glaze, and Rayne edged over to snag a chocolate dip, passing Champ a treat as he resumed his chair.

*How long will the other eight pastries last? I'm starving.* Still, a coffee and the donut would take the bite out of the hunger.

We consumed our donuts in silence, all using the napkins to wipe our hands.

To my surprise, Champ lay quietly at Rayne's feet. Not begging. Not even looking at the donuts. No, he kept his eye on Colton.

*Interesting.*

Gil eyed Colton. "What do you know?"

Colton, clearly in the process of retrieving his pen and notebook, stilled. "I was hoping you could tell me."

"We don't know anything." Gil held his dark-brown eyes steady on the police officer.

"Okay, we all know that's not true." He passed his gaze from each of us. He pointed to me. "You're Farrah's attorney."

I nodded.

"You were involved in the incident last night—"

"What incident?" Gil scowled.

"Driving while Black." I eyed Colton. "You think the cop last night had something to do with this?" I nearly said *racist* cop, but I still didn't know Colton's full relationship to the man. Yes, they worked together in the same detachment. Were they friends? I was ninety-nine percent certain Colton didn't judge either Gil or me by the color of our skin—but how well did I really know the man?

How could someone know anything in another person's heart?

*You know Rayne's attracted to you. You know as soon as he's healthy that you want a repeat of Halloween. That, despite everything, you still crave him.*

Yep. All true.

"I don't know if Janic would do that. He's been suspended—"

"With pay, I'm sure." Rayne snickered. "Like that's a punishment. Oh, look, here's a punishment—sit home and watch SportsNet all day. Oh, or go out and earn more money while we twiddle our thumbs and decide if a racist asshole like you deserves another chance."

"Well, that's not quite—"

"*Driving while Black?*" Gil glared back and forth between Colton, who'd spoken, and me.

I straightened, making it clear I wasn't going to cower.

"An unfortunate incident—"

"Unfortunate?" Gil again glared at Colton.

The police officer didn't cower.

"Are we talking about human-rights violations? Should we be suing?"

The police officer shifted in his seat. "Look, I'm pushing for a full investigation—including into his past. Nothing came up in the background checks before he joined the force."

"Not good enough." Gil pivoted to me. "Spill."

"Maybe later?" *Please, let's just move on*.

"We have all the time in the world." He eyed Rayne. "You know how to make a pot of coffee?"

"Uh, yes, sir."

"Great. I assume you know where the kitchen is."

"Uh, yes—"

"Don't *sir* me. I'm younger than Everett."

I rolled my eyes.

Rayne grinned. He snagged another donut and headed downstairs with Champ hard on his heels.

"He already knows the story. He was with me last night when I recounted it to Colton. Uh, Corporal Pritchard."

Colton leaned forward to grab a vanilla dip donut with sprinkles. "We're friends here."

"And yet this is an investigation and, when you're finished with the donut, you're going to take notes." Gil wasn't going to be lulled into a sense of false security. "Now, what the fuck happened last night?"

So I told him.

# Chapter Sixteen

Rayne

*B*eing sent out of the room like a child. Jesus.

Still, given Gil's reaction, he clearly assumed I didn't know everything and shouldn't be privy to anything more than what I already knew. Still, he could've *asked* rather than *assumed*.

The man was impressive. And sort of...dorky? Certainly not hot, like Everett.

And the cop could be considered good looking as well—all tall, dark, handsome, and super broody. Like mega broody. He had a story. Guys like him always did.

*So do guys like you. Handsome, black eye, bruises.*

I sighed.

*The coffee's brewing...no reason I can't go back upstairs.* I eyed Champ. "You think we should go back upstairs?"

I could've sworn the dog nodded. I almost gave him the last bite of donut, but Torah's words of warning about *snacks* and *treats* rang though my mind. Being the best dog owner ever was top of mind. She'd given me the tools I needed—I just had to execute the follow-through.

On that thought, I headed back upstairs.

"I don't like this." Gil's growl carried into the hallway.

*Oops, Forgot to close the door all the way.*

"Gil—" Yeah, Everett trying for a reasonable tone.

"I'm not thrilled either." Prichard—hell, Colton, since I was now on first-name terms with a cop—had a nice deep voice. A bit rougher than I'd noticed before.

Everett, his tone tight. "Can we move on? I've rehashed this several times, and it doesn't get easier with each retelling."

My heart lurched.

Everett's upset last night had been clear. I'd hoped it would've eased by today.

*Right, like you're no longer angry at the guys trying to kill you. Isn't it about the same?*

Okay, yeah, that was true.

"What's the deal with Rayne?" Colton's voice rang loud and clear.

*Does he know I'm listening? Maybe.* Although I'd been quiet on the stairs.

"He's just...a mistake." Everett sighed. "But he's with me for now. I don't think this is related to him."

"But you don't *know*." Gil sighed. "Honestly, my friend, I expect better. What do you really know about this guy? Except that you hooked up at a party and he disappeared—"

"Gil." No missing the warning tone in Everett's voice.

"Okay, I need to hear about this." Colton cleared his throat. "And don't leave anything out. Because in no way do I believe he walked into a wall."

"No, you wouldn't." Gil, speaking quietly. "Belief is not one of your strengths."

*Likely that has to do with being a cop. With that sex crimes job. Jesus.*

Colton's voice again rang clear. "Rayne? Are you bringing us the coffees or just going to stand there lurking? We heard the dog's paws on the stairs coming up."

"I can't carry four mugs."

"Then ask someone to help you. In fact, why don't you leave the dog with Everett while you and I get them?"

*Yep, that's a trap.*

"Nope. I don't know how he'll do with Everett."

To my surprise, Everett appeared at the door. He held out his hand for the leash. "In my world, we do what the police ask." He said the words quietly.

I handed him the leash. "Only if you wait out here where he can hear me." Champ was *my* responsibility. I was the one he trusted. Torah had drummed that into me.

Champ gazed uneasily at me.

Or at least that was how I chose to interpret his sad eyes. "I'll be right back, okay buddy?" *How often have people said that to him, and it hasn't proven to be true?* From breeder to first home to second home to Torah? At least four, and the dog wasn't even a year old. That broke my heart. "Sit." I made a hand motion.

Champ sat.

"Stay. Stay with Everett."

He didn't lean into Everett's leg the way he did to me, but he didn't look too spooked.

"That's a beautiful animal." Colton emerged and gestured for me to head back downstairs.

"Torah's a good trainer. Torah Dixon." *Right, because poking the bear is a good idea.* Maybe mentioning Colton's ex-sister-in-law wasn't the brightest. But Everett had mentioned something in passing when we'd been getting Champ secured in the SUV. Just a casual thing. In fact, I wasn't certain he would even remember.

But I had.

Because I'd known, in my gut, I wasn't finished with the cop.

"Torah is an excellent trainer. And I'm certain you're aware she's my ex-sister-in-law."

"Oh?" I affected my most innocent expression as we entered the kitchen. Thank Christ, the coffee was finished. We wouldn't have to stand around chitchatting while it continued to brew.

Colton opened the cupboard above the coffee machine and retrieved four mugs.

I really was hankering for another hot chocolate—but anything that might delay me was a hard *no*. Remembering I wasn't the only one who would take milk in his coffee, I scoured for that and sugar.

Colton poured the four mugs. "What's your last name?"

I heaped sugar into my coffee. Then more sugar.

Colton choked. "Holy shit. I know it's cliché, but you'll rot your teeth. My dentist would have a fit."

"I guess it's a good thing he's not *my* dentist." Which reminded me that I was way overdue to see one. I didn't even have a regular one anymore since I'd left West Van. I'd find one, if I survived the next few weeks.

Colton watched as I added tons of milk to mine and a dash to the others, remembering in time he took his coffee black.

"Last name?"

"I'm like Madonna. Or Lady Gaga. I don't have a last name."

To my shock, Colton grasped my wrist as I tried to head back to the fridge to put the milk away.

I froze, glaring down. "Uh, I don't think you're supposed to be touching me." I managed a steady voice, no sign I was a millimeter from punching him and running.

He blinked.

"I have rights. You not touching me would be one of them." I didn't have a clue what the rules were, but I was willing to do my best to get him to let go of me. His touch disconcerted me—and not in a good way.

Finally, he released my arm. "Why do I get the feeling you'll be in a database?"

"I have no idea because I can swear I've never been arrested."

He continued to stare.

I broke the stare to put the milk back in the fridge. "Think what you like about me, I don't give a flying fuck. But I'm not lying when I say I've never stepped foot in a police station. Sorry to disappoint." Sometimes I could tell the absolute truth.

*Sometimes.*

"There will come a time when you'll tell me everything."

I snorted.

"Did it ever occur to you that by running to Everett, you've likely put his life in danger? Or Gil and the other people who work here? Even Champ and..." He wrinkled his nose. "Torah, if you're working with her. And anyone else who might associate with you."

*Kennedy, Rainbow...plus whoever was up there. The person Everett went to see.*

"Nice try. No one knows I'm here. Unless you snitch to the wrong person. No one's going to get hurt."

"You're delusional if you think that. Even with the burner phone Everett bought you, you're bound to make a mistake. You're just not that smart."

I blinked. "Are cops allowed to insult people?"

"I'm not insulting you—I'm just stating a fact."

*Something tells me he was the reason for the marriage failure.* "Look, I'm missing my dog. Can we just go back upstairs?"

He held my gaze. Unblinking.

*Don't back down. Don't back down. Never let them see you sweat.* That was my grandfather's expression and, until this moment, I hadn't truly understood.

The office was cool enough that the ambient temperature wasn't making me hot...but his cop glare certainly triggered all kinds of negative physical reactions. Like churning gut. Tight chest. Trembling hands. Totally clichéd, but not without justification. "Look, you don't like me—I get that. I'm not your number one fan either. But—"

"Seriously? These coffees are going to get cold." Gil entered the room and moved toward the coffees. "Which one is Everett's and which one is mine?"

Colton grabbed his black coffee and stalked out of the room.

"Uh, this is yours and this is Everett's." I pointed. "Thank you."

He eyed me. "I didn't do it for you. I did it for Everett. He was sweating and panicking at what you might or might not say. He begged me to intervene."

"Well." My nose twitched. "I'm still grateful."

"Show that by answering Colton's questions, for fuck's sake. Only honesty is going to get us out of this mess."

I wanted to assure him I agreed, but I didn't. Sometimes, sure, honesty could be important. Today? Nope, I could totally survive by not telling the truth. I only hoped, in the future, that Everett understood.

To be polite, I allowed Gil to grab the two coffees without argument. I followed him up the stairs, carrying my own drink that was nearly a latté.

Gil hadn't commented.

Champ whined when I arrived back at the room.

Before Gil could give Everett his coffee, I relieved him of Champ's leash. I put my coffee on the bookcase, then sat. I allowed the dog to move in between my legs.

He laid his chin on my thigh and gazed up at me—balefully.

I said, "Sit," and rewarded his obedience.

He paused before lipping the treat off my fingers. Either he was too stressed, or he was holding out for a donut.

"Down," I told him. "Bingo. Good boy." My treat pocket was almost empty. "I'm sorry, buddy. But, you know, at some point I'll have to take a leak without you."

Gil chuckled as he handed Everett his mug. His gaze focused on me. "You haven't taken one in all this time?"

"I might've brought him into the bathroom with me. But I might not be able to do that here."

"Seriously, you can do whatever makes the dog happy." Gil sat in his chair. "Just as long as Everett sweeps up the dog hair afterward."

"Shedding season isn't for another couple of months."

Everett stretched out his arm, eyes on Champ to make sure he didn't mind, and plucked a strand of fur from my thigh—ensuring his hand lingered.

*Possessive or does he not realize he did it?*

I peeked at Colton and was left with no doubt he'd caught the little interaction. I couldn't figure out why Everett was staking his territory. Gil was happily married, and I didn't see Colton as competition. Hell, I didn't read an ounce of queer in him. Not bi and not gay. My gaydar had failed in the past—sometimes spectacularly—but I was pretty certain. Unless he was buried in a closet under the ground.

Everett tucked the dog fur into his pocket. An odd gesture, but unless he dropped it on the floor, held onto it, or put it on Gil's desk, he'd have to rise and scoot past Colton to the garbage can.

I didn't blame him for not taking that route.

"We should also consider our client at Healing Horses." Gil tapped his fingers on the table. He glanced at me.

"You want me to leave?" Jesus, he'd been the one to drag me back up here.

He shook his head. "We're not talking specifics of the case—although your complete discretion is appreciated."

Colton scoffed. "I don't think we can count—"

"Hey." I cut him off. "I'm discreet. I haven't told anyone about my amazing night with a sexy lawyer. I could share—"

Everett glared at me, and he might've whacked my shoulder if Champ hadn't stirred at my side. "You need to know when to shut the fuck up."

I grinned. "See, I can be discreet."

"Go walk the dog, Rayne. Keep your head down, avoid people, and stay out of trouble." His expression softened. "We can't take the risk."

*That* I understood. I rose carefully, then guided Champ out of the office.

Only as we were walking along Fourth Avenue did the enormity of this clusterfuck really hit me.

*I might die.*

*I might get Everett killed.*

And I hadn't yet found the courage to tell him how I really felt about his kindness to both Champ and me.

# Chapter Seventeen

Everett

By the time we hit my townhouse, I was so exhausted I couldn't keep my eyes open.

After Rayne's perky reminder, we'd stopped by the KFC drive-thru and gotten a bucket of chicken, fries, gravy, corn, and mashed potatoes. And two large drinks. Way more food than we needed, but at least we'd have leftovers for a couple of days.

We ate, then, as Rayne took Champ for a long walk around the neighborhood, I showered and crawled into bed.

Only to find myself joined an hour later in bed by a very naked Rayne.

I sighed. "What are you doing?"

"Picking up where we left off."

I sighed as I turned to face him. "Rayne"

"Yep?" He was lit only by the minimal light from the streetlamp farther down the street. He had a weird pink tinge to him.

*I should buy blackout blinds.* A thought I'd had numerous times, but that struck me now as incongruous and totally off track. "You ditched me last night once you got what you wanted. So why are you back? Doesn't Champ need you?"

"Shh." He pressed his index finger to my lips.

I rolled my eyes, uncertain if he could see me in the dark. *Like that's the most important thing...* I pulled back. "Are you shushing me because you don't want the dog to hear his name—and perhaps get agitated—or do you not want to admit you walked out the door?"

"Thank you for buying me the phone."

"Completely not the point."

"It is." He drew in a breath and let it out slowly. "No one's ever done something so sweet, and knowing what happened on that trip...." He winced and something flashed into those otherworldly eyes that were clearly visible despite the crappy light.

"Nothing happened." Even as I said the words, though, I could acknowledge something could've happened. I was within inches, or seconds, of losing my life. Well, at the least of being shot.

"I hope he rots in jail."

"He's not going to jail. He committed an administrative offense—not a crime."

Rayne regarded me. "You're bullshitting me."

"Whether I am or not is of no relevance." The truth was I hadn't gone digging into the RCMP handbook on possible punishments for pulling a gun. On racially profiling someone. But odds were not much. If he'd shot me...

"I still maintain you could go to the press—"

"Off the table. Now, Champ—"

"Shush." He hissed that.

"—needs you. So off you go."

"He told me he hopes I get lucky tonight, and to have fun."

I scowled. "I can one hundred percent guarantee your dog did no such thing."

"Do you really want me to leave?"

"Yes." I breathed. Repeatedly. "No."

Where I expected triumph, though, he gave me only tenderness. I just couldn't find another word for it. *Tendresse* as the French would say. And I didn't need to sink into the romantic language, but it fit. Possibly because I felt the same way.

*Ridiculous. You* know *better.*

I did.

And yet...that didn't matter. So I drew my finger lightly down his cheek—mindful of his bruises. "You still haven't told me the whole story. You know who did this."

"Of course I do." He said the words on an exhalation. "But I'll always protect you."

"I don't need your protection. You could've told Colton—"

"Do we really have to bring the police into the bed? Because as cute as he is—and I'd never toss him out of my bed for eating crackers—he's not here."

"And not likely to be."

"You sensed that too, eh?"

"Even if he wasn't Sunshine's ex-husband, I'm certain he's not gay."

"And that's almost too bad, huh?"

"Not really. I wouldn't want to date him."

Rayne frowned. "Why not? He's one of the good guys, right? All noble and self-sacrificing and, I dunno, kind of like you."

"Okay, first of all, you barely know me."

"I know the important things—"

"Secondly, I would have to be attracted to Colton. I'm not. And I don't try to convert straight guys." Boldly, I stroked down his cheek again. "Bi guys are a different story."

"You're trying to talk me out of my love of women?"

"Absolutely not. You're free to see whomever you want."

"I want to see you."

I sighed. "I'm convenient. I've always been...convenient."

"Everett, you are the least *convenient* guy I know."

*Okay, that's interesting.* "Why did you pick me at the party? The party where the host didn't know you, and no one remembered you? Why me?" A question I'd asked myself about a million times since that night just over two months ago.

His eyes flashed. Something I couldn't identify that was there one moment and gone the next.

*Whatever he says next is going to be a lie.*

This time, I placed my finger against his lips. "Never mind. I really don't want to know."

Unexpectedly, he kissed my finger.

I pulled it back.

"You don't want to hear how you were the most attractive person in the room? Men, women...everyone. I only wanted you."

"That doesn't answer my question. But I don't want you to. We'll move on."

"Oh, yay." He snuck his hand under the covers so fast I didn't have a time to react. Unerringly, he found my cock. "Oh. Already interested. *Fabulous.*"

The campy way he said the word made me smile—despite myself. "So, you're already...hey." He snagged my hand and drew it down to his rather impressive—and very interested—shaft. "You found that conversation a turn-on?"

He stroked me through my sleep pants.

I grasped his naked cock.

He surged into my hand as he moaned. "Everett, you could be reading me the phone book and I'd be turned on. Your sexy voice, your—"

"I don't own a phone book. Haven't for years."

"You're missing the point." He chuckled. "But I'll get you in the mood soon enough. You have condoms?"

I blinked. "Uh, yeah." *And they're not even expired…I think.*

"Your side table or mine?"

"Mine."

"Cool. You grab the lube and hand it over. Then you scoot out of your pajama pants, nab a condom, and fuck me. That sound like a good plan?"

I blinked. "What if I don't think so?"

"Well, I'm not *making* you fuck me. If you didn't want to, then you wouldn't be removing your pants or handing over supplies. Now, if you don't want anal—which is totally legit, and some guys don't—"

"Uh—"

"But you've fucked me before, and I *know* you enjoyed it, and it was pretty much the best I've ever had, and since we're here and both horny, why not just enjoy ourselves? So, grab the lube and let's get at it."

I blinked again. Had that just been one run-on sentence? Had he drawn breath? "No discussion?"

"Nope. That's, like, for post-coital. Although I might fall asleep. I've set an alarm because I don't want Champ to be upset, and oh fuck, I just said his name." He held himself still.

"I'm pretty certain he can't hear us separated by two closed doors and a long hallway." But I wasn't positive. No clicking nails sounded down the hall, though.

"Great. Grab the lube, toss it over, and let's get on with it."

"How romantic of you." *Sarcastic much?*

He stilled the hand stroking me. "You want romantic? I can do that." He stared into my eyes. "You're the smartest man I know. Gil's pretty close, but no cigar. You're perceptive and know when to speak and when to shut up. You're strong—and I don't mean in the physical sense. You maintain you had a plain middle-class upbringing and a simple education. The truth is you worked like hell to get into one of the toughest law schools in Canada. You're charismatic, but it's subtle. You champion the downtrodden and abused when no one else will. You're kind to total strangers and take in stray animals—"

"Champ's not a stray—"

"Shush." Another gentle whisper.

Without an iota of doubt, I knew he wasn't shushing me because I'd said the dog's name. His words were beyond cheesy, and undoubtedly exaggerations...except he clearly saw me in a way few did.

Gil knew all that. He treated me as an equal and a colleague. Nicole asked for my opinion on legal matters, and we got along well. My parents loved me. August and Julian adored me in a platonic sense. Simeon, Maddox, Stanley, and all our other friends knew they could rely on me and, in turn, I knew I could count on them. My clients always got everything I could give.

But Rayne?

He *saw* me.

Unbidden, a tear leaked and ran down my temple to the pillow.

"Oh, baby." Rayne moved his grip away from my privates and, with both hands, grasped my cheeks. "I didn't mean to make you cry."

"You didn't." I sniffed. "I'm fine."

He pressed a broken kiss to my lips. "You are fine. You're...perfect." He let out a long breath. "I'm the one who's a master clusterfuck who brings chaos wherever he goes."

I held his gaze. "Are you really always this bad?"

He bit his lower lip in a show of indecision I wasn't accustomed to from him. "Yeah, I can be. I mean, I chose my profession because I could be all over the place. Satisfying each client means getting paid, but each day is different from the next. I'm barely eking out a living, but that's not from lack of effort on my part. I do my fucking best to hustle all the time. And I make enough to live on. But you're right—taking on a dog is a hell of a responsibility. Especially with my erratic work schedule. But he needs someone, Everett. He needs a champion. And if I can't keep him—which would break me—at least he'll be trained and well-behaved and better able to integrate into a new family."

*What clients? What work schedule?* I didn't want to break the flow of his confidences to ask.

Instead, I cupped his cheeks. "We'll figure out a way to make this work." I wanted to say that my schedule was pretty regular. That between the two of us, we could help Champ. That we could hire a dog walker. A myriad of potential solutions to the problem existed...and I didn't have the right to offer up a single one. "We'll...figure something out."

He kissed my temple. "I love you for saying that—even though we both know it's not true."

"We can make it true." Pure fiction...but what he needed to hear right now.

I pulled away from him, rolled, then grabbed the bottle of lube from my nightstand. As requested, I tossed it at him.

As he positioned himself on his back, I scooted out of my sleep pants and snagged a condom. Finally, I made my way between his spread thighs.

He'd already coated his fingers in lube and was pressing them into his hole. His cock curved up toward his belly—hard and leaking a drop of precum.

I leaned down to lick it.

The purple head pulsed.

"Jesus, you want me to come before you're even inside me?" He said the words through gritted teeth.

"Sweetheart, I want to make you come over and over until your balls are empty. Until you're breathless. Until you're boneless. And then I'll do it again." Questionable whether I'd have the stamina to do any of that—but for him, I was sure willing to try.

He moaned.

"Prostate?"

He nodded.

I grinned. He'd been responsive that night two months ago. Hell, he'd been pretty damn awesome last night before he'd run away. I had no doubt I could bring him pleasure. That wasn't arrogance—that was experience.

Not wanting to wait any longer, I rolled the condom onto my very excited cock. I snagged the lube from where he'd abandoned it and slathered my shaft.

Slowly, he eased his finger out.

Our gazes met.

"Don't go easy on me."

The words should've disconcerted me, but they didn't. He had an inner strength I admired so damn much. But then I glanced at his torso—covered in bruises, bandaged along his side—and I faltered. He didn't appear to have broken ribs—which was truly remarkable—but he had contusions everywhere. *He was shot. I shouldn't be doing this. No fucking way should I be touching him, let alone drilling him the way we both want.* Except stopping now would likely hurt him even more than it would hurt myself. "Turn on your side."

He blinked. "No."

"Yes. Or this doesn't happen. We give each other blow jobs and then I gently hold you all night. You want sex? We do it nice and easy with you on your side." I squinted. "Will the left side be less painful?" God, everything looked painful. And yet he'd carried on all day as if he'd been fine. Not once had he flinched or blanched or hesitated. If not for the bruise on his face, I could've forgotten he was injured at all.

"Everett, that's not what I want."

"Well, it's all I'm willing to give." I placed my hand at the base of my cock—right by the end of the condom.

He clearly saw the threat—that I'd remove it—and he sighed. "You're a shit."

"I thought I was your *baby*."

"Whatever." He mumbled the word as he turned onto his left side. He adjusted several times—clearly trying to find a comfortable position.

*This is such a bad idea.*

"Fuck me already, or I'll go find someone who will."

I rolled my eyes. "And where, precisely, are you going to find this mythical man who will fuck you?"

Even as I said the words, though, I realized I didn't want to know the answer.

"There's a bar, down near Commercial Drive. I know a guy. Works rebar on skyscrapers in Vancouver. Man, his cock—"

"And how are you going to get to Vancouver?" Even as I asked the question, I stroked myself a couple of times to maintain my erection. Talking about other men wasn't a turn-on for me.

"I'd figure it out." He pulled his right leg toward his chest, giving me a tempting view of the most fabulous ass I'd ever seen. I wasn't a guy who had a ton of past lovers—but I'd seen enough bare asses to know when I was in the presence of something rare. So firm and—

"Jesus, Everett. Pretty soon I'll be limp and uninterested."

A hollow threat if ever one existed. One thing I knew for certain about Rayne—he was *always* up for sexy times. Even injured, he could totally be a horn dog.

So I slid in behind him.

He settled back against me.

With gentle fingers, I guided his right thigh back over mine—opening him for me.

As I gripped his hip, I positioned myself and started to press in.

He relaxed.

I thrust harder.

My crown made it in.

He sighed and pushed back against me.

I slid in gently. Oh, so slowly.

"Oh God, baby, you *are* going to kill me."

"Yeah, but what a way to go." I kissed his neck.

He sighed.

From there, our bodies knew what to do. I'd never used this position before, but the depth of penetration was pretty incredible. I continued to thrust and withdraw and thrust again at a steady pace. I wanted him to enjoy this as much as I was—without his pain increasing. Okay, increasing the least amount possible.

"I need more, Everett. Please give me more."

"Jack yourself." I would've tried to reach around, but I had a firm grip on his hips, and that kept him from moving too much—and risking injuring himself again.

He did as bade—and his frantic jerks were much harder and faster than the pace I set. Still, I didn't increase my strokes. Didn't chase the orgasm I wanted with any more speed than necessary. I'd come...in due time.

Even as I had the thought, he snapped, "I'm coming."

"Go ahead." I was proud at how steady my voice was.

His body went rigid as he let out a long groan.

Then he contracted around me, even as his breathing turned ragged.

I continued my unrelenting pace with a steadiness I truly admired in myself.

"Oh God, baby, seriously?" He whined the words.

"Am I hurting you?"

"No." Another whine. "I just...I need you to come." He squeezed my cock. "Please."

I chuckled as I picked up the pace. Whether my self-control came from years of discipline—or because I was older—I was able to stave off orgasms more easily.

Some partners enjoyed that talent. Others, who wanted simultaneous orgasms, found me frustrating. But I'd had guys from both camps come back for more, so I was obviously doing something right.

Even as I had the thought, though, my control snapped. I snapped three successive hard thrusts, my balls drew up, and I came.

Hard.

My breath stuttered.

Rayne laughed.

All was right in the world.

If only for this moment.

# Chapter Eighteen

Rayne

"You're sure you have nothing better to do?" I eyed Torah.

"My therapy dog class is tonight." She petted Champ, scratching rhythmically on his chest. He eyed her, but seemed to relax into her touch. So different from that first day. "So we're going to do another couple of hours of training." She grinned. "I understand you were given the choice between staying at the law offices and the ranch."

I stuck out my lower lip. "I would've been fine at Everett's house. He's got a few streaming services—"

"And think of all the mischief you could've gotten into."

"Hey."

She laughed softly. "Six younger sisters, my friend. A couple who've been responsible from birth. A couple who kept their trouble to teenage years. A couple who will never fully grow up, I fear."

"Is that so bad? To be a child at heart?" Even as I said the words, though, I understood Torah had the wrong impression of me.

Everett had implied I'd simply gotten into *mischief* and was lying low until things cleared up. That I wasn't a threat. Which I wasn't. As long as the bad guys didn't know where I was, everyone was safe.

But the idea that I didn't take things seriously grated. I had a client I'd left in the lurch. Contacting her was too risky, and so she'd think I flaked when she'd really needed help. The client who Everett was connected to—even though both were unaware of my mutual involvement—also would wonder where the fuck I'd gone.

Still, I wasn't ready to correct any misperceptions. Not yet. In the meantime, the choice of the ranch over the law offices had been easy. Sitting bored in a kitchen with nothing to do versus working with Champ and being in the great outdoors?

No-brainer.

And work we did.

Torah put us through our paces, and by the end of three hours, I was exhausted, Champ was in great shape, and we broke for lunch.

Rainbow happily gave Champ the green light to hang in the kitchen with us as she served some kind of casserole that smelled amazing.

Torah coached us so he ended up happily by my chair, chewing a toy, while I chowed down. I'd never tasted anything like a homemade casserole, as my family only did fancy gourmet everything. Most of that stuff I couldn't name either, but it wasn't comfort food.

We were about halfway through the meal when an attractive woman entered the kitchen with a labrador trailing behind her. Tiffany, the ranch's official therapy dog, was already seated under Kennedy's chair.

The newcomer and her dog halted.

Champ, whose leash I still clung to, stiffened.

"Oh." The woman petted her dog, shortening his leash.

Torah rose. "Avery, this is Rayne and his dog Champ. Champ's in training with me, and he's doing amazing, but he's new and a bit unpredictable."

Avery brightened. "Oh. Hi, Rayne. This is Rex." She again petted the dog. "He's a cream Labrador and super friendly with other dogs, loves kids, and sometimes struggles with strangers. Hence, he's not a formal therapy dog."

"Okay." I could appreciate Avery's good looks. She wasn't stunning, like Kennedy. She didn't have ethereal eyes and dark hair like Rainbow and Torah. Instead, she had cute blonde hair, green eyes, an attractive body, and a wide smile.

And, although in the past, she would've been my type—good looking, breathing, and nice—I didn't feel anything toward her.

Nope, I wanted some grumpy Black lawyer dude who knew how to nail my prostate very effectively.

I turned to Torah. "Can the dogs meet?"

"We'll try them out. Rex may be wary of you and Champ of Avery, so go slow." She beckoned me to rise. "Short leashes."

I stood, and Champ came to attention.

Under her direction, we brought the dogs together so they could sniff each other. Rex flicked a look at me, his tail clamped down, but seemed okay with Champ.

My beloved pooch tried to nose his way around to Rex's ass.

I gently coaxed him back.

"Well done. Praise your dogs." When we'd rewarded them, she added, "Avery, why don't you sit near Kennedy?"

Tiffany sat by Rainbow's feet and, obviously, Champ remained at my feet.

"Sure." She sniffed, then spotted the dish. "Oh my God, is that your grandmother's recipe?"

Rainbow grinned. "Of course."

"It's amazing." I sat and, to my relief, Champ dropped beside me and laid his snout on his front paws.

Avery plopped into a chair and was in the process of serving herself when another person appeared.

Champ stiffened.

*Fuck, what is this, Central Station?* I didn't need more strangers seeing me, and neither did my dog.

The attractive, tall ginger with a beard and stunning blue eyes stopped in his tracks. His gaze traveled from me to Champ and then back again.

"The Shepherd is Champ. He's in training." Torah, who'd just sat, rose again. "Justin, ignore him and let him get used to your scent and voice. Sit over there. He's better with men than women, but don't react if he grumbles."

"Never let them see you sweat." He grinned. "I'm a counselor, a father, a husband, rescue dog owner, and a PhD student. Nothing fazes me."

Yet even as he said the words, his gaze flickered to me.

I nodded. "We're getting better at this."

"Great." He made big eyes at Kennedy. "Tell me there's casserole left."

I petted Champ repeatedly, whispering praises as Justin joined the table and, in turn, piled casserole on his plate.

Then he eyed his hands, rose, hustled over to the sink, washed his hands, and then returned to the table.

"So, how's Will doing?" He eyed Avery.

"Isn't that against the rules?" Her cheeks pinkened in a truly adorable way.

"He's been discharged as my patient." Justin grabbed a roll as well, broke it open, and slathered it with the honey butter.

*He must have some kind of exercise routine to be so fit. Oh, wait. Father, husband, student, and...dog owner?* Yeah, that'd keep someone busy.

"I..." Avery cleared his throat. "Things have been...unexpected."

"You mean you fell for him when Rex tackled him?" Rainbow grinned. Then she met my gaze. "Tackled in a good way."

"Will does have a way with Rex." Avery gazed affectionately toward her dog.

"Will has a way with you." Kennedy met Avery's gaze.

"He says he's staying. He's buying the ranch with the trail-riding business." She also grabbed a roll. "Do I think this is too good to be true? That he'll take off back to Alberta and the wide-open range? Sure." She buttered her roll. "But he says he's staying. That he's over..." She eyed me.

I mimed zipping my lips. Attention on Avery and Rex meant more anonymity for me. I forked up more casserole.

At my feet, Champ went back to his toy.

"Well, it's not a secret Will's a widower." Avery ripped off a piece of roll. "He loved her, but she'd been gone five years. He's ready to let go of that part of his life and start a new one here." She fingered the roll. "His sister's thrilled. And I think Will is, too—he'll be close to his niece and nephew. And..." She hesitated. "And might even want kids of his own." She shoved the piece of roll in her mouth.

"Woo-hoo." Rainbow clapped. "That's awesome."

Champ stirred.

Torah said, "Softly, now, people."

I petted him.

Then realized I should wash my hands before eating my roll.

Oh, the world wasn't going to come to an end if I didn't. I wasn't touching other people's food. And Champ had Frenched me this morning while I'd been praising him and he'd been giving me cheek-aimed kisses.

We needed to work on our timing. Because as much as I loved him? Gross.

"Sounds like everything worked out." Kennedy offered Avery a grin. "The magic of Christmas."

"Well, rumor was the wedding went well and the grooms are enjoying Europe." Avery grinned.

My ears perked.

Kennedy caught my gaze. "Everett's friends Dean and Adam. He was here for the wedding on Christmas Day. Quite an affair."

"Sleigh rides and everything." Rainbow pressed a hand to her chest. "And now Foster and Arnav are going to get married here as well."

"What?" Avery's jaw dropped.

"I know, right?" Justin grinned. "Another Healing Horses success story."

Rainbow pointed to me. "If Rayne and Everett stay together—"

I coughed. "Uh, yeah, no."

Justin regarded me. "Apologies. I met your dog, but not you."

"Such is the way when you have pets," Torah piped up.

"Yes, but I feel like we should be properly introduced. I'm Justin Bridges. A good friend of Everett's. Or so I thought." He added that bit with just a bite of humor.

Just a bite of warning.

"Hey." He glanced over at Rainbow and bent to rub his shin.

I actually burst out laughing.

She winked at me.

Justin poked at his food.

"I'm a recent addition to Everett's...life." I took another mouthful of the most delectable, creamy concoction. I tasted peas, ham, and several flavors I couldn't identify. Probably because my palate was accustomed to KFC, burgers, and pizza. *I need to do better.* Yeah, like vegetables and fruits. Working out might keep me looking decent, but my metabolism wouldn't always be that of a twenty-four-year-old. And I needed to get nutrition from food rather than supplements and vitamins.

Justin tilted his head. "How recent?"

*That way lays danger...*

*Oh, fuck it.*

"We met at Quinton's Halloween party."

This time, Rainbow snickered.

Justin and Kennedy exchanged confused looks right up until...

*Wait for it...*

The counselor poked his fork at me. "You."

I shrugged. "Maybe."

Avery slowly raised her hand. "Curious minds...?"

Justin's eyes narrowed. "Everett met a guy at Quinton's Halloween party. Asked all of us...well, shit."

This time, Kennedy arched an eyebrow at him.

He winced. "Sorry."

"She doesn't care." Torah grinned. "She just has to pretend because, you know, clients."

"Of which there are none right now." Avery leaned closer. "What did Everett ask?"

"If any of us knew a guy named Rayne." Justin narrowed his eyes. "None of us did. And we didn't ask any other questions because, you know, respectful."

"Oh yeah." Rainbow grinned. "I saw Everett that night." She pointed to me. "I suspect after you...?"

"Took off?" Because just about everyone at this table knew—or could figure out—what had happened. I was just giving them information that would've come up eventually. I'd already figured Everett had asked about me. And we hadn't thought to give me an alias when he'd brought me around here. Anyone could've put this together.

"He didn't give me your name." She tilted her head. "But he was damn..." She glanced at Kennedy.

"Perturbed." Kennedy buttered her roll. "I seem to recall hearing the name *Rayne*. Things have been so chaotic around here that I didn't put together the pieces. And those two have been remarkably tight-lipped."

Justin held my gaze. "You didn't have to say anything. Hell, maybe you shouldn't have. None of our business."

"You honestly think no one was going to put it together?"

"If Everett hadn't asked any of us..." He narrowed his gaze. "Quinton."

I laughed. "Yep. Not a guy exactly known for discretion." From everything I'd learned about the nurse, I'd assumed a notice on the internet looking for *Rayne* should've appeared mere moments after I'd bailed from the party without leaving my contacts. I still couldn't figure out if I was insulted he hadn't, or impressed at his restraint.

"Well, I say we don't tease Everett or Rayne." Avery surveyed the group. "Because that's exactly what *some* of you would do."

Four people sat a little straighter.

"Oh, I didn't mean Kennedy."

*The boss. Probably a good catch.*

Justin pressed a hand to his chest. "I would *never* tease one of my dearest friends."

Avery narrowed her eyes.

Torah snickered.

Rainbow outright laughed.

He shrugged.

"Avery's right." I sat a little straighter myself. "Well, not just about teasing Everett. I'm...a sore spot with him. I wasn't good to him—and that's on me. I didn't realize..." I held Justin's stare. "You're right. I shouldn't have said anything."

He dipped his head. "And you're right. Certain friends would've put things together." He gestured to Rainbow. "He might not have given your name to everyone, but it's safe to say a bunch of us saw the change after Halloween. I'd hoped he'd be recovered by New Year's but..." He frowned. "When did you, uh, reappear?"

"The morning of the first."

"Holy shit. Sorry, boss." He cut Kennedy a quick glance then refocused on me. "So you've been back for three days?"

"Technically four, to those who can count."

"I don't suggest you mouth off to Justin." Torah nudged my shoulder.

"I wasn't—"

"And she's teasing you." He cut his gaze to her. Then refocused on me. "Where, precisely, are you living?"

"Uh..."

"And when did you get the dog?"

"He rescued Champ three days ago. Got him from me." Torah buttered another roll.

*We can take two rolls? Score!*

"Right." Justin shook his head. "So you and your dog are...living with...Everett?"

"Temporarily...?"

Avery shook her head, undoubtedly trying to warn me I was up to my neck in shit. Completely my own fault. Naturally.

Justin caught Kennedy's gaze.

After a very long moment, she gave a slight nod.

He took a deep breath, then refocused on me. "Now, Everett's older than me."

Which I'd figured. That this guy was halfway between the two of us.

"And he probably wouldn't thank me for sticking my nose into things—"

*Then why do it? Oh, right, because you're...wait for it...nosy.*

"—but he can sometimes be more fragile than he appears."

"Is that a clinical diagnosis? Should you be sharing it with me?" Because I wanted to tell the guy to shut the fuck up. He had no idea what Everett's life was like. At least based on Saturday night, it could be super shitty.

"He's not speaking as a clinician." For the first time in a while, Kennedy spoke. Her husky voice carried the authority which she was due. "I was unaware of your history with Everett when you arrived. Truthfully, it's not any of our business. He's asked us to watch out for you today while, in the same breath, assuring us that you won't bring trouble up here."

"I won't."

Justin cocked his head. "That's a decent makeup job."

"Thank you." Rainbow preened.

"God knows I wasn't going to try." Torah snickered that.

I wouldn't have pegged either woman as huge makeup users—both were fresh-faced and favored jeans and plaid shirts. They worked with dogs and horses.

But looks could be deceiving—and I knew better than most not to make assumptions. Rainbow had offered her help the moment I arrived, and not asked questions.

"Where did you get the shiner from?" Cool bright-blue eyes from an adorable ginger were laser-focused on me.

"A wall."

I could've heard a pin drop. Only Champ's panting caught my ear. When had he started? Was he sensing my increasing discomfort?

Justin swallowed. "You realize you're sitting at a table of counselors, therapists, and siblings of therapists?"

"Uh, yeah." I pushed a stray pea around the plate with my fork. "If I say Everett didn't do this to me...is that good enough?"

"It's not a matter of what is *good enough*." Kennedy examined me. "We're against people living in denial—especially if they're in danger."

"Everett didn't do this to me. An abusive partner I might go back to didn't do this." My gaze shot to everyone at the table. "Everett knows what's going on." *Mostly and please don't ask questions.*

"Then we'll respect that." Kennedy met the gazes of everyone at the table before finally settling those piercing eyes on me. "Ask for help if you need it. If there's one thing this place is known for, it's helping those in need. If we can't do it ourselves, we know people who can." She offered a small smile. "Including ex-husbands."

"Oh, fuck Colton." Torah bit off the words.

Everyone laughed.

The tension dissipated and, mere minutes later, Rainbow served brownies.

Justin's quick glances didn't ease my stress, but something had shifted, and I found I couldn't regret that.

# Chapter Nineteen

Everett

I sat across from Gil in my office and tried to stay calm.

"You did everything you could." He offered a sympathetic smile.

"She shouldn't have had to go through that." Acid churned in my gut. I'd never unsee the terror Farrah had endured in the courtroom—having to testify against those men.

She'd also given new details—which worried me. Her story was horrific enough if she'd stuck to what she'd shared with the crown prosecutor. Remy Stevens had guided Farrah through the questions. Just like we'd practiced.

But Farrah added things I'd never heard. Some were little details that didn't matter. Other things—like implicating several women in the planning of the attack—had come out of left field. Had left me with hundreds more questions. Like, if Colton and Remy had known, might some of the women been charged? Could they have turned into witnesses and saved Farrah the stress of having to spend hours on the stand while being grilled by the defense attorneys?

The judge kept things moving forward and, in answer to my fervent prayers, Farrah's testimony had wrapped up just before the end of the day. She might be recalled to the stand but, for the moment, she was finished.

Seth Jacobs had driven her to my office as planned.

Spring Dixon, with the same height and hair as Farrah, had sat in my office with her back to the window for an hour.

Nicole, with Farrah wearing Spring's clothes, had escorted her around to the back of the building. Colton and Dorrie, in their un-marked vehicle, had watched Farrah get into Ryan's car and be driven away.

They'd followed Ryan until they were certain no one was behind them. Ryan peeled off and had driven around the hills north of Mission City for half an hour before delivering Farrah to Healing Horses.

I owed Ryan a lot. I had hardly spent any time in his presence since he'd arrived in Mission City two months ago. He'd kept to himself except when he was around my friend Simeon. They'd fallen in love. When Ryan asked me why I was so stressed last week, I'd spoken in generalities.

He'd spoken in specifics and offered to help.

Kennedy made it clear that Ryan was up to the job. Emotionally, he was on much better footing. Physically, he was good as well. He wouldn't have been able to fight off thugs, but we'd made certain he didn't have to face that. As an ex-soldier, he had a protector vibe Farrah had reacted positively to.

The plan worked.

"I hate waiting."

"She's with Kennedy." Gil nodded. "And Rayne's up there too. With Torah, Rainbow, Justin, and Stanley. It's a party."

"But will that attract attention?"

Gil cocked his head. "Almost everyone on that list either works there, is related to the owner, or is married to someone. I'm glad Stanley and Justin left the kids with Maddox and Ravi for the night. Just to be safe."

Their two kids, Angus and Opal, adored Maddox and Ravi's twins. Pretty much guaranteed chaos with two dogs thrown in for good measure.

"You can head out." Gil checked his phone. "Colton says no one's been near the back alley all night. If they follow you like before, you…" He made a weird motion with his hand.

"Drive all over the place?"

"Yeah, that."

The hills north of Mission City were such that someone had to drive close or they'd lose you. If I was careful—as I was obviously going to be—everything should be fine.

Gil tossed me his keys, which I barely caught because I wasn't expecting them. "It's snowing. Wear my overcoat and hat. Take my car. I'll text Colton we're changing up the plan."

"Don't you think that's a little excessive?"

"Has your SUV been checked for a tracker?"

I blinked.

"It just occurred to me that while you were in court today, someone might've put a tracker on your car."

"You think…?"

"You just rehashed everything they did to that poor woman. Do I think them capable of tracking you to get to her? Yes. Hell, if I'd been on top of things, I would've hired someone to watch the cars."

"You're thinking a bomb?"

"Well, nothing blew up, so obviously that was a little paranoid. But yeah…" He tapped his desk. "I think Colton was on to something when he said the family might be responsible for the blood on the door."

Although forensics confirmed pig's blood, no trace of the perpetrators had been found. Our cameras only picked up a shadowy figure. They'd been careful to keep their face hidden from the cameras—the ski mask helped—and they obscured their footprints in the snow.

We had precisely nothing.

"The height and build resembled Janic." I didn't want to think of the racist cop, but he had to be a suspect.

Colton let it slip the guy didn't have an alibi for the time of the vandalism.

"And Rayne still hasn't given me an adequate explanation as to why he feels it's not because of him." Gil again tapped the desk.

"If they wanted him and knew he was with me, they could've taken him out that first morning—he'd been here for a couple of hours."

"Yeah, but how'd he know you'd show up? The first is a statutory holiday, and this is a business. Plus, we were closed over Christmas."

"We didn't put up a sign we were closed."

"Because we would've been inviting people to break in. Downtown Mission City doesn't see many breaking-and-entering events, but I didn't want to invite them in."

I scratched my cheek. "I don't want to say that he knows me, because that would be ridiculous…"

"But he knew you'd be in the office on a holiday."

"I almost wasn't." Which stressed me out in other ways. What if he'd fallen asleep? What if he'd died of hypothermia?

"But you were."

"Yeah."

"And now he's living with you. And that dog—"

"Champ's a good dog."

"Didn't say he wasn't. Just...you're not exactly a German Shepherd kind of guy."

"What does that mean?"

"Don't take offense—"

"That doesn't sound good."

"—but I see you with, I dunno, a beagle."

"A beagle? Like Ben's?" The teacher lived in a condo a couple of streets over, and I'd met him not long after he'd moved in.

He liked to walk Buddy the beagle with his boyfriend—now husband—Isaac. They made an adorable couple.

"A dog who would walk into a wall because his nose is always plastered to the ground?"

Whatever I might think of Champ, he was always on alert. Not one to obliviously follow a scent on the ground. Unlike Torah's search-and-rescue dogs Bishop and King—both labs—Champ didn't have the disposition to search that way.

Gil laughed. "Okay, maybe a mutt. You've got a good heart. You might go to the shelter and find...some dog of indeterminate breed."

"Something calm? Like Maddox's Princess Sofia?" The rescue—whom his beloved nieces had named—was the bane of his existence and the light of his life. She was hell on wheels despite being a little white fluff ball. "Anyway, Champ *is* a rescue."

Gil gestured to his jacket. "Get going. And give me your keys."

I yanked them out of my pocket and tossed them over. "That's all?"

"You've got the care package Cullen put together for her, right?"

Because Gil's husband was just that amazing. He'd heard only that we had a survivor who had little of her own, and he'd put together a huge care package with gift cards, baked goods, and little things meant to make the woman smile.

I had no idea how Farrah would receive the basket—but I'd happily deliver it.

My phone buzzed with an incoming text from Kennedy.

—*Olivia's here. Giving you the heads-up.*—

I frowned.

"What?" Gil sat straighter.

"Olivia has gone to see Farrah."

"You worry she might've been followed."

"She's Farrah's best friend." Logical the family might've had eyes on her.

"Did she drive herself?"

Before I could answer, another text came in.

—*Tristan drove her in his car. They say they weren't followed.*—

"Uh, the barista swears no one followed them. I think we can trust that."

Gil and I exchanged a look.

Tristan was a good kid.

Well, not exactly a kid. He was twenty-four and getting close to finishing university.

*Rayne's age.*

But while I saw Tristan as young, but responsible, I viewed Rayne as immature and damn reckless. Yet they were the same age.

"Rayne's up there too, right? Did Ryan stay?" Gil again tapped his desk.

—*Who's up there?*—

A moment passed.

—*Me, Rainbow, Farrah, Olivia, Tristan, Torah, Justin, Stanley, Simeon, and Ryan*—

"Jesús, they're having a party."

—*Oh, and Rayne. How could I forget Rayne?* —

Except, for a heartbeat, I had.

—*Torah, Justin, and Stanley are leaving. Are you on your way?* —

—*Yes.* —

—*Great. See you then.* —

"A party?" Gil frowned.

"Well, a whole pile of people. I'm kind of surprised all eight Dixon sisters aren't there." I said this only in jest—where one was found, often all could be within earshot.

I loved my own sisters but didn't go searching them out all the time. Perhaps a loss on my part, but I'd had enough of them growing up.

"So you don't need to go up."

My gaze shot to Gil's.

"Except, oh shit, your boyfriend is up there."

I growled. Yep, actually growled.

He laughed uproariously. "Go, buddy. You deserve a night of..." He sobered a bit.

"Yeah, it's not a celebration. That'll come with the guilty verdicts."

"How soon?"

"Crown will finish tomorrow with Dorrie testifying about the psychological trauma victims suffer. Remy felt buffering Farrah with the cop who found her and then the cop who investigated would sort of insulate her testimony. Farrah's telling of the story is critical—but professionals around her could verify her assertions. Especially the stuff she said to Seth as he waited for the ambulance. She believed she was going to die. Hell, she almost did."

"Yeah." Gil winced. "Hard to celebrate even if the bastards get serious jail time."

"We'll see. I'll be in the courtroom."

"She's lucky to have you."

I didn't have an easy answer for that. I was doing this work pro bono after Colton and Dorrie approached me when they worried Farrah wasn't strong enough to advocate on her own behalf. I hadn't hesitated.

Gil made room in the accounting ledgers to ensure I got paid from the firm's pro bono funds and did right by the young woman. I'd have done it without payment, but I was deeply grateful.

So I remained mute as I grabbed his coat. I was a bit broader in the chest, but not so much I couldn't do the thing up. I put his trilby cloth hat on my head. Ironic, because I'd teased him mercilessly about the *grandfather* hat.

Then he told me it had indeed belonged to his grandfather.

Knowing what high esteem my friend held the man in, I'd stopped the teasing. Somehow the weight of that generational brilliance felt good on my head.

Gil's grandfather started this law practice when Black men were barely admitted into law school, let alone settled in a small town and hung out a shingle. He'd fought plenty of prejudice over the years, but the law practice—passed down twice—thrived.

"Thank you." Because, really, what else was there left to say? I tipped my hat to him, then headed out. I unlocked the door downstairs and glanced around the street before relocking it. I didn't spot anyone as I walked quickly around the side of the building. Ostensibly against the snow, I pulled the hat lower and the flaps of the coat higher.

Using Gil's remote, I disarmed his car alarm. Moments later, I slid into the plush seat. I hit the starter, the defrost button, and then secured my seatbelt.

After a minute, when the windshield and windows were clear, I backed out of the spot. A car pulled in behind me. I couldn't see whether Dorrie or Colton was behind the wheel, but it didn't matter—both were incredibly competent drivers.

I drove to the end of the alley, hung a left onto James Street, and began the steady climb up the hill that would take me away from downtown Mission City.

Given the late hour, traffic was sparse as I headed over to Cedar Street—the main road that would take me into the hills north of the town.

Gil's favorite jazz played low on stereo.

I chanced a glance at the console.

Ugh, too complicated to try to change things.

*You'll live.*

True enough.

I finished climbing the next big hill and emerged into the flat part of town where many home and townhouses had been constructed in the last ten years. The subdivisions were completely different from the fields that had been here when I'd first come to town.

While I'd saved for my townhouse, I'd lived in a condo near the office.

I checked my rearview mirror, comforted to see the same headlights behind me.

Soon I was driving into the hills where properties were often multiple-acre and the distance between houses could be substantial. People who lived out here tended to be more independent. More able to look after themselves and their properties. More self-sufficient. They had to be because these electrical power lines were the last to be fixed if they came down in a storm, and these roads were the last to be plowed after major snowstorms.

My phone rang.

*Shit. I can't answer it.* Not only was that terribly illegal—and the police were following me—but the hairpin turns made taking my eye off the road, even for a moment, incredibly dangerous.

The phone stopped.

*Oh thank God.* I'd check my messages as soon as I got to the ranch.

My phone started ringing again.

*Fuck.*

Making a quick decision, I pulled over to the shoulder.

What constituted a shoulder—which was barely the width of Gil's car. If a cyclist and another vehicle came by, then we were all fucked.

I put the car in park and angled myself so I could pull my phone out of my back pocket.

*Gil*

I swiped to accept. "What the fuck, bud. I had to pull over to take the call."

"Where are you?"

"Heading to the ranch. Why?"

"Colton texted. They're here waiting for you."

"No, they're right behind me."

Even as I said the words, the car, which had pulled over behind me, revved its engine.

"Oh shit."

I dropped my phone as I tried to get the car into drive. If I could just get moving, then I might—

"Everett!"

Gil's voice was the last thing I heard before the crunching of metal and the smashing of glass exploded around me.

# Chapter Twenty

Rayne

*B* *less me father, for I have sinned.*
 *It's been...*

Fuck.

I couldn't get my brain to emerge from the fog of panic. Because I could not, for the life of me, calculate the however-many-odd years since I'd attended confession.

Having attempted to erase everything to do with my bigoted priest after he'd accidentally discovered I was bi and had threatened me with eternal damnation, dates became fuzzy. Math—never my strong suit—had become impossible.

"He's g-going to be okay." Simeon repeated the words he'd uttered six times since we'd gotten on the road.

"He's being medevacked to Royal Columbian Hospital." I tried to speak past the lump in my throat. "They don't medevac people who aren't in serious condition."

"RCH's trauma center is better than Abbotsford's. They're just being safe." Ryan squeezed my shoulder. He'd generously offered to sit in the backseat of Simeon's roomy pickup truck so I could sit in the front.

What I wanted was to be in Everett's townhouse with him, Champ, and a couple of beers.

Instead, Champ was hunkering down with Torah—something I still didn't understand how had happened—and I was in a pickup truck with two very kind, but strangers to me, men.

*They're friends of Everett's.*

Colton planned to question Everett, but based on the little Gil had provided when he'd shown up—driving Everett's SUV—there wasn't much Everett could likely tell.

From his call with Gil, he'd believed Dorrie and Colton were behind him, and about the time he realized he was wrong, the other car had rammed him and, eventually, pushed his car into a tree.

The firefighters had needed the jaws of life to extract him, and the paramedics decided to fly him to RCH as a *precaution*. I didn't really believe that he wasn't gravely injured. On top of whatever crush injuries he'd suffered, he'd also been unconscious. Something about a gash on his head.

I hadn't been able to take it all in. Frankly, I was terrified.

"We should call his family."

"Gil's called them. They just live down the street from the hospital, so they're probably already there." Ryan with his soothing voice.

I knew almost nothing about these two men. Except Ryan had fought with the Ukrainians—against the rules, since Canada wasn't a party to the war. He'd been injured and had come back to Canada.

Simeon was a handyman.

They'd met at Healing Horses, and the rest had been a sweet courtship, and now they were together.

"How do you know so much?"

"He has a knack f-for these things." Simeon offered a smile. Pure pride.

Ryan chuckled softly. "Colton and Gil didn't realize I was eavesdropping. Not exactly aboveboard."

"You got information I need—I don't care how that happened."

"You know that Gil and Colton are coming to the hospital, right?"

I nodded at Ryan's question. "Yeah, I did catch that much." In fact, they were directly behind us. I was adamant I was going to be by Everett's side when he woke up.

Both men, in turn, pointed out I wasn't kin.

I maintained I didn't give a shit.

In all the confusion, though, I had taken Ryan and Simeon aside and let them know a minute chance existed that I might be the reason Everett got hurt. That giving me a ride might risk them.

Both men decided to live on the edge and not to worry. Plus, with Colton following, we were safe. Heading home would be an entirely different story. That said, my only other alternative was getting a ride with either Colton or Gil—and that wasn't going to voluntarily happen. Because until we knew what was going on, I was sort of viewed as...a witness? A suspect? I wasn't under the impression either particularly saw me as a victim.

Bruises notwithstanding.

I wished my ass had been a little sorer. Everett's gentleness had been sweet—but I'd wanted passion and violence. I'd wanted to forget all the shit that had come before.

Basically, I wanted a repeat of Halloween.

Instead, he'd given me a whole new set of memories. Of tenderness. Of kindness. Of holding me into the night.

I hadn't run from his bed last night. Maybe I'd been too tired. Too wrung out. Or maybe I'd acknowledged Champ would be okay and what I really needed was the reassurance Everett could give me.

That everything would be okay.

Now, he was fighting for his life, and I was panicked.

As we raced along the Mary Hill Bypass and then merged onto the TransCanada highway, my mind whirled. I couldn't fathom what was happening. Somehow, Everett was injured. Was this my fault? Had I brought this down on him? I couldn't gauge. Couldn't orient myself. I was one-hundred percent certain no one had followed me to Mission City. They could've easily taken me out as I'd huddled in front of Everett's office. My phone was long dead, and I hadn't tried to revive it. So that was out. I hadn't made contact with anyone I knew, hadn't touched my car.

So I wasn't the problem. *Can't be, right?*

We exited the highway and merged onto the road that would take us to the hospital.

The real question was why had the disguise not worked? Gil had explained, and again, more questions than answers remained.

Things we'd only have an answer for if they caught the perpetrators.

A phone rang.

"I'm p-putting it on speaker. It's C-Colton." Simeon hit a button. "N-not alone."

"I figured." Colton's voice rang through the truck's sound system. "And you're driving. Just wanted to let you know they found the car that hit Everett. On fire. Up near the Stave Lake Dam."

"Shit." Ryan against squeezed my shoulder. "They get the fire out?"

"Yeah. With the time of year, and the snow on the ground, nothing else caught. A forensics team is on their way—"

"They're not going to find anything." I sighed.

"No, probably not. Still worth trying, though. I'll let you get back to driving—just thought you'd want to know."

"T-thank you." Simeon kept his eyes on the road as we neared the hospital.

The line disconnected.

"So much for knowing who did it."

"The car will be traceable, right?" Ryan's voice carried a touch of optimism.

"Not if it was stolen."

"Oh."

"We're h-here." Simeon pulled up to the front entrance.

"Thanks."

"We'll p-park and then come in." He offered a small smile.

"Thank you." I gazed between the two of them. "You're okay to stay?"

For the umpteenth time, Ryan squeezed my shoulder. "Chia, our dog, is home with Nanny and Bops. No one else is waiting for us. She'll be pampered to bliss. The longer we're gone, the more baby carrots she's going to get."

Somehow, even though I didn't understand everything about dogs and family, I understood this. "That's great." I undid my seatbelt, opened the door, and slipped out of the truck.

After I closed the door, Simeon drove away.

I stared at the entrance. What if things were worse than they'd said? What if—

"You okay?" A tall man in some kind of dark green approached me. His blond hair and blue eyes made him damn attractive. He was on the slender side while the woman next to him, also wearing the outfit, was curvier.

I blinked. "Yeah. They just brought a friend in. I'm...stressed."

"These are awesome doctors." He cocked his head. "I'm Tex. This is Samantha." He had an accent that sounded vaguely Texan to me.

"Okay." I squinted. "And you are...?" I couldn't figure out why this guy was talking to me. Did I really look so lost? I should've moved on, but something held me in place. Some attempt to understand.

"Oh, we're a flight crew that does runs around Cedar Valley."

Ah, flight suits.

"My friend just got brought in via helicopter. From Mission City."

Tex puffed his chest a little. "That was us."

"Oh. How is he? Sorry, I'm a bit freaked out. He's...it's important. I appreciate anything you can tell me."

"Well, he's headed into surgery—"

Samantha elbowed him in the ribs. Her dark-blonde hair swished in the ponytail, and her eyes narrowed on Tex. "You know you're not supposed to say anything." She offered me an apologetic smile. "He's usually pretty good." She glared at him.

He winced. "You just..." He cocked his head.

"Yes, I'm a *friend*. I don't know if they'll tell me anything."

"Yeah. I'm glad I married my husband, Davey. So I don't have to worry about any of that. We, uh, live in Mission City too."

"Okay." I waited.

"He's being operated on by one of the best cardiothoracic surgeons in the region." Samantha offered me a sympathetic smile. "He's in the best hands."

*Okay, so she gets it. They both do.* I wasn't family. I didn't have any rights.

"We were just grabbing a soda before heading back." Tex pointed to the sliding glass doors.

"And you came outside?"

Samantha shrugged. "I'm from up north. I like brisk."

"And I was originally born in Texas, but was raised in Mission City." Tex exhaled on purpose, and I could see his breath "This cold weather doesn't suit me, but I do whatever my copilot wants." Even as he said the words, both their phones rang.

"Shit." Said simultaneously, although Tex's deep timbre was louder.

Within moments, they were sprinting back into the hospital.

"Best of luck. Your friend will be fine." Tex threw the words over his shoulder as they disappeared.

"You okay?" Ryan, to my startlement, tapped me on the shoulder.

I blinked. As if that could somehow clear the fog of the last five minutes. I cleared my throat. "I just met the pilots who brought Everett here. They weren't supposed to tell me..."

"T-tell you what?" Simeon's hazel eyes appeared greener in the neon light of the emergency entrance sign. His blond hair contrasted with Ryan's bright red—and those thoughts were completely incongruous with what they'd just asked me.

"Uh...surgery. With a cardiothoracic guy? One of the best?"

Ryan frowned. "I wonder if it's the same guy who operated on me? Probably not, since I was at Vancouver General." He shivered. "Is there a reason we're standing out in the cold? They're predicting more snow. I don't remember a winter with so much of the white shit."

Simeon nudged him with his shoulder. "It's magical, and I seem to remember you liking being snowed in."

"Uh..." Ryan's expression turned first pensive, then he got a lovesick look on his face. "Yeah, okay."

"I don't want to go in." I wrung my hands. "I don't know his family. What if they—"

"What's going on?" Gil approached.

He faltered when he spotted me.

"No." I held up my hands. "I don't know anything. I'm too scared to go in."

"Okay, well, Everett's family is here, and they're expecting us."

"Sounds good." Colton jogged over, clearly having overheard the conversation.

I debated telling him about the cardio guy, but they'd find out soon enough. I had no doubt if Everett's family was going to share, it would be with the cop investigating and the partner at the law firm. That felt logical. If I stuck close, I might eavesdrop.

Ryan linked his arm in mine. "We won't know until we go in."

Fifteen minutes later, after Everett's mother, Janisse, had provided us with a thorough update, I dropped to a chair in the waiting room.

*Chest wall injury. Compression. Damage...*

Oh, and Ryan had introduced me as Everett's boyfriend.

To what end, I had no idea.

As Everett's dad approached me, he held out his hand. "Melville."

I shook. "Rayne."

"Well, Rayne, seems we have some things to discuss." He dropped into the chair next to me. "So how did you meet Everett?"

*Oh shit.*

# Chapter Twenty-One

Everett

"You're okay, just open your eyes for me."

A soothing voice whispered the words near me, but I couldn't grasp them. Any clues to the speaker escaped me as I struggled. *Where am I, how did I get here, and why the fuck am I in so much pain* crowded into my aching head.

I tried to lift a hand to that head, but gentle pressure held me down.

"Don't try to move right now. You're doing great. But I do need you to open your eyes."

A persistent beeping permeated my pain-laced brain.

I tried to lick my dry lips.

*I'm in a hospital.*

But why?

Realizing answers wouldn't be forthcoming if I didn't open my eyes, I cracked my left one open a sliver. "What...?"

"I'm Theresa, your nurse. You're in recovery at Royal Columbian."

"How...?" I tried to search my memory, but I kept coming up with nothing. Then, "Rayne?" I closed my eye again. Relief flooded me as the light was blocked.

"Your partner? He's in the waiting room with your parents, a business partner, a couple of friends, and a police officer." She pressed a hand to my shoulder.

I was trying to process Rayne and my family in the same room when the rest of her words connected. "Police?" Another croak.

"Do you remember anything?"

Thinking hurt, but I tried to piece together my life over the past few days.

*Rayne. Driving while Black, Farrah. Rayne. Court...*

*Gil.*

*Car.*

"Was I in a wreck? In my boss's car?" I had no memory of a crash, but dread overtook me. Surely he'd understand. Had I spun out on black ice? The roads could be treacherous, and if one was tailgated—

Memory returned in a painful flash. "I was rammed." The sound of shattering glass and crunching metal had my breath catching. Which contracted my chest. Which seized me with a blinding pain. "Fuck." I couldn't get air behind the word.

Theresa placed a hand on my chest. "Keep breathing. Your surgeon will be here in a few minutes. He's going to check you over. If he gives his approval, we'll move you up to ICU."

"Which police?"

"Uh..." A long pause. "An officer from Mission City."

I assumed Colton or Dorrie, but it might also have been Seth.

"Surgeon?" My chest hurt like a son of a bitch, and my head was a close second on the pain scale. I was able to move all my fingers and toes—for which I was extremely grateful—but I still didn't have a concept of what had happened.

Except someone had rammed Gil's car.

With me in it.

So, had I been the target, or had it been him? Or had it not mattered as long as they got to the firm?

Janic the cop seemed less likely, and Rayne's predicament still weighed on my mind. Still, if a cop was here, then Rayne was safe.

*For now.*

"Everett, Dr. Rodgers is here." Theresa's soft voice penetrated my thoughts. "I don't..."

*Focus.*

Slowly, I opened my left eye.

A tall man stood beside my bed. Or maybe that was simply my perception of him. His close-cropped brown hair suited him. The glasses were a sexy addition to his green eyes.

*You're thinking sex appeal? Right now?*

I shouldn't have been, but under those navy-blue scrubs and white lab coat lay an attractive guy. I squinted to see if the hint of muscle was real or just a figment of my imagination.

*You've got Rayne in your bed, someone tried to kill you, and all you're doing is ogling your surgeon? Maybe you should ask him for a neural consultation as well.*

I tried to ignore my snarky inner voice. Ogling the doctor distracted me from what he was about to say. Or so I told myself. "What..." I swallowed. "How...?"

Nope. Not a single coherent sentence to be found.

"I'm Doctor Leopold Rodgers. I specialize in cardiothoracic surgery. Your crush injuries were such..."

I closed my eyes as his explanation washed over me. Fixed this. Checked that. All okay.

At that, I cracked my eye open again.

He offered a clearly empathetic smile. "That was a lot. Yes, you're going to be okay."

*Barring any complications.* My friend, Arnav, had recently handled a medical malpractice suit. Because shit could happen.

Doctor Rodgers stood a little taller. "My patients have excellent recovery rates."

*Jesus, either he can read my mind or I'm way too expressive. So much for a poker face.*

*Or did I say something out loud?*

*No, my voice isn't working properly.*

*Oh God, my head...*

"Theresa will oversee your transfer up to the ICU. I've briefed your boyfriend and your family about your status. I'll allow one person to visit you tonight, and then we'll see about tomorrow. I don't want you taxing your body. You've had a hell of a crash, and recovery's going to be slow. You're on heavy-duty painkillers. I was worried about the gash on your head, but your intracranial pressure is normal. If the headache gets worse, let a nurse know. I'll be back in a few hours." He checked his watch. "Any questions?"

*Yeah, about two dozen, but my mouth doesn't seem to be working, and my head hurts too much—* "Uh, no." I tried to shake my head, but that brought on a wave of pain and, oh fun, nausea. I closed my eyes.

"Then rest. I know it sounds trite, but you need rest."

His voice faded as I sank into that darkness.

I sort of woke as my bed was moved, but I sank back into oblivion as soon as Theresa wished me luck.

Luck? My chest ached, my head hurt, and I felt like I'd been hit by a truck.

Or a car.

Or whatever.

My mind muddled the dreams, as Rayne was the one in the accident, and I stood over his body laid out on the cold, icy asphalt. I tried to reconcile that image with the fact he was okay.

*Or is he? What if they're targeting him? What if the bad people find him?*

I drew in a ragged breath—bringing agony to my chest—as panic seized me.

A hand stroked my forehead. "Rest, baby boy. The doctor says, rest."

I'd recognize that voice anywhere. "Mom?"

She chuckled. "And you don't even need to open your eyes."

"No, I don't. I'd know your voice anywhere." I cracked an eye.

At nearly sixty-five, my mother was a handsome woman. Distinguished—both in her work life as well as the fact she'd raised four kids. My sisters were all successful—each in their own way. Be that motherhood, career, or the arts. Yet...my thoughts splintered. Mom hadn't done that alone. "Daddy?"

"Waiting room. Along with half-a-dozen other people or so."

I frowned even as I closed my eye. "Do I want to know?"

"Well, your father, Denali, Ursula, Gil, Simeon, his boyfriend Ryan, some cop named Colton and, of course, your boyfriend." No missing the teasing tone.

My eyes shot open.

Pain hit my brain.

Hard.

"My b-boyfriend?" I managed to stammer out the word.

She laughed. "Lovely young man named Rayne. Swears there's a story behind his black eye and that you weren't involved—which I'm grateful to hear." She grinned. "I know you're going to be okay, so I'll tease you. He's cute. Denali keeps eyeing him."

My sister. The actress. The gorgeous one who'd recently nabbed a role on some series. A big deal I should've paid more attention to.

"Rayne's…" I closed one eye as if that could make my brain work.

"Well, if I had to guess, I'd say bisexual." She winked. "But he's also clearly besotted with you and not interested in your sister beyond that first appreciative look. Ursula's been teasing them, and he's just not listening. Too busy worrying about you."

My other sister. Who'd invented some kind of hair product for Black women and was in the process of getting a patent and then planning to start her own business. She blew my mind.

Hell, all three of them did.

I was glad Laila hadn't come. She was very pregnant with her third child and had been ordered to rest.

*That word again.*

"Mom, I'm worried."

"I know, baby." She stroked my hand. "Colton says everything is under control. Gil doesn't seem upset—"

"Gil's good at saying that." I wrinkled my nose. "His car. His clothes."

"So he said. Colton says the investigators are looking at all angles, and you don't need to worry about any of this. Now, Daddy's chomping at the bit to see you, but I think Rayne is going out of his mind."

"Only one visitor." A young man in scrubs breezed in. "I'm Dominic. Your nurse. You're in the ICU, in case you haven't figured that out. So, one visitor at a time. Fifteen minutes maximum—and that's if you're up to it. I'm a lioness, in case you wondered. Fiercely protective of her cubs."

*Lioness? Is that some kind of weird...?* Too much brain power required. "Rayne, please, Mom. Dad'll understand...right?"

She smiled. "He will if I tell him to."

Which was a joke in the family. Mom ran a tight ship, and Dad was fun. He could step up to the plate—and did all the stuff that kept the house clean and the kids fed—but he was fine with sitting back and letting Mom rule both her school and our house. He admired and loved her.

We all did.

"Thank you."

She kissed my forehead with the lightest of touches. "That cute surgeon says, *rest*." Then she was gone.

Dominic stared at the IV machine and the multitude of lines. Looked like spaghetti noodles to me, but he seemed to know what he was doing. He obviously caught me staring. "Fifteen years at this. I'm the best."

I nearly burst out laughing. Guy didn't look a day over thirty. Still, I found myself believing him. "Thank you." More like a croaked whisper.

He grinned. "I take it your parents hadn't met your boyfriend?"

"Uh... I didn't know I had a boyfriend either."

A laugh burst from him. "Oh, you're going to be a fun one, aren't you?" He smiled. "I just started my shift—so you've got me for the day. Ring the bell, okay?"

I tried to take stock of my body.

Dominic must've caught my eye roll toward my groin. "Catheter for now. It'll come out, and we're going to get you moving around. Prevents blood clots. Your chest is going to hurt like a son of a bitch, and we've got you on the good stuff for a while longer. If it hurts too bad, you let me know. You're going to nap for most of the day and hopefully have a solid night's rest at the end of it. Be good, and we'll get you up to a ward soon—away from the chaos of this place."

"I'll lose you..." My attempt at teasing because I liked this guy and, as I waited for Rayne, I could admit the pain had lessened a bit after he'd fiddled with a device.

"I'll keep you in my heart." He winked. "Speaking of..."

Rayne stuck his head in the room. "You, uh..." He noticed Dominic. "Hey. I'm Rayne."

"So you are. Behave or I boot you." With that, Dominic left.

My *boyfriend* took the seat my mother'd recently vacated. Tentatively, he took my hand. "You're going to be okay."

He looked awful. I managed a smile, even as fatigue threatened to drag me under. I had to speak softly, with minimal breath behind it, but he leaned close. "I'll do my best."

In turn, he managed a smile to match mine. "I know you will. You're the most stubborn man I know." He glanced over his shoulder. "Dominic is cute, but that surgeon? He's a looker."

"Oh?" I'd noticed, of course, but this was fun, and I was managing to stay awake, which was what I wanted. More than anything, I just wanted to look at my beloved's face.

*Beloved? What the actual fuck? You fucked twice. You don't even trust him—*

And yet I saw myself falling for him—almost like I was an observer. Outside of my body and looking in. Falling all the way down that slope to *beloved*.

*Okay, maybe these drugs are making me loopy.*

"Yeah. I mean, he's hot. Really hot. And those glasses? Sexy as fuck." Rayne grinned. "I know you noticed."

I breathed, "I might've been at death's door...ogling my surgeon wasn't high on my list."

His face fell.

"I'm teasing. I'm surprised I'm doing so well. Well enough to recognize a hot man." I squeezed his fingers.

He perked. "Yeah. A few days in the hospital, and you'll be ready to come home—"

"To what?"

"Huh?" He furrowed his brow.

I cleared my arid, aching throat. "Are you still going to be here? Are bad guys still going to be chasing us?"

"Colton thinks his coworkers are going to catch whoever did this to you. I mean, the car was left out of town and burned out, but that doesn't mean they can't still figure out who did this."

I closed my eyes briefly, then licked my chapped lips. "What happened?"

He blinked. "You don't remember the crash?"

"Sort of."

"They rammed your car off the road. You hit a tree. Thank God you were driving Gil's car and not your SUV—the impact wasn't enough to topple the tree, and the engine didn't explode. Apparently someone driving the other way saw what happened and hit their horn hard. That must've scared the bad guys off."

"But which bad guys?"

"Well..." He rubbed his forehead as if in deep thought.

I found it adorable. Yes, adorable.

"Janic was in a meeting with the higher-ups at that time. He's off the list unless he hired someone, and no one thinks he's that..."

"Smart?"

"Something like that." He rubbed his forehead again. "I still maintain no one knows where I am."

"Except you've been seen, Rayne. By lots of people." Some of which was my fault. My head throbbed. "You're here now."

"But in a different context. No one here is going to go out to Cedar Valley with my picture and tell everyone where I am."

"You never know." Even the thought of that left me short of breath. Well, that or the chest injury. Could've gone either way.

"So that leaves Farrah." Rayne blew out a long breath. "You and Gil do have similar builds. The night was dark. Maybe they figured they could get to her via whomever. Or maybe they thought scaring you—or Gil—was enough."

"Huge risk with very little reward."

"They might've thought she was in the car with you. Spring had left not long before that."

"But they would've seen she didn't get into my car."

"I don't know, and you're getting upset." He laid his hand over mine. "You're alive. Colton's arranged for someone to watch your room. From the New West police department."

Worry and pain and meds and lack of breath were catching up with me. The room swam, but I clung to Rayne's hand. "They can't watch me forever. I don't believe I'm the target anyway."

His eyes narrowed. "Colton says we have to assume you were. Although Gil's house is under surveillance as well. Hell, he might be the target because he pissed someone off."

"Gil doesn't piss people off."

"He's a lawyer, Ev. Someone always loses."

His words brought me up short. I knew that. I *knew* that. Yet I'd forgotten it for a moment. Because I was always on the side of right. Even if we lost, we were still on the side of right. "Don't call me *Ev*."

"Well, I could call you *Evey*." He said the word like *Ev* and *ee* as opposed to the way a woman might call herself.

"Not helping." I pressed my free hand to my chest. Probably because, despite my frown, I wanted to smile.

"Time's up." Dominic entered the room with a serene smile on his face. "Out you go." He directed the words to Rayne.

"I just got here."

"Nice try. Seriously, it's time to go. Everett needs some rest. You can come back later."

"I'm staying." Rayne set his jaw.

"Oh honey, nice try. I have the wand of permanent banishment. Don't make me use it."

I had no idea of what the *wand of banishment* meant, but Dominic clearly cared about me. "It's okay, baby. Do as the man says."

Rayne grinned. "I'm your baby? I like that."

"You would." Dominic gestured to the door.

My *boyfriend* pressed a delicate kiss to my lips. "Get better soon—Champ needs his other daddy." Then he bolted.

Dominic raised an eyebrow. "*Daddy?* You got a kid—"

"Rayne owns a dog."

"Sounds like you own a dog as well." Dominic moved to the IV machine. "How's your pain?"

"It hurts."

"I'll see what I can do about that."

Within moments, I was gone.

# Chapter Twenty-Two

E ight days later, Everett was finally sent home.

Conveniently, the day after Farrah's brother was arrested.

Turned out the guy wasn't as clever as he'd thought.

The cousin he'd convinced to steal a car hadn't realized the family he'd stolen it from had a doorbell camera that caught him driving away with their vehicle.

It took the police a few days to track down the thief, as he didn't have a record and was, in fact, Farrah's third cousin by marriage. Still, dogged determination by Colton and Dorrie nabbed him.

He'd given up Farrah's brother's name in a heartbeat.

So much for family loyalty.

Everett *had* been the target. The clothes switch and car hadn't fooled the guy.

Still, Everett had come a little too close to death for my liking.

As August drove us back to the Glencairn townhouse, Everett let out a long sigh and leaned against his pillow on the passenger door. "I really appreciate—"

"Stop." Julian grinned from the backseat beside me. "We agreed to allow three. So every time you try to thank us after this gets a buzzer sound. This is your warning."

I sat next to him, in the middle, with Champ harnessed and seated between me and the door. August had the honor of driving while we'd tucked Everett into the front seat so he had the most room. Aside from the multiple thanks, he'd been silent.

"Torah's set up a training session with Champ and Chia," I told him. Chia being Ryan and Simeon's rescue poodle.

"Oh?" Everett scratched his chin with its ten-day-old stubble.

I'd offered to shave him. Hell, that would've been sexy as fuck.

His two nurses had offered to shave him.

Nope.

He didn't want to *bother* anyone.

His mother threatened to drive to *visit* us tomorrow and do it herself. Apparently Everett had always hated stubble. *Has he noticed those couple of silver whiskers? Oh God, so fucking sexy.*

Except sex was off the table for a long time. In fact, Dr. Leopold had provided three pages of instructions. The nurse had gone through them, and I planned to reread them once we got home, and to follow every single one.

"You think Champ's up for the challenge of a stubborn poodle?" Everett managed a chuckle.

"First, how do you know she's stubborn? You haven't even met her." I took vague affront he didn't think Champ was up for the challenge. Every moment I hadn't been in the hospital, I'd been working with Torah and my dog, as well as—near the end—two of her Labradors.

"Ryan confided to me about Chia when he came to visit the day before yesterday. Or was it yesterday?" He pressed a hand to his temple.

"They came on Monday. Today's Wednesday. You're doing fine." He didn't have a head injury, but surgery sometimes messed with people's minds. He still got confused.

And I was glad he hadn't actually asked how I was driving back and forth to the hospital every day. In his SUV, no less. For reasons I couldn't fathom, Simeon figured out I was short on cash and had floated me—a total stranger—almost a thousand dollars to pay for gas and parking and food. He said I was good for it.

Given I barely had enough in my bank account to pay my rent for January, I wasn't convinced of that. Fourteen days off the grid meant no money coming in. Truthfully, I was in big trouble financially. *I'll deal with that later.*

I told Everett, "Champ's come a long way. Torah says he might wind up being one of her best pupils. It's unfortunate he was badly trained to be a guard dog, because when he's not hyper alert, he's actually a big softie."

Everett turned his head to meet my gaze. "He's been sleeping on the bed."

"We missed you."

"Oh God, please tell me he hasn't been sleeping on *my* bed." Exasperation of the first degree.

August chuckled.

Julian guffawed.

Champ snuffed.

He hadn't, of course. No, I'd done the adult thing and laundered Everett's sheets in anticipation of his return. Champ and I had slept in the guest room each night. "Uh..." This might prove fun.

"Ask him about the sofa." August took the turnoff for the Haney Bypass.

"Seriously? My leather sofa?"

"It's faux leather." I wrinkled my nose. "And he was on top of a blanket."

"Which blanket?"

"So, I think we should look at the pretty Fraser River and shelve this conversation for another day." Julian eyed me.

"The old one from my bedroom that you gave me for this exact purpose. And I've vacuumed every day. He's going through a shedding phase. Might have something to do with stress since it's not really the right time of year for it."

"Well, keep vacuuming," he grumped.

"Your mom likes Champ..."

He turned with an astonished expression on his face—raised eyebrows and gaping mouth.

"I might've brought Champ into the city to visit with them yesterday. They adore him, and for some reason he doesn't seem to see your mom as a threat. Maybe because she's older."

"Didn't Laila bring the baby over yesterday?"

In the rearview mirror, I saw Everett frowning.

Child number three had made his appearance two days after Everett had been injured. He'd yet to see his own nephew.

"Yes. Adorable. Champ was fascinated. Wary of Laila, but not the baby."

"Please tell me—"

"I had a tight grip, and they were far away from each other. Don't worry, I'd never put the kids at risk. The older two kids weren't interested, so Champ and I sat in the corner. He's really good with kids, though. I wonder if he misses—" I cut myself off. Thinking about Champ's previous life always upset me.

Julian put one hand on my thigh. He knew. He understood.

"Laila's a sensible woman." August eased into the merge onto Highway Seven. "Your parents were there. And Rayne didn't leave Champ for a moment."

"How do you know this?" Everett sighed. "Am I always the last to know?"

Julian barked out a laugh. "That's my line. People forget about me because I sort of blend into the furniture."

All four of us laughed. Julian, with his red hair and vibrant personality, would never *blend in* anywhere. And that was a good thing—his personality suited August's more sedate and contemplative nature.

Just like I complemented Everett.

Or so I told myself. "We have a surprise for you."

My *boyfriend* pressed a hand to his chest. "I think I've had enough surprises."

"You'll like this one."

Champ licked my ear.

Okay, gross—and probably against a rule of Torah's—but super adorable.

Everett closed his eyes. "I just want to crawl into bed and sleep for a month."

"You've earned it." I leaned forward so I could squeeze his shoulder.

Farrah's male relatives had all been convicted at trial and were in jail awaiting sentencing. The women who'd facilitated were unlikely to make a move on their own. She'd moved back into Olivia's basement suite at Marnie and Jake's house. Which was fine because Olivia spent much of her time at her boyfriend Tristan's house. Farrah had the safety of being in a busy household while also some peace to contemplate her future. The new semester had just started, and her academic counselor was trying to coax her back to school—even if only for virtual classes. Just something to return normalcy to her life.

"You're going to be okay." August downshifted as we ascended a hill. "And work will be waiting when the doctor okays you to return. Or you can just take more time off and loll about sipping cocktails."

Everett groaned.

Everyone laughed.

He'd already been restless and wanting to get hold of his case files.

Gil had put his foot down. At least another week of rest.

I had the feeling this was going to be a *very long* week.

Julian squeezed my thigh again—undoubtedly in sympathy. If August was down for a couple of weeks, he'd be going squirrelly as well. Our men were doers—uncomfortable with just sitting around.

In fact, I didn't figure Everett had stopped more than a handful of days in all his years since starting at the law practice. Gil had intimated as much. Which was why he'd deputized me to ensure Everett took the time off he needed.

Eventually we neared Mission City.

"Straight home?" August turned off the highway.

"Yes." Everett said the word quietly.

My heartstrings tugged. Weariness was evident.

"We'll get you settled and then take off." Julian stretched a hand across me for Champ to sniff.

Champ leaned into his fingers for a scritch.

"Actually, August and Rayne will get you into bed. I want some quality time with my nephew."

"Nephew?" Everett's disbelief was clear. "How do you figure?"

"Well, you're practically August's brother. So that makes you my brother-in-law."

Both Everett and August groaned—but neither refuted the assertion.

Julian continued. "And you're Champ's other daddy—"

"Oh my God." This time only Everett groaned.

"What?" Julian affected shock. "Rayne's your boyfriend, so—"

"Do I get any say in this?" Just a touch of exasperation from Everett. Mixed with a bit of humor.

"No, not really." Julian grinned. Absolutely impishly. "I think you make a lovely family."

Everett turned stiffly to gaze back at me. "Later. We're discussing this later."

My right eye socket ached. The bruises that had mottled my body were mostly faded or fading. I still had a couple of nasty contusions which would linger for a while, and the graze on my side had a small moist spot I kept covered with gauze...but I was a thousand times better than I'd been two weeks ago when I'd shown up on his doorstep.

Unfortunately, the biggest issues hadn't been resolved.

And I knew it.

More importantly, he knew it.

# Chapter Twenty-Three

Everett

I fingered the heavy parchment in my hand. No one wrote letters by hand anymore, let alone on this classic stationary—yet Farrah had. Although I could've shrugged off an email of thanks, this missive, delivered by Jake and Marnie, weighed on me.

Undeserving.

I'd just done my job. I agreed to help her, and I'd helped her. Now she was able to move on with her life. Hopefully when her scumbag relatives got out of prison, she'd be living the best life possible. That was all I could wish for her. I didn't need her thanks.

And yet I had it. In a form I'd never be able to disregard. I had a little safe in my closet. For personal papers, my passport, and a watch my grandfather had gifted me upon my graduation from law school. A watch I dared not wear—which would've irritated the shit out of him. Still, I kept it safe. Admired it whenever I was adding or swapping documents out of the pile. I just couldn't get over the thought I might lose it or break it or something equally unlikely. Yet I couldn't bring myself to wear it. So it stayed precious and protected. And…maybe I needed to pull it out and put it on. Tomorrow wasn't guaranteed, as I'd discovered. My treasure might as well be used as he'd intended.

Now I had this letter.

I blinked.

"Too much?" Rayne sat on the side of my bed. I'd wanted to be in the living room, but August and Rayne insisted—for today at least—that bed was best.

Given how exhausted I was, I couldn't really argue. "Just right?" I sniffed.

Gently, he extracted the paper. "I'm going to put it on your dresser. If you want to see it again, you just let me know."

"I'm capable of getting it myself." I pointed to the bathroom. "Been doing the back-and-forth trip for about eight days now." At the hospital. But recovery was slower than I would've liked. Dominic kept insisting I was doing well. Hell, Dr. Rodgers said the same thing. But I wanted to be better. I wanted to get back to my old life. I eyed Rayne. "You've put your life on hold for almost two weeks. Don't you have somewhere to go? Someone who might be looking for you?"

"You mean aside from the goons who tried to kill me?"

"Well…yeah. I mean, if I disappeared for two weeks, a few people would notice."

He grasped my hand. "That's because you're important to them. You call your parents every Sunday. You text Denali every other day. You send cat videos to Laila, and business articles to Ursula."

I cocked my head.

He laughed. "Oh, I've gotten to know your family well over the last week. Hell, your parents have asked me to call them Janisse and Melville."

A sigh escaped. "You're a charmer."

He puffed his chest. "Which is why you love me." His eyes widened. "I didn't mean—"

"Yeah, you sort of did." I tried to purse my lips, but I couldn't summon the energy. "I'm screwed, Rayne."

"How so?" He shifted closer. "Are you in pain? We've got the—"

"I don't need painkillers. I need to understand how you wound up in my life."

He grinned. "A certain epic Halloween party, as I recall."

"Rayne."

"Yeah?"

His eyes shone that incredibly breathtaking color I struggled to identify. "Why me? I was certainly not the only single guy there that night. You could've had your pick."

"Well..." He tried to look bashful.

I didn't buy it for even a fraction of a second. The man was damn near perfect. I cleared my throat.

He bit his lower lip. A real tell for him. "Okay...I'll tell you everything."

I let out a breath.

"When you're healthy enough."

"Hey!" Indignation laced my voice even as a ripple of pain moved through my chest.

He scowled. "You might, I don't know, kick me out. Then who will take care of you?"

"Uh, me?" I didn't need any damn nursemaid.

"You won't, though. And then you'll end up back in the hospital, and your parents will have to put their lives on hold to worry about you while they should be enjoying their new grandchild—"

"Are you trying to make me feel guilty?" I gaped.

"—and then Denali won't be on set for her big debut, and Ursula won't fly to New York to pitch—"

"Ursula's going to New York?"

He bit his lower lip. "Well, no. But she could." He rolled his hand in some weird motion I didn't understand. "Like, she might get the call at any moment, and she'll be worried about you and she'll miss her flight—"

"My sister never misses a fucking thing, and you're so far off topic, I can barely remember what it was." I glared.

He sat silently. Clearly chastened. *Not.*

"Rayne."

"Everett."

I arched an eyebrow.

He bit his lower lip.

I waited.

"Okay, I think I need to go down to the repair shop on First Avenue and get my phone looked at. I have something super valuable on it. If it can be retrieved, that's...important."

"Is that safe?"

"Is anything safe?" He gesticulated. "I could trip over Champ on the stairs, fall, and break my neck."

"Okay." Not what I'd had in mind. I shook off the distressing image. "Will you at least talk to Colton? He knows something—"

"No."

Right. We'd been over this. I just kept hoping the response might change if I tried asking the question in a different way. "Okay, so when do you propose to go?"

"Later this afternoon. I don't want to leave you right now. And your surprise is coming soon."

"I don't like surprises. Surely you've figured this out by now."

"Oh, but you'll *love* this one."

I doubted it very much, but I'd hold my tongue. Clearly this was something he'd put a lot of thought into. Although what he had up his sleeve, I could only guess.

"What would you like for dinner?"

"Anything other than hospital food." I couldn't entirely complain. The past three days my family had been sneaking in things Dominic definitely wouldn't have approved of, had I still been under his eagle eye.

"Pizza?"

My salivary glands kicked in. "With peperoni, mushrooms, and olives."

His eyes widened in evident horror. "No. Ham and pineapple."

I gagged. Well, mimed gagging.

"Well, you're stuck. I'll just..." He eyed his phone, then tucked it away and nodded at mine. "Can you place an order for two pies that I'll pick up in a couple of hours? That should be enough time for me to figure out if the data can be retrieved."

"You didn't upload them to the cloud?" I snagged my phone off the nightstand—slowly—and opened the pizza shop app. I did truly love pizza. One of my few treats.

And Rayne knew it.

My weakness.

He grinned. "Yeah. You're okay with me picking up Domino's? Over by the connector?"

I nodded. Then considered. "And how are you getting there?"

"Oh, I'm driving your SUV. Gil and Cullen brought it over from the office the second day you were in the hospital. How did you think I was getting back and forth?"

He winced. "Clearly I didn't think. You do have a license, right?"

He grinned. "I even aced my test. With zero accidents."

Then he bit his lower lip.

*So what's he hiding now? Do I want to know? Nope...probably not.*

"At some point you need to retrieve your own car. Where is it?"

"Probably the impound lot in Abbotsford. It's safe for ninety days." He squinted. "Or thirty. Or...something..."

That should've worried me. Truthfully, I was too tired to care. "Maybe make a phone call?"

He yanked his phone from his back pocket—then hesitated.

So I pulled up a web browser until I found the number for impoundment, and I dialed.

"Abbotsford Bylaws Office." A pleasant woman's voice.

"Hello, my name is...well, that's not important. Uh, theoretically, if my car were towed, how long would you keep it?"

"What's the name?"

"Oh, this is just a hypothetical."

The line remained silent for an uncomfortable amount of time. Finally, "thirty days."

"Great, uh, thank you."

"Are you certain—"

I cut the line. "Your time's half up."

He winced. "Yeah, I know."

"You've got sixteen days to fess up and get help to retrieve your, car or you're going to lose it. I get the feeling your job is reliant on a vehicle."

"Uh, yeah."

"Rayne."

His gaze shot to me.

"Look, I almost just died—"

"But you didn't."

"But I didn't. I do, however, have a different perspective than I did ten days ago. I didn't want to die. Those amazing medical people kept me alive. I want the amazing law enforcement people to keep you alive. Could you..." I swallowed. "Could you do this for me?"

Slowly, he shook his head. "I'm sorry, I really can't. Why don't you order the pizza, and I'll be back in a couple of hours?"

I nearly shouted in frustration. Except that would just wind me up with a sore chest and he might just go and not come back. "Right, pizza." I opened the app. "Pineapple and ham?"

"And maybe some of that cheesy bread stuff?"

"Right. Cheesy bread." Finally, I met his gaze. "Come home safe."

"I will."

Then he was gone.

# Chapter Twenty-Four

Rayne

I wasn't happy about leaving Everett, but he also would've been grumpy if I stayed and hovered.

Well, grumpier.

I couldn't blame him.

He was accustomed to regular physical activity and to doing things for himself. He was a get-up-and-go kind of guy.

Now he struggled to get out of bed to go to the john. He was sometimes breathless. Mounting the two sets of stairs this morning had nearly done him in.

I'd been tempted to give in to his demand to be allowed to stay sitting up in the living room. Except I would've had a hell of a time moving him come evening when he was even sorer and exhausted. No, we'd done the right thing by putting him straight to bed—where he'd dozed much of the morning.

*How will he cope without me? He's right...I can't stay.*

I focused on driving safely. The last thing I needed was to be pulled over by the cops. Or to be in a crash.

Soon enough, I was on the main drag and, fortunately, found a parking space just in front of the electronics store. The outside wasn't anything to fawn over, but the reviews were solid and, as I tracked back, not likely from bots or family and friends. Not that I had much choice. The big retailers would want my personal information before I could touch a computer. Likely this guy wouldn't.

So imagine my surprise when a young woman waved as I came into the store.

*Sexist. Women can do tech shit too. Probably better that you.* I had a lot of digital equipment, but I wasn't good at servicing it. "Hey, I need help."

She grinned. "I'm here to help. Name's Marita. What do you need?" Her voice was pleasantly melodic.

I yanked out my phone.

"Ouch." She took it from me. "Did you run it over with your car?"

I burst out laughing. "Uh, no. Just my hip hit it when I slid on the ice and landed on it."

"Wow, that must've been quite a fall."

"You have no idea."

"Huh?"

Damn. Thought I'd said that under my breath. Clearly I'd said it aloud. "Yeah, bad spill. Banged up pretty bad." *From a beating, but she doesn't need to know that.* "I need to retrieve what's on there."

"You didn't back it up to the cloud?"

I sighed. "I thought it happened automatically." *And if I check, I might be located, so that's out.* "What do you think?"

She glanced around the store. "I don't have anything that can't wait."

"Oh, I was hoping you'd say that."

"This isn't going to be cheap."

*Which is why Everett gave me his credit card. Which was an insane thing to do.* "I'm good for it."

"Great. Let me get some cables and a laptop, and we'll see what I can do. Do you want to upload it to your new phone or just to a stick?"

"Stick's fine. You, uh, won't look at it?"

She grinned. "Sex stuff, eh? No, I'll do the data transfer. You can watch it here—" She pointed to a desk in a corner facing the store so the laptop screen would be hidden. "—or you can take it home. Your call. Whether I retrieve it or not, you still have to pay."

"You want payment up front?"

Her gaze traveled up and down. I was still surviving on Everett's *spare* clothes. He'd mentioned something about paying for me to buy new stuff but, again, that involved a store with surveillance cameras or buying online and shit never fit properly. I had weird proportions. But I was about the same size as my *boyfriend*. Well, I had more muscles, which was why the T-shirt I wore under my jacket was tight. I'd unzipped the coat when I stepped inside the warm store.

After a moment, she nodded. "I trust you. Plus, you don't get the stick or the phone back until you pay. And we're wired to the police department. One too many burglaries."

"Ouch."

"Times are tough. People think we're an easy mark. They learn the hard way we're not, but their attempts cost me money and that pisses me off."

"Marita?"

"Mmm?"

"I never intend to piss you off."

"I like the sound of that. What's your name?"

"Rayne." Wasn't like she could do something with it or anything.

"Okay, Rayne, you have a seat and let me work my magic."

"Yeah." I yanked my new phone out of my back pocket, made my way over to the comfortable lounge chair, plopped down, and started scrolling. I hadn't checked the Abbotsford Police Department website since Everett's crash.

Nothing new. No arrests. No further information about the shooting.

Hesitantly, I entered Sonny's information in the browser—after going incognito. Nothing about him. Except how he was an upstanding citizen. In fact, Citizen of the year in Abbotsford last year. *Yeah, aside from all the illegal stuff.*

My client had been screwed by Sonny. Or so they contended. They'd hired me to dig up the dirt, and I had—the most damning coming the night before Sonny and his goons had tried to kill me. But instead of just offing me first, they'd tried to get the evidence back.

The evidence I desperately hoped was on the phone. The evidence I hoped Marita could retrieve. The evidence I hoped would bury Sonny. *That's a lot of optimism. Something you're not known for.* No. In my line of work, things rarely had a happy ending. Okay, so I found proof a spouse was cheating, and my client got a better divorce settlement. That really wasn't a huge win unless there'd been abuse or something. Which had happened. A local shelter passed my name around to people who needed help. I gave a discounted rate.

See? I wasn't entirely a mercenary.

I also needed to put food on the table and pay the rent.

Which meant I needed to add some funds as soon as possible, or February's rent payment was going to bounce. I had two weeks to figure that out.

"Done."

My head snapped up. "That easy?"

Marita nodded. "Really, you just needed power. The screen's beyond repair, but the inner workings were—mostly—intact. I mean, the phone's not worth fixing at this point. Especially since it's two models behind and the new ones are so much better."

"Good thing I'm not attached to it."

She laughed. "Oh, I get it. Some people are in tears when they come in here. People are so devoted to their phones."

"I used to be one of those people. But these days, not so much. How much do I owe you?"

She gave me a very reasonable rate.

I tapped Everett's credit card, accepted the phone and stick, and then headed out with a final wave and thanks.

Now I needed to see if anything on the recordings would be helpful.

*And I have to tell Everett the entire truth.*

*He's going to hate me.*

*Still has to be done.*

I texted him that all was good, then hopped into his car and headed over to Domino's.

The retrieval had been so quick, they hadn't even started the order.

I was happy to wait. I continued to scroll online, desperately looking for something—some scrap of information—that would help me get out of this mess. That didn't exist, though, and I knew it. I'd have to be honest, and that didn't sit well with me. Not because he didn't deserve honesty.

He did.

But that I'd hidden several important things from him.

Like why I'd scoped him out and then let him fuck me at the Halloween party.

Like why I hadn't been honest the morning he'd found me.

Like why I'd been reluctant to tell him about what was on the phone. Well, hopefully on it. If the recordings hadn't been retrieved, and weren't in the cloud either, then he'd only have my word for what I'd seen and my word was worth about ten cents at the moment.

*Hell, you still haven't told him your full name.*

Luckily, his friends and family were fine with just *Rayne*. My last name was on a couple of dedications throughout Vancouver. Likely not anywhere Everett's people might know, but I could never be certain.

When I'd discovered the full story behind my family's wealth and legacy, I'd nearly asked the various institutions to remove the name. They could keep the money, but why should *Iverson* be associated with charitable endeavors when, in reality, the name was so... I shuddered. I tried to thrust the images from my mind. The labor my family exploited over the years. The people on whose backs their wealth had grown. And, mostly, how they'd never been called to account. Only when I'd cleaned out my grandparents' house, had I discovered the truth.

My phone buzzed with an incoming text from Everett.

—*Dominos texted. Pizza's ready. I'm starving. Come home soon.* —

Huh.

*Come home soon.* Of course, he meant *his* home. Not *our* home. Tonight, I'd sleep in the guest room.

—*And you have to get our dog off my bed.* —

I smiled. He likely hadn't meant to type *our* dog. His finger just slipped over the *y* key. I liked the idea of Champ keeping him company and lying on the bed. Torah had given us the go-ahead once we were sure he was safe with Everett and me. The shedding problem hadn't gotten any better, though.

Torah thought he was settling well, at least with those of us he knew.

God, I hoped so.

*You're going to have to find a new place to live anyway, can't go back. Maybe letting the rent payment fail isn't the end of the world.*

Yeah, except I had a few things I wanted to pick up from my apartment. If anyone went in my stead, they were risking themselves.

Although...the blinds were drawn, and my apartment was only accessible through a private entrance. So I could maybe ask August and Julian to swing by. No one would know who they were, and unless the goons were waiting around in the hallway, no one would know they were getting the few things I actually needed.

I exited my car and sprinted over to the pizza store. I tried not to get too excited because a million things could go wrong with that plan—including that I was putting Everett's friends in danger.

Hell, I was starting to see them as my friends.

The smiling kid handed me the two pizzas and the cheesy bread as well as a bag full of my favorite sodas. *How the hell did he know? Or is this for him?* What were the odds we both loved ginger ale?

I couldn't do math like that in my head. So I put the pizzas on the seat next to me and drove carefully back up to Glencairn.

*Am I being followed?*

*No, can't be.*

*But still...*

I was surprised when a car followed me into the townhouse complex. Well, there were two hundred townhouses, so maybe that shouldn't have been a huge surprise. Especially since the road the complex was on dead-ended not far ahead.

*Shit.*

I pulled into a row that didn't have access to Everett's. I slowed as if I was looking for a particular number.

The car followed.

I tried to get a look at the driver but the sun glared off the windshield.

After another row, I made a slashing motion as if tremendously frustrated. I turned and headed out of the complex.

Whomever was behind me didn't follow.

I drove up to the top of the hill that was the dead-end of the street. I pretended to eye the new complex being built. A guy standing near the gate eyed me. I waved back, turned the SUV around, and headed back.

*Go back to downtown Mission City? Try to figure out if the guy was following me?* If he was, he certainly hadn't followed me up this far.

Slowly, I eased my way back down the hill and turned into the Glencairn Estates. I drove the farthest row away from Everett's and kept an eagle eye out for the car that had followed me. I hadn't gotten a license plate, but I remembered the make and model.

I found it in a visitor parking spot with no sign of the driver. Relief wasn't complete as he could be lurking.

*Or she. Don't make sexist assumptions.*

Still, I only spotted some kids in the little playground park area with parents who weren't paying me the least mind. Finally, I headed to Everett's. When I didn't spot anyone, I turned onto his lane.

*Phew.*

Okay, so we were safe.

I hit the remote and happily pulled into the garage. Once the door was down, I grabbed all the food. I had to put it on a bench while I unlocked the door. Some people—who were just a little unparanoid as far as I was concerned—didn't lock their house door from the garage. I liked that Everett did. He had nice things, and I would've hated to see him lose them.

That said, nothing was absolutely safe.

I put the pizza and drinks on a bench on the inside of the house. Then I reactivated the alarm. I ditched my coat, grabbed everything, and headed up the stairs. "Honey, I'm home."

Somewhere from upstairs, a *woof* sounded.

Moments later, nails clacking on laminate signaled Champ running down the stairs.

"Hey, buddy."

He barreled into me.

"I missed you too." I gave him serious scritches. "Now, treat for you. Then I wash my hands and take food upstairs. How does that sound?"

He backed up and sat on his butt before I got the command out, clearly having understood the word *treat*.

My heart sang. I gave him a kibble bite for calmness, then told him to stand, then sit again on command, to get his appropriate reward. He listened, ears pricked forward, not an ounce of anxiety in his posture.

*Yeah, it'll all work out.*

*It just has to.*

# Chapter Twenty-Five

Everett

"Should I go down and help him?" Denali grinned.

I winced. "I should've texted that you're here."

She shrugged. "I surprised you. He's expecting me later tonight. So I'm surprising him too. I'll run down. You got cheesy bread, right? Because I won't eat pizza that's been sullied by olives."

"He loves Hawaiian."

"Oh God, a man after my heart. I'll be right back." She kissed my forehead like I was a child.

"Wait, let me give him a heads-up." Champ was still leery of her, sitting in the hall rather than in the room when she was here. I texted and saw Rayne had seen it. "Okay, go on."

Denali clomped off, following Champ's path.

For a former dancer, she sure wasn't light on her feet when she wasn't performing.

The happy sounds from downstairs—from two people—made their way up to me. I heard a huffed bark from Champ, but it sounded more like his greeting than fear. *God, I want to be down there with them*.

I almost—almost—did just that.

Except I had to piss and wash my hands. Because I'd been petting Champ for the last two hours while worrying about his owner. And I'd winced when I'd reread my texts.

*Our dog*.

That implied somehow I had a connection to Champ. Some kind of responsibility. But I didn't. He wasn't mine.

*Neither is Rayne*.

Nope. They'd leave together when the coast was clear, and I'd never see either of them again. I felt that certainty down to the marrow of my bones. They'd go. I'd be alone.

Somehow I managed to relieve my bladder and wash my hands and was just easing back into bed when Denali bounded in, juggling plates and sodas.

She handed me a plate with two slices of heavenly smelling pizza, a napkin, and a bottle of ginger ale—which I put on the nightstand.

Moments later, Rayne appeared with Champ walking obediently at heel. Champ hesitated in the doorway, eyes on Denali, but then walked forward at Rayne's side. Rayne came around to the far side of the bed with his own plate and sat next to me, leaning against the headboard. He sighed as he sniffed the grotesque pizza in front of him.

Champ sat beside the bed eyeing Rayne, then Denali, then me. He whined a little, his *asking-for-something* whine, not his *I'm-worried* whine. I wasn't sure how I felt about the fact I could easily tell the difference.

"What?" Rayne asked him. "You got your T-R-E-A-T."

Champ whined again. His eyes seemed to be fixed on me, not Rayne.

"Don't tell me he can spell now," Rayne muttered.

"I think he, um, wants up on the bed." *Did I just say that?*

Rayne glanced between the bed and where Denali sat in my bedside chair. "That would be a step forward, I guess, if you're cool with it."

"For the dog's confidence progress, just this once, I guess," I lied.

Rayne patted the spot by his feet. "Up, Champ."

A single powerful leap landed the big dog on the covers, as far from Denali as he could get. Still, a lot closer than he had been.

"Down." When Champ settled, Rayne dug in his pocket for a kibble. He'd have to learn to turn all his pockets inside out before doing laundry. "Good boy." Rayne settled his shoulders stiffly against the headboard.

I told him, "You need a pillow. I have a spare one in the walk-in closet."

He furrowed his brow, eyeing Champ thoughtfully. "I'll grab mine from my room. Leave him here. See how he does without me." He scooted off the bed and strutted out of the room, jiggling his butt.

Denali laughed. "I like him."

I gazed down at my olive, mushroom, and peperoni pizza for a long time. "Yeah, I like him too."

She reached over and squeezed my leg. "You're allowed."

At Champ's raised head and ear-flick, I slid my leg out from under her hand. "Maybe no touching."

She sat back. "Sorry, dog. Hands to myself. Got it."

He settled again, nose on paws, eyes on her.

I glanced at the door. "Rayne's not staying."

"Have you asked him to?"

Rayne strutted back into the room. "Okay, this is going to be so very awesome."

He put two pillows against my headboard then settled beside me. "Yeah...awesome."

And it kind of was. Between the two of them, they had me laughing to the point I begged them to stop because my chest hurt.

Eventually they went downstairs, ostensibly to put the plates in the dishwasher and the leftover pizza in the fridge—although little had survived the hungry masses. I might've eaten a third piece.

Champ raised his head to watch them go, but when I murmured to him and scratched his shoulder, he stayed with me. I felt proud, such a huge step from when he used to follow Rayne to the bathroom.

Within a couple of minutes, they were back with white-chocolate cheesecake with heated chocolate sauce drizzled all over it.

Suddenly, I had room for just a little bit more.

Rayne and I shared.

Before, I might've found that gross. Now, though, I found it charming. Endearing. Intimate. Which, given my cock had been up his ass a couple of times, meant I was warming up to this relationship thing.

*Watch. You might just fall in love with him.*

I snuck a peek at him.

My heart stuttered.

I gazed at Champ.

My chest seized, in a way that didn't have anything with the surgery.

"That was amazing." Rayne grinned.

Denali preened, swinging her head over her shoulder in that flirtatious way she had. She did it with everyone, but I suddenly became aware my very available sister might consider flirting with my very bisexual boyfriend.

*She wouldn't. He won't. You're just being silly.*

Yeah. I was. Still, I needed to pull the attention away from my very considerate, attractive sister who'd brought the cheesecake and syrup and get it back on the matter at hand. I turned to Rayne. "Were you able to retrieve your files?"

His gaze shifted to Denali before settling back on me. "Yeah. I haven't looked yet, but Marita said she got them."

I cocked my head.

"The woman who owns the repair shop?"

"Ah. Repairs. I have a habit of either driving over to the electronics store where I bought my stuff or, worse, just taking it to the disposal place for e-waste and buying new."

Denali wagged her finger at me. "You should at least check with all of us first. It might be something worth fixing, and then one of us might use it. You know better."

Go figure, getting lectures from the woman who loved fast fashion all through high school. The environmentalist only started to poke her head up when Laila had her first child. Then suddenly we were all looking at carbon footprints and how we did everything. I might not have kids of my own, but I wanted to do my best to leave them a habitable planet. "Apologies, sis." I turned my attention back to Rayne. "So?"

"They're on a flash drive. I need a computer—"

"Oh, I'll grab mine." Denali was off the bed and out of the room before I could draw a breath.

Rayne chuckled. "Did she say how long she was staying?"

"Uh, you were the one who knew she was coming."

"Where's her car?"

"In a visitor spot. She needs to move it to my garage. The advantage of having room for two vehicles."

"That's true. I'll go mention it to her."

I snagged his wrist. "No, you're going to show me whatever's on that drive."

He tried to give me a hangdog look.

"Well, Denali and I can watch while you're gone."

"I'm not certain Denali needs to see this at all."

"Oh, she's so watching." Said woman pirouetted with socked feet on the laminate floor while clutching her laptop to her chest.

I chuckled.

Even Rayne cracked a smile. Then he sobered. "It might not be anything."

"Bullshit." Denali handed him the laptop and then perched very gently on the edge of the bed beside me.

Champ raised his head again, his ears and lips signaling anxiety.

"This could get a bit high-emotion," Rayne mused. He told Champ, "Go to your bed." When the dog jumped down and made his way to the plush dog bed in the corner—yes, he had one in my room now too—Rayne said, "Bingo," and tossed him a kibble. "Okay, Denali, get us into this thing."

Denali snagged back the laptop, opened it, entered her password—where both Rayne and I could see—and held out her hand.

After a long moment, Rayne pulled the stick out of his pocket and dropped it into her palm.

She accepted, stuck it in the slot, and grinned.

Soon a window opened.

She frowned as she manipulated the mouse trackpad. "Looks like a pile of video files." She clicked on another folder. "And messages."

"Let's skip those, shall we?" Rayne cleared his throat. "They're, uh, confidential."

"What did you say you did?" She moved the mouse back to the first file.

"Oh, not that one!" His panicked voice filled the room and Champ whined.

"He hasn't said," I replied cooly. "Still, you will respect his privacy. But I suspect we're going to know by the end of this little adventure." I glanced at him over Denali's lowered head.

After a long moment, he met my gaze. Those tawny-brown gold eyes had lost their sparkle. Finally, he let out a breath. "I'm a private investigator."

"Ooh." Denali grinned. "I can't wait to ask more questions. My new character—"

"How about you show her which video is safe to watch? And later you can explain to me why there are some that aren't safe." I gave him my best scowl.

He swallowed hard. "It's revenge porn an asshole downloaded to the internet after his girlfriend broke up with him. She thought she'd found it all, but I came across a stash she didn't know about. After I told her, I turned it over to the police. I should've deleted it, but I started working the next case and I forgot." He looked past me at Denali. "No sex on camera. Ever. With anyone. I don't give a shit if you're even married to the guy—"

"Or gal."

"Or gal." He said the words without missing a beat.

My brain screeched a little. *Did my little sister just come out? Or is she just correcting his assumptions because he shouldn't be making them?* I just didn't know, but Rayne pointed to a file.

Denali double clicked.

We all leaned in.

The image was so dark, Denali had to adjust the screen trying to get a better view.

Two people were meeting in a parking lot.

They exchanged something.

They shook hands.

They each took off in different directions.

The video cut off.

"Uh..." Denali tapped her chin. "That didn't look good."

"Look at the next one."

She double clicked.

One of the guys was the same but the other...

I grabbed the laptop. "When did you take this?"

"September 30th."

"Son of a bitch. That's one of my clients. Allyson." I double checked the time stamp.

"Yes."

"She said she met a guy on the thirtieth."

"She did."

"So when they arrested her for robbery that night—at that time—you didn't think I might want to know about it?"

He cleared his throat again.

And didn't look at me.

"I didn't know, at the time, that she was going to be arrested for something completely unrelated."

"But you knew she'd been arrested when you let me fuck you on October 31st."

"Jesus, you two." Denali glanced between us. "I wondered why Everett was all mopey at Christmas. So you like, fucked on Halloween?"

"Denali." I used my stern voice. My friends pretty much knew the details of the half-a-one-night stand, but I didn't want to think of my sister knowing about my sex life.

She glared back. "When did you come back?" She stared at Rayne.

I couldn't see her expression, but given the look of terror in his eyes, she was obviously shooting daggers.

"Uh, first day of the year."

"So...what..." She waved her hand. "You had evidence that exonerated his client, and instead of handing it over you, what, fucked him?"

"Well, technically he fucked me—"

"Jesus, Rayne, this is my *sister*." I didn't need her knowing my preference in sexual positions.

She laughed. Actually laughed. "Everett, you're adorable. Of course I knew you preferred to do the fucking. My God, I'm younger, not innocent."

"Apparently not." I grumbled that. Then glared at Rayne. "Allyson's being held in pretrial. She's in jail right now."

"I know." He pointed to the screen. "That's shady shit. Maybe not as bad as armed robbery, but still shady shit. Look—" He drew in a deep breath and let it out. "—my client needed me to nail the guy. That meant keeping quiet about Allyson. I figured, I dunno, that you'd get her out of jail. And put off the trial as long as possible. By then I figured I'd have this guy in jail and I could, you know, slip you the recording."

"I'd need you to verify it. Put your name to it. You know that."

He winced. "Which is why, despite me having the recording on a thumb drive, I didn't give it to you that night. I couldn't."

"You could have at least told me that Allyson was innocent. That you knew she'd been elsewhere. You could have told me what she was up to." I pointed to the screen.

Denali swatted my hand away. "No fingerprints. This baby's new."

Rayne snickered.

I glared.

He bit his lower lip in that way I found so endearing.

"What?" I might've snapped that.

After a moment, he pointed to the final video.

Denali clicked.

The guy who'd been in the previous two videos pulled a gun on a guy and shot him in the head.

He dropped like a stone.

"Hey, is someone there?" A voice from someone off camera came through clearly.

The video ended.

"Oh." Denali closed the file, her voice admirably steady. "Do we need to look at the others?"

"They're all like the first two."

"So he only killed one guy?"

Yeah, that got a wobble. I rubbed her arm.

"That I know of." Rayne's voice was quiet. "I ran, and I was sure they didn't spot me. I was out the next day, debating going to the police." He cleared his throat again. "But one big impediment existed."

"You didn't want to wind up dead?" Denali clicked to eject the stick.

"Make a copy for me before you eject," I told her. "Go into my office. Top right drawer, there's a ten-pack of thumb drives. Bring two, and we'll make two backups."

"I could just email—"

"No! That's not secure at all. And we don't want it in the cloud, either, if someone is looking for it."

Denali nodded, lower lip between her teeth, then handed me the laptop and slid off the bed.

Champ watched her go out and come back with the sticks, tracking her movements, but stayed in his bed, looking alert but not too nervous.

As she settled back at my side, Rayne told Champ, "Bingo," and tossed the dog a treat.

I made two clean copies of the relevant files including the "like the first one" clips we hadn't watched, then ejected the original and held the stick out to Rayne.

He went to take it, but I didn't let go.

"He's a cop, isn't he? The guy with the gun?"

"Yeah, Abbotsford police."

"Ah."

*Well, shit.*

# Chapter Twenty-Six

Rayne

Everett was pissed.

Legit.

His mostly innocent client had been sitting in jail for almost three months for a crime she hadn't committed. The asshole who *had* done it had tried to kill the poor clerk in the liquor store, so on top of robbery charges, Allyson was facing attempted murder charges.

She was innocent.

And I'd known.

I had, to my defense, tried to figure out who'd actually done the crime. If I could've handed the actual guilty party to the cops, then they might've given Allyson a second look.

Except without, like, access to evidence and shit, I hadn't made much of a start. None of my few informants knew anything. I wasn't like a police detective, linked in to the Abbotsford underworld, such as it was.

So I'd bided my time. Gathered more evidence about Sonny. Tried to figure out the right time to approach the cops here in Mission City or even in Vancouver. Just some police force that wasn't connected to Abbotsford. Blue protected blue, but I wanted to believe they'd take down a truly dirty cop. If not, I planned to send the bribery videos to CNC, the Canadian News Channel, and let the broadcaster decide how to deal with what I handed them.

Until Sonny had killed the guy.

"Do you know who the victim is?"

I shook my head. "I didn't know any of the people. My client just knew Sonny—Officer Menendez—was dirty and asked me to collect said dirt. That night was my last surveillance. I planned to hand everything over to the cops the next night."

"New Year's Eve."

"Yeah. I figured maybe Mission City, since they're RCMP. I knew they'd be busy, but I was prepared to wait. I was just trying to figure that out when they ambushed me."

"Why the hell were you in Wellington Park?" Everett's tone bit.

"I was...thinking."

Denali snorted.

I sighed. "Okay, I was meeting a guy. But it's not like it sounds."

"You had evidence of a murder on your phone and you were off getting laid? In a public park?" Everett's clipped voice cut.

I sighed. "The guy was cheating on his husband. I was trying to see how far he'd take it. I planned on recording everything, wrap up that case before I got sidetracked, and then you know what happened."

Denali held up her hand. "I don't know what happened."

"Some guys tried to kill me. Your brother saved me." *Please don't ask specifics. Please don't ask—*

"What guys? I only saw the one guy. Well, and the one who shouted..." Denali eyed me. "Do you have more evidence? Can the cops arrest them?"

I winced at her words. "I know Sonny. I don't know who the other guy is."

"Jesus." Everett let out the word on a harsh exhalation. "You've got nothing."

"You mean aside from Sonny shooting that guy? Cause that felt like something."

"Has a body turned up?"

"Nope." I hesitated. "Well, not that I know of." A reason I'd been waiting. Easier to say, *This cop's a murderer*, when there's a body to point to.

Everett clenched his teeth. "This is why you've been so paranoid about everything."

"Well, yeah. He's a cop. He has access to literally everything. He obviously knew who I was. If I hadn't had the meeting with the cheating spouse, I wouldn't have been anywhere near the park."

"Did the guy show?"

"Huh?"

"Did the cheating spouse show?"

"Well, if he did, I didn't see him. I mean between me getting beat up and then them shooting at me when I ran away... Oh."

"Yeah."

"You think?"

"Yeah."

"So if I give up the information about my *client*..." I put air quotes around the word.

"Yeah."

Denali vibrated with excitement. "So, we can call the cops? Oh, will that cute one show up? Colton? He was all dark and brooding and—" She seemed excited, but I saw her hands shaking.

"Not for you." Everett bit out the words, apparently missing her nerves. "I don't ask for much, sis, but I'm asking for this. He's bad news. Just ask his ex-wife."

"Everyone—"

"No. Denali...just no."

I tried for a smile. "I'm starting to come to trust him as a cop. But as a romantic partner? That's a hard *no*, hon."

She huffed. Then pulled the laptop to her chest. "Are we doing anything tonight?"

"No." I said the word with force.

"Yes." Everett being just as defiant.

"Well, I'm going to my room to memorize my lines. If things change, just let me know. Dark and brooding can be fun for a fling—"

"Denali." Everett's tone was part exasperation and part warning.

"He's right, hon." I winked at Denali. I needed to help keep things light. Being around me was a danger to them. If she kept smiling, I was okay with that. "Sometimes things are best left alone. You've done enough flirting with him—"

"Jesus fucking Christ, what else happened while I was..." He flailed.

Denali kissed his cheek. "You probably don't want to know." She slid off the bed and did another pirouette on her way out.

"Oh God." He let out a long breath.

"Nothing except for flirting." I leaned back against the pillows.

"That you know of."

"That I know of. Truthfully..." I tried to find the right words. "Colton played along, but—to me at least—he wasn't interested."

"Should I be offended on my sister's behalf?"

I chuckled. "One minute you're worried he might be interested in her, and the next, you're offended because he might not be?"

"Huh."

"It's not..." I squinted. "I honestly don't think it's because she's Black. I mean, she's damn attractive—"

"Hey."

I laughed. "I'm with you, Ev. Keep your pants on."

He frowned.

I waved him off. "Never mind. I'm just saying..." I hesitated. "There's something about him. You're right—he's dark. I met Dorrie, and she's, like, his opposite."

"Okay, but you know what, she plays bad cop. She's the one who goes after perpetrators. Interrogates them. Colton's the soft one. He's great with victims."

"What?" That sort of blew my mind.

"Which is why you can't...I don't want to say *trust*. He's incredibly trustworthy. But he's also got deep secrets. I don't know how else to put it."

"I'll steer Denali away from him if you're not around."

"That would be appreciated."

"Okay, so we need to get you ready for bed—"

"Not so fast."

*Fuck.*

"You need to go to Colton and Dorrie. You know you do. I would trust them with my life. Hell, maybe not with my sister's heart, but everything else, I would put in Colton's hands. He can sometimes be overbearing, but it's only because he cares."

"What if he knows Sonny?" Tingles ran up and down my spine every time I said the fucker's name.

"I don't know, Rayne." He scratched his beard. "Okay, what the fuck is your last name? Because I think we're beyond games at this point. Clearly Sonny knows who you are. And how did you get away?"

"A couple walked by. Sonny's goon had been beating the shit out of me. He wanted my phone. Obviously. But I wouldn't give it up. Sonny was having a good time watching until the couple strolled by. I'm sure they didn't see anything, but I used the distraction to run. That's when he shot at me. But with a silencer. I'm sure the couple figured it was some random thump."

"A silencer."

"Yeah. They were prepared for murder. God, Ev, I've never run so hard in my life."

"Even with all the bruises and a bullet wound."

"I was running for my life."

"Yeah, I guess you were."

"The rest is true. I really did hitch a ride to Mission City with a bunch of young women. I really did spend the night hanging out at Fifties with Sarabeth keeping an eye on me. I really came to your office hoping to Christ you'd show. You'd been in on Remembrance Day and Christmas Eve, so I figured you might on New Year's Day."

He sighed. "A little creepy you know that. As well, that was a hell of a risk."

I waved my hand around. "Better than showing up here."

"Well, that's true." He twitched his nose. "You're going to have to emerge, Rayne. You can't live in the shadows for the rest of your life."

"I need you to be safe."

"I am safe. I have nothing to do with anything. You show Colton and Dorrie the video. No one ever needs to know Denali and I saw it. We'll just...move on with our lives." Everett shrugged, as if that meant nothing to him.

My heart shattered. *And so it goes.* The kiss off I'd expected. Just hadn't been prepared for. I pressed a hand to my chest. "In the morning. I promise in the morning." I'd laundered my clothes the day before. I could wear my own stuff and be prepared to leave immediately after that. Or I could have Denali drive me down to the police detachment. Save Everett the hassle of having more people invade his safe space. His refuge. His home.

He sighed. "Last name?"

"Iverson. My name is Rayne Iverson."

"As in..." He frowned. "Not *the* Iversons. The ones who endowed—"

"Yep."

"Okay." He met my gaze. "They're wealthy."

"They *were* wealthy. Most of those endowments were made in the seventies and early eighties. They lost everything in the crash of eighty-seven and lived off credit until they both passed. Somewhere in there, my mother had me. That, like everything else she did, didn't work out well. She dumped me with my grandparents and moved on. When Gran and Grandpa died, I assumed she'd crawl out of the woodwork, looking for her inheritance. Nope. Just me—the gay grandson they'd disavowed. They left me everything. Knowing, of course, the joke would be on me. Nothing remained of their legacy. Everything was mortgaged to the hilt, and a bunch of stuff—all the family jewels and antiques—had been sold off, with bad knockoffs put in their place. I think I netted about fifteen thousand when the estate was settled last year. I invested that in my private investigation business—equipment, advertising and all that shit. Money's gone, but I'd started to make enough money to live off of. Until this."

"Until this." He echoed the words. "I had no idea. I hadn't even heard of your grandparents' passing."

"I didn't make any announcements. Didn't even have funerals. I worried if the newspapers found out about everything, my family's name would be destroyed." I rubbed my hands up and down my face. "Turns out the legacy was all shit anyway. I found my mother's journals. She talked about her crazy Aunt Judy—my grandmother's sister. How the woman used to rail on to my mom about all the illegal labor practices my grandparents engaged in. The exploitative business...stuff. Truly, if half of what Judy said was true, my grandparents should've been locked up. Instead, they'd been treated like damn near royalty by the elite of Vancouver society."

"I had no idea." Everett repeated himself.

"And no one ever will. Restitution is damn near impossible—I have nothing to give. Even if I could track down all the people they swindled, to what end? There's nothing. All I'd do was destroy the Iverson name. Hell, after the grief they gave me for being gay, I was sorely tempted. Almost wrote a check to an LGBTQ charity and asked for a big thank-you recognition. But..." I sighed. "I needed the money. They didn't give me anything *but* the name. I'd change it if I could."

"You can, you know. It's not tough. But you'd need something to change it to."

*Williams. I'd change it to Williams, if you asked me. Because your family is amazing. I wish they'd been mine growing up. And that's only the side benefit.* Yet I said nothing.

"Well, you could always get married. Then you don't have to pick a new name—the option will be picked for you."

*Williams. I could marry you and take your name.*

Which sent all kinds of warning signals off in my brain. We barely knew each other. He'd been laid up in the hospital for more than half of our official courtship—his father's words, not mine. I sighed. "I'll figure something out."

"First the police and keeping you alive."

"Yeah." But I wasn't convinced his course was the best. I nearly suggested just asking August and Julian to pick up my stuff. But Sonny might have other eyes on the condo I didn't know about. If he'd had any doubt about my identity, the beating I'd taken rather than just handing over my phone, probably proved it. And the goon was just getting started when I got free.

Or some shit like that.

"I need to piss." Everett tried to shift.

I was off the bed and around to him just as he swung his legs over.

He growled.

I grinned. Then I helped him stand.

He swayed.

I steadied him.

Our gazes clashed.

"Stay the night with me?" He blinked those brilliant dark-brown eyes at me.

"Yeah, okay."

Because there was nothing in the world I wanted more.

# Chapter Twenty-Seven

Everett

Rayne hadn't seemed overly enthusiastic about my request. In fact, I expected him to be gone by the time I finally got my ass out of the bathroom and back into bed.

The opposite was true.

All the dishes had disappeared, and he was now in my spare T-shirt and sleep pants. The ones with the frayed pant cuffs.

Now I was glad I hadn't tossed them.

Me—too thrifty for my own good.

Denali's words came back to me. Yeah, I'd have to do even better about recycling my electronics. About leaving behind a better world for my sister's kids.

Champ was missing, which suggested he'd been walked and put to bed in Rayne's room. My *boyfriend* stood uneasily by the side of the bed. "Get in." I might've barked that.

He laughed. "Glad to see grumpy bear is back. With all that tenderness and caring, I thought he might've disappeared forever." He offered a wicked grin.

"You're incorrigible."

"And you love that about me." Then, as if unaware of what he'd said, he plumped my pillows, then moved around to the other side of the bed. His side of the bed. He slid in.

After a long moment, I did the same. I was grateful he and August had suggested getting undressed and into pajamas when I'd first come home. I'd been so fucking exhausted, but they'd assured me I'd be appreciative later.

I hadn't been convinced.

Now I was.

I turned off my lamp.

Rayne didn't.

*Okay, apparently there's more to say. I don't think he wants to hear me nagging about Colton—*

He cleared his throat. "How are you feeling?"

I frowned. "Like I was in a wreck just over a week ago?"

"Right."

"Why?" He had me damn curious.

"I dunno." He flopped on his side facing me. "I have a hankering."

I sighed. "I'm tired, and I have no idea what you're saying."

"I'm saying my cock's been very lonely the past ten days."

"Uh...you realize you have a right hand, don't you?"

"I'm a southpaw."

Something I hadn't realized and wow, talk about a way to derail us quickly. "Same logic applies."

"But what if...?"

I sighed yet again. "Baby, it's not getting up. Even if I were allowed—which I'm not—it is *not* getting up."

He swatted the air. "I know that."

"Then why—"

"How about I put on a show for you?"

Again, I blinked. "A...show?"

"Yeah, something to keep you entertained. I'd hate for you to get bored."

"Rayne. Baby. Being around you is *never* boring. Like...ever. I have to be vigilant because you're *always* up to something."

"Hey."

I arched an eyebrow.

He winced. "Okay, fair point. I just...I think you'll like this show."

Somehow, in my heart of hearts, I had no doubt. "Okay, show me what you've got."

"Yippee." He slid out of bed and, in the blink of an eye, was naked.

"Nice trick."

"Scrawny kid in gym class. The quicker I could get changed, the easier my life."

"Someday you'll have to show me the other half of that equation. Getting dressed quickly," I clarified.

"Yeah." He winked.

My gaze traveled from his dear face, down his muscled chest to his excessively amazing abs to his happy trail and, finally, to his very erect cock. "You're that turned on?"

"Everett, I'm perpetually horny around you. Oh." He bit his lower lip. "That's sounds bad. I mean, you're injured and, like, while I was worried then of course I wasn't thinking about...well, yeah, I kind of was. I mean not *when* you might be able to again. Because like Dr. Leo said a month, right? Or something like that? Well, he said you need to work with the physiotherapist first. And we've got an appointment for you with the guy the day after tomorrow. What was his name? Marcus something? And like, he'll assess you and follow your progress—"

"Rayne."

He blinked.

"Breathe."

He did that.

"Yes, I start physio with Marcus Branigan next week. Yes, it's going to be a while before I can do anything sexual. Logistics alone would be a nightmare. Even if I could get it up." I gazed down my blanket-covered body. "Which I absolutely cannot."

"Yeah, I figured."

"But, baby, you have a beautiful body. One you clearly spend a lot of time taking care of. I think it's amazing, and I can't believe you've shared it with me."

"Uh—"

"I'm still mad about that, and we have to get Allyson out of jail. She might be willing to say why she was with Sonny."

"Yeah."

"But you didn't have to let me fuck you."

"No. That's true."

"And you didn't have to show up at my doorstep."

"That's also true."

"So I'll take what you're offering. A show? Yes, please. But...could you toss down a towel? You were the one who pointed out jizz on someone else's floor was bad taste."

He laughed. Then hustled over to the bathroom, made a big show of getting a towel, then dropped it before him.

I reached out to snag.

To squeeze.

To tug.

"Hey." He batted my hand away. "No touching until you're better."

"Uh, Dr. Leopold said *no sex*. He didn't say *no touching*."

Rayne appeared to consider. "Nope. No touching until I can touch back."

"So I'm going to get a show every night? You know eventually I'm bound to pop a woody."

He hesitated. "We'll deal with that when we get to it."

*Oh God, I just implied he was going to still be here after tomorrow's meeting with Colton and Dorrie. What if he doesn't want that?*

I didn't have an answer to that question. We'd never once, in the entire fourteen days we'd been together, talked about the future. Everyone else seemed to assume we had one—but we didn't seem to. Were we just being pessimists or ostriches? Sticking our heads in the sand?

He stepped back, still in my line of sight. In fact, whether out of his consideration or out of happenstance, I didn't even have to crane my neck to get the full show.

Our gazes met.

"You ready?" He offered the grin I was getting to know so well.

"Bring it on." Only now did I realized he couldn't jerk himself—the condom would snag. "Oh, shit, you can take the condom off. We can just clean—"

"Hush." He elongated the *s* into a hiss of sorts.

I relaxed. With just one word, he could soothe some of my anxiety.

He ran his hand from his lightly stubbled jaw down his neck to his sternum. He tweaked each of his nipples.

His cock, sticking straight out, jerked.

He moaned.

I pressed a hand to my chest. Not because I was in pain. The painkillers I'd taken were decently effective. No, I was trying to hold in the words of affection. Not so much the compliments—although I could wax poetic about his beautiful body. This time, I wanted to talk about his soul. He was a good man caught in a tough situation. Hell, the fact he was still alive spoke to his strength of spirit.

His bruises appeared to be mostly healed. The fresh scar on his side was clean and dry.

He slid his hands down his abdomen. One snagged his cock while the other—with a little help from being able to contort in an interesting way after he set a foot up on the edge of the box spring—grabbed his balls.

Another moan.

This time, from me.

My spirit was definitely willing. Alas, my cock lay nestled contentedly with zero interest in making an enthusiastic appearance.

Dr. Leopold would be very proud of me.

Or so I told myself.

Because this was definitely not getting shared with him. The man had an ex-husband with whom he had a *complicated* relationship. I was so not stepping in that. And I aimed to make certain Rayne didn't either.

*You don't own him. You can't dictate who he does and doesn't spend his time with.*

I hated when my inner voice was right.

Still...

He twisted his wrist, squeezed his sac, then rocked up onto the balls of his feet. "Holy fuck." He went rigid and held himself still. His cock jerked, spurted.

When I'd been fucking him against the desk, and I'd come, I'd needed him for support.

He had no such need. Somehow, he managed to stay upright through the orgasm. His breath stuttered, and he shook, but he stayed on his feet.

My breath hitched in a whimper.

His eyes shot open.

I held up my hand. "I'm fine. Just...you're magnificent. Truly. I'm...stunned."

"But okay?" His voice came out as a croak.

"Better than okay. You...you heal me."

He chuckled. "I think that might be a little much. I need to get rid of the condom." He offered one more impish grin before sauntering off to the bathroom.

I pressed a cool hand to my heated cheek. I was pretty certain Dr. Leopold wouldn't have approved of the rapid breathing I was doing, but I had no intention of telling him. Just my little secret with Rayne.

*Well, along with all the others.* Too many to count. So much deception. And he wasn't safe. I had to make him see that only the police could put an end to this. As much as I wanted to, I couldn't just keep him here with Champ forever. He had a life he needed to get back to. A fledgling business he'd invested his inheritance in.

"Hey." He hotfooted back into the room and, in the blink of an eye, was dressed in my sleep pants again.

"That was quick."

"This house is cold. Reminds me of my grandparents' place."

The place where he'd been so unhappy. "Turn up the heat."

"Nah, it's bedtime. And you're comfy. Right?"

"Uh, yeah. Very."

"Great." He started for the door.

"Where are you going?" Panic seized me, but I tried to rein it in. I wasn't going to lose my shit just because he left.

"Back to my room." His look of uncertainly was accentuated by his furrowed brow.

I patted the bed next to me.

"I can't." He gestured to my chest.

"I'm not moving. I'm good on my back." Because side-sleeping still hurt too much, even though I normally slept that way.

"Oh, you need your knees raised." He moved to my side of the bed. "And you should be lying flatter. Here. Scoot down. Do you need help?"

"Jesus." I muttered the word. Yet he was right, I was feeling strain on my lower back. Within a moment, he had me flat with one orthopedic pillow under my neck and a pillow under my knees. *God, I'm old. No, not old. Just badly damaged. No, not badly. Ten days in hospital wasn't too horrendous. My body just needs time—*

"Everett, I can hear the gears grinding all the way over here." Rayne stood at the end of the bed.

"Now will you please get in?"

He bit his lower lip.

"I promise you, no hanky-panky will take place in this bed." *Although if you put on another show, I won't complain.*

Finally, he moved to the other side. He slid in and lay on his back.

"Now *you* need a pillow under your knees."

He rolled onto his side, facing me. "I've missed you."

"You've seen me every day."

"I mean...I missed this."

Which was nuts since we'd only done *this* once.

But I felt the same way.

"Where's Champ?" I couldn't believe I'd lost track of the dog.

"I took him out for a walk, and he's in his crate in my room. Good thing he loves his crate."

I yawned. "Good thing."

"Rest."

"If I hear that word one more time..." Then my eyes shut, and I was out.

Not until I woke much later, did I realize Rayne hadn't stayed.

# Chapter Twenty-Eight

Rayne

I opened my door, and Champ uncurled to look at me. "Might as well come out for a bit," I whispered to him, tiptoeing in and unlatching the crate. "But no waking Everett." I had some thinking to get through, but Champ might as well get a little attention too, while I decided how to protect Everett.

I would do anything for my man. And my dog.

Amazing how possessive I'd become in such a short period of time.

I put on a pair of wool socks, then pulled a blanket over my shoulders like a shawl. Slowly, I eased my way down the stairs. On the second floor, I looked around. The television might be on the opposite side of the house from Everett's bedroom, but I couldn't be certain of the acoustics—or even what volume we'd left it on. Knowing Everett, probably low. He didn't do anything loudly.

Still, I crept down to the first floor. Feeling a little guilty—but not enough to stop myself—I made my way into his home office on the ground floor. Why he had a den upstairs with a desk and an office down here was a little beyond me. Man, did the guy ever work hard. Except the room down here didn't have a door, unlike the room upstairs. I didn't feel like I was intruding as everything was under lock and key. I wasn't snooping anyway...I just wanted a break.

From the intensity.

From Everett's pain.

From my feelings.

Which, in retrospect, would've been better addressed if I'd just gone to bed and tried to sleep. *Oh well, I'm here now.* I opened the blinds, then settled into the very expensive ergonomic chair to just gaze outside.

His lawn glistened in the moonlight as the pristine-white snow came into focus. I loved his little garden with the path leading to the little gate. A gate Champ could easily hurl himself over—if he had enough running space.

We'd have to fix that, if we stayed. If Everett kept me, and I kept Champ. Zephyra had told Torah that the abandonment waiting period was over, so I could adopt him formally now, if I was ready. He loved his life with me...right?

I gazed down at the pooch who'd settled at my feet. Within moments, he'd gone to sleep. *So trusting now despite his history. So honest. Wears his heart on his sleeve. His paw. His...whatever.*

So very different from me. I'd learned to keep everything bottled up inside.

Until Everett.

The uncorking started at the Halloween party. Each time I was with Everett, it loosened a little.

Then had come his crash.

Hearing he was being medevacked had done me in. That cork had shot out of the bottle and my contents had flown everywhere. My heart had shattered. Only seeing him alive, albeit hurt, had given me strength to keep going.

And to swear to be more honest.

I could've told him Marita hadn't been able to retrieve anything. I could've gone to the library or a public café to watch the videos. I'd had tons of less-honest options.

Well...maybe not *tons*. But I'd made a series of choices tonight—including letting Denali stay. So I didn't chicken out.

Ev had been pissed. Appropriately so. Except his client was up to her neck in other shit. She could've told the police about Sonny—but she hadn't. Clearly, she'd decided to roll the dice about being convicted of a crime she hadn't committed rather than face the wrath of the dirty cop.

Now it was my turn to roll those dice.

I wanted answers to questions I could barely formulate.

What would happen if I turned my evidence over to the cops?

What would happen to my relationship with Everett if I didn't?

What would happen if I tried to go home?

Was I willing to walk away from my car, my equipment, my possessions, and—most importantly—my life as I'd known it?

How could I keep both Everett and Champ safe?

*Christ, that's a lot of shit to wade through, and I have no idea where to start*. Somehow, I couldn't see a way out of this mess. Even if I went to Colton—whom I didn't entirely trust—what would the ramifications be? Even if they arrested Sonny—which was a big *if*—he had associates. I didn't know if they were on the police force or if they were just buddies. Would the money flow to them stop? Would they come after me?

This all felt super impossible.

I laid my elbows on the desk, let my head fall forward, and supported myself on my arms. I hadn't worked out in more than two weeks. First my body had been healing. Then Everett's had. I missed the excitement of that first fuck we'd shared...but I also remembered how tenderly he'd taken me. It'd be a couple of months before he was strong enough to fuck me like that again. I wondered what he'd feel like under me, taking it easy, letting me care for him. I wasn't a great top, but if he asked, I'd totally do it for him. But we were a long way from him being healed enough for anything. Chances were I'd be long—

Champ bolted upright.

My gaze shot up as well. Instinctively, I gazed outside.

And saw nothing.

I squinted.

Still nothing.

Champ darted from the room into the hallway, barking his head off.

I followed, hard on his heels.

To come face-to-face with a man holding a gun at my head.

*Well, okay then.*

He'd come from the garage.

*How did he get in? Denali didn't lock the door? Where's the fucking alarm?*

My mind whirled.

Champ snarled at the man, hackles raised, although he pressed his rump against my shins.

"Shut the fucking dog up." The man's voice carried menace. But was also sort of high-pitched and...whiny?

I'd never heard Sonny speak, but I was facing him. I just… He didn't seem like the type to leave the dirty work to someone else. Clearly he had no issues with getting down in the muck.

"Champ, hush, it's okay, he's not hurting us." I tried to steady my voice. "See, nice man, not a woman. We're fine."

Champ's loud rumbles softened.

"Sit," I told him. "Good boy."

His rump landed on my foot, and although he kept an intent gaze on Sonny, he quieted. "Bingo." I didn't have treats in my PJs. *Everett's* PJs. *And let him not have heard, not come downstairs.* "Good boy, Champ. Sit quiet."

Sonny's gun was still trained on my head.

"Let the dog go." My voice was unnaturally steady. "I can send him upstairs."

"Just hand over the stick and I'll, uh, be on my way."

I didn't, for even one moment, believe that. He wasn't wearing a mask. No way was I getting out of this alive. But maybe I could keep Denali and Everett safe… "How do you know about the stick?"

Even in the semi-darkness, with just the light coming from the outside, I saw him roll his eyes.

*Uh, rude.*

"Just hand it over. And tell me where the copies are."

"I don't have copies." Slowly, I reached for my pocket.

Only to realize of course I wore the sleep pants—no treats, no pockets— and I'd left the stick on the dresser in the guest bedroom.

"I need to go upstairs to get it."

He frowned.

"Look, you can follow me up. The guy who lives here's sleeping. It'll just be us.

"I know who's here. Some guy just out of the hospital, a skinny little woman, and you with your soft heart for your dog—"

I rambled, trying to keep him off balance, "You know, I wouldn't let that *woman* hear you describe her that way. The derision in your tone tells me you don't have respect for women. So is that all women or just, uh—"

"I'm not a racist, fuckface. All woman are idiots." He gestured with his gun toward the stairs.

"Wow. So, like sexist. Misogynist. Or both? I never understood the difference between—"

An almighty crash and then a gunshot with the shattering of glass ended my babbling against the vagaries of language.

Sonny dropped like a stone—felled by a massive clay pot planter that had been dropped down the stairwell on his head.

I turned to find the glass window in the front door cracked with a bullet hole in the middle of it. *Fuck. That could've been my head.*

The light in the front hallway turned on—nearly blinding me.

Champ whined and leaped up, barking toward the stairs, then snarling and lunging at Sonny's still form. I was torn between Sonny, the gun, and the dog, but the first two were motionless. Champ was the loose cannon. "Hush, boy. Sit." I grabbed his collar. "Sit. Easy."

"Is he out? I had to wait till he wasn't aiming at you." Denali clomped down the stairs. She bolted over to Sonny and, when she got to him, slid his gun toward me with her bare foot.

I hung onto Champ. "Watch out for broken glass. How is he...?"

"I'll be fine." She cleared some dirt off Sonny's head. "He's alive, but you better call an ambulance. He's got a hell of a contusion and he's out cold. Oh, and police too, I suppose."

"Let me find something to tie him up with. He might, you know, wake up." Keeping between the shaking, growling dog and Denali,

I grabbed Champ's leash. I tied him to the doorknob of the closet, away from the glass. The I nabbed a scarf from the coat tree and advanced toward the weapon, I used the scarf to grab it by the silencer. Fingerprints were going to be super important. I put the gun on the desk, well away from Sonny, Denali, and Champ.

Denali grinned fiercely. "If he wakes, I'd be more than happy to drop another plant on his head."

"You might've killed him."

"Good riddance."

I grabbed a second scarf, because of course Everett had two scarves, and tied Sonny's hands. Then I patted him down to see if he had another weapon.

He didn't.

Champ vibrated, ears down, panting hard, but still sat obediently. "Such a good boy. Okay, phone."

She pointed. "There's a landline in Everett's office."

I didn't ask how she knew—clearly she was very comfortable in the townhouse.

"Hey!" Everett yelled down the stairs, I realized, not for the first time. "Hey, was that a shot? Rayne! Denali! Are you okay? I'm coming down."

I pointed at Denali. "You keep your brother from hurting himself. I'll call the cops." I made my way to the phone and called 911.

# Chapter Twenty-Nine

Everett

"I want to see for myself." I was beyond exasperated. This was my home, for fuck's sake. But Denali blocked any attempt I made to go down to the ground floor. So I sat on my couch, seeing the flashing lights reflecting off my neighbor's homes, and feeding Champ reassuring treats. He'd been pacing and whining, growling at Denali, who was probably going to have to start winning him over again from the beginning. But now, he lay tucked close beside my feet. I handed down another bit of kibble, and this time he took it without hesitation.

Apparently a crowd had gathered outside. Even below-freezing temperatures weren't enough to get rid of the looky-loos. The owner's association was going to have a shit fit.

Rayne was downstairs—dealing with the police, the paramedics, and the firefighters. Because of course they'd shown up. They were faster than the ambulance and had medical training.

"That redheaded fireman is gorgeous." Sitting upright with her feet tucked under her butt, Denali fanned herself.

"Firefighter." Because language was important. Because precision—in this moment—was all I had.

"Oh, but he's all man."

"He's also gay."

She frowned. "Not bi?"

"Nope."

"And you've never tapped that?"

I snorted. "I don't *tap* every gay man in Mission City, thank you. I'm...discerning. Finn, however? Yeah, not so much." Which was way more than I should've been saying about the guy, but my mind was muddled. I was aware he often went into Vancouver to hit up the gay clubs on Davie Street. Personally, I wondered if he wouldn't be better off just moving to Vancouver. God knew, the city had way more options than Mission City. Then even Cedar Valley. But Finn was a hometown kid. He loved his mom—a nurse at the hospital—and he loved Mission City. So he stayed.

"Well, if he's not discerning, maybe he and Rayne might hook up."

"Hey! Fuck no."

She grinned. "Yeah, you *so* have a thing for Rayne."

"I...might resemble that statement."

"What are you going to do about it? If Sonny talks and his associates get taken down, then Rayne's free to move on with his life. To take Champ and go home."

"His apartment doesn't allow big dogs." I seemed to recall having that conversation with him.

"So he'll find a new place." Denali smiled at Champ who backed farther away from her, his butt half under the couch, and whined. Poor dog was traumatized. Denali knew better than to approach him but she crooned, "He's such a good boy. A brave boy. I never would've known someone was here if he hadn't barked."

"Did the asshole say why he came alone?"

"No, he never did. Kind of stupid."

"Well, he wasn't expecting to have a planter dropped on his head."

"Nope." Denali grinned. "That was fun."

"You might've been shot. Rayne nearly was. Champ was in danger. You need to rethink your definition of fun. For fuck's sake, Denali. You could've gotten Rayne shot. What if your timing had been off? Planter versus gun. You had time to call the police. You said yourself that Rayne wasn't in immediate danger. Sonny wanted the thumb drive first."

My beloved sister straightened and gave me her *oh, it's on now* face. "For the record." She held up her index finger. "I waited till the asshole wasn't pointing the gun at Rayne."

Her voice trembled a bit, but I couldn't tell if that was leftover stress or a new wash of realization. "Not the point."

She added her middle finger. "The gun wasn't pointed at Champ."

The dog snuffed as if he couldn't believe her rashness either.

"Still not—"

She added her ring finger. "You were upstairs, defenseless."

"Jesus."

"Hey, I wasn't armed either. Just because I was some *skinny woman*—"

"He said that?"

"Yep."

"No wonder you took him out." I shook my head. "We're getting off topic."

"What I'm trying to tell you, big brother, is that I didn't have a better choice. The moment came, and I seized it."

"You always were too smart for you own good." I muttered that.

"Admit it, you love me."

I pursed my lips.

She swatted my biceps. Then added a hearty laugh. "We're all fine. Bad guy's on the way to the hospital. Cute fireman spoke to cuter paramedic...I think his name is Sawyer...? Anyway, apparently they're running the douchebag over to Abbotsford as he might need surgery." She dusted her hands.

*If he dies, I doubt you'll be so cavalier. You, who escorts ants out of the house rather than killing them...*

"He deserves worse." As if reading my thoughts, Denali jutted her chin out. "Scumbag. Slimeball. Degenerate—"

"I get the picture. And a cop to boot. I overheard Colton saying the guy got Officer of the Year a few years back. How can he be so corrupt and people not know?"

"He's been on the crown prosecutor's radar for a while." Colton strode in from the kitchen, through the dining room, and into the living room. Which was all just one long space. Champ barked at him, and Colton paused a few feet away.

"Oh?" Denali puffed her already poofy hair. When she wasn't on set—or at least when she wasn't required to have more-sedate hairdos, her curls were wild. *Glorious and natural* my dad loved to say.

"Yes." Colton didn't miss a beat, apparently either not noticing the flirtatious pose my sister was taking or, just as likely, ignoring it because he was on duty. "Zach Finnegan, the crown prosecutor, was approached by a member of the Abbotsford police force. That officer was promised anonymity—and they provided plenty of evidence. Zach's been planning something with my boss to move on Sonny. Was supposed to happen next week. They were going to read in some

Mission City police officers for the op on Monday. Likely not me, given I'm in sex crimes—"

"And yet you're here tonight." Denali fluttered her hand.

*God save me.*

"Well, since I was part of the investigation with Farrah, and you—" He pointed to me. "—were injured as part of that, the dispatcher thought this might be related. They called me and, since I don't live far away, I came. Becoming the investigating officer sort of makes sense, so Greg approved it." He snagged his notebook. "Now for your statements. Normally we like to separate victims, but since you—" He pointed to me again. "—really don't have much to add..."

I shook my head. "I woke to the gunshot. I didn't even know Champ had barked. Good soundproofing." Apparently Rayne had closed my door, but Denali's had been left partly open. She'd heard Champ bark and...saved the day.

The impotence I felt rivaled the rage toward this yet-unmet Sonny. I looked forward to testifying at his trial. I'd seen the video Rayne had shot. He'd invaded my house. I wanted him taken down for ever putting Rayne and Denali in danger.

Oh, and Champ. My dog and my man. That was pretty much the worst of the worst.

Colton turned to Denali. "Can we go over the events of this evening again?"

And so they did.

A chill ran through me, and I hadn't realized I'd shivered until Denali wrapped my throw blanket around me.

"We've put cardboard over the broken window downstairs." Colton eyed my baseboard heater. "You want to turn up the heat?"

Denali said, "What we need is to get him back upstairs."

"I'm fine—"

"You're anything but fine." Denali put her hands on her hips.

I sighed.

Champ's ears flattened and he half sat up.

"Down. Bingo." I fed him a treat when his chest hit the floor. I was certain I wasn't doing this properly, but I'd watched Rayne enough to have some idea.

He vibrated with unleashed energy—as he had the entire time he'd been separated from Rayne.

Perhaps I was also stressed.

Colton chuckled softly.

"I'm also going to make you some chamomile tea." She eyed Colton. "Watch him."

She flounced away.

Yes, flounced.

"You are surrounded by some strong women."

I was going to ask how he knew, but then I remembered he'd been at the hospital with my family. Denali was stubborn—my mother even more so.

I narrowed my eyes.

He shrugged, clearly aiming for nonchalance. "I should've said people. Your sister's a dynamo—I noticed that at the hospital. And Rayne? Didn't see him coming. I knew he was hiding something—"

"You're not gay."

He burst out laughing. "Yeah, not. I'm not going to make a move on your man."

"You're not going to make a move on my sister either." I tried for righteous anger—and promptly shivered.

"I should see how Denali's doing with the tea—"

"I'm fine." Said through chattering teeth. I pitched my voice lower. "We need to talk."

Colton remained seated, but also pitched his voice lower. Almost to a whisper. "I'm not looking to start a relationship right now. And I suspect, although your sister comes off as flirtatious, that she's a *relationship* type of person. I respect that. Maybe another time—"

"Colton." As much warning as I could inject.

"She's an independent woman, Everett. Hold her too closely, and she'll rebel for the hell of it. I'm surprised you haven't figured that out yet."

"How's that going with Mallory?" Colton's younger sister.

"She's happy with Darius. I'm hopeful they might marry. God knows, they've been together long enough..."

Mallory's stubborn streak matched her brother's. Likely if she knew he wanted her to marry, she'd just do the opposite.

*Like if Denali knows you don't want her to date this eligible police officer she just might...?* "You're right. I'll try to loosen my grip." I hadn't spent much time with her since leaving home—but she'd visited me enough that I liked to think I might have some influence. Some sway. Even if only backward if I pushed too hard.

"Okay." Denali entered my line of sight.

*Damn. I'd assumed she'd clomp across the space like she always does. How much did she hear?*

She held a steaming mug of fragrant tea.

Champ eyed her while pressing himself against me.

She pivoted to Colton. "Can you help him upstairs? I'll follow. He's got Champ as well." She wasn't hurt the dog didn't trust her yet. Understood he might never.

"What about Rayne?" Damnit, I wanted him with me.

"The investigating officer is getting a statement. And you're not going to interfere, or he'll be taken down to the station tonight. He probably should be, but given your state—"

"Yes. I'm very tired." I cut Colton off. Because if they thought I needed Rayne here then maybe they wouldn't drag him down to the detachment.

Denali eyed me.

I jerked my head while Colton positioned himself by my side. The guy was damn good at helping me up without putting pressure on my chest. Soon, as a group, we were ascending the stairs with Champ by my side and Denali following at a distance.

The cold from below was coming straight up the staircase.

"I've called a glazier." Denali spoke as she followed from behind. Almost like she could read my thoughts. Although, really, they weren't complicated.

"Thank you."

"I offered them double if they come out as quickly as they can."

"Your insurance might cover the cost." Colton unerringly pointed me toward the solo door at the far end of the hall.

"I'm not filing a claim. I really don't need to be explaining gunshot damage." I shot a glare over my shoulder.

Denali pursed her lips.

*Let it go. You said your piece. Making her relive that moment isn't likely to earn you any favors in the future. She's a kickass, and that'll stand her in good stead in the future. Be grateful she saved everyone's life.*

Colton pointed to the ensuite.

"Uh, yeah." I considered trying to coax Champ over to his bed, but he'd gone through enough. I'd be okay if he joined me in the bathroom.

"I can take things from here." Denali placed my mug on the side table. She moved to my side.

Champ let out a low growl.

I couldn't blame him. He was beyond stressed with everything that had happened.

After a moment, Colton stepped back. "Yeah, I believe you can take care of just about anything. I'm going to say next time *please* call the police. But I'll also say that was a gutsy move that probably saved three lives—"

"Four." She jutted her chin.

"Four?" He squinted as if trying to sort out the word.

"Champ." Her mouth took on a grim line as she gestured to the dog with her chin. "I don't believe that Sonny asshole would've let the dog live."

"You're probably right." Colton eyed all of us. "Don't go downstairs until the techs are done and they tell you it's clear. Better yet, once they're out of here, hire a cleaning crew. There are experts who specialize in cleaning up crime scenes. There's a team in Cedar Valley. Out of Abbotsford. They're the best. I can—"

"We're good." Denali gave him a defiant look. "I can search *crime scene cleanup*. Frankly, I can do it myself. Everett doesn't need to spend—"

"If you can text me their details, Colton, I'd be appreciative. I'll call them as soon as you're gone." I squeezed Denali's arm. "I need to piss."

She pursed her lips—well aware I was being manipulative.

I was too fucking tired to care.

By the time Champ and I made it back from the bathroom, Colton was gone.

I guided the dog over to his bed. "You'll be okay." I couldn't remember the command to tell him to get in the bed, but when he did on his own, I managed, "Down," and "Bingo," and dropped him a treat since bending over hurt too much. He lipped it off the floor, then lay in a lion pose instead of curled up, his head tensely raised, ears at half-mast, not looking sleepy or settled. I told him, "Stay," and dropped him another kibble.

Then reluctantly, with Denali's help, I climbed into my bed. I didn't want her help, and I wanted Rayne by my side.

*Oh well, we don't always get what we want. Everyone's safe. Nothing else matters.*

Denali leaned on the wall by the head of the bed.

Champ whined, but didn't get up.

I tossed Champ another treat. "You're such a good boy." Then I checked my phone and found a text from Colton. I made a call to the cleanup people and secured a promise from a very alert-sounding woman that they'd have a crew on my doorstep the moment the police cleared the scene.

"You promise you'll call her?" I eyed Denali as I sipped my tea.

"You're not going to?"

"I had to take my painkillers." I'd slowly been slowly lowering the dose, but my chest was screaming in agony. I'd had no choice.

"You're about to pass out."

"Between the pills and the tea, I'd say that's a safe bet."

She pressed a kiss to my cheek. "I'll wait in the living room for Rayne. I'll make sure he's okay."

Which should've been my job. I wanted to know why he'd been downstairs when Sonny broke in. Had he been planning to run? That didn't make sense because, according to Denali, he'd still been in my pajamas. At least the police had let him change into street clothes so he wasn't freezing.

They were taking those spare pajamas for forensic analysis.

Fine by me. I didn't want them back.

"Hey, careful." Denali snatched the mug from my shaking hands before it tipped over.

Whether from fatigue or delayed panic at what could've been, I wasn't certain.

She pressed another kiss to my forehead. Then she helped me settle.

Within a moment, despite the night's events, I was out.

# Chapter Thirty

Rayne

I shook Colton's hand, as he was the last person to leave. I wasn't certain he'd needed to stay and supervise the crime-scene techs, but I appreciated his diligence.

The shot-out window had been covered with several layers of cardboard and Colton had explained that Denali had hired a glazier.

And said glazier had shown up moments after the forensic people had packed up and left.

Almost like she'd been waiting.

So I'd supervised that.

Denali wanted to help, but I'd insisted she stay upstairs. She didn't need to see the blood or shards of pottery. Head wounds bled like a sonofabitch, and although Sonny'd been moaning, he needed to go for scans to make certain there wasn't bleeding on the brain. I wouldn't have felt bad, but Denali didn't need a death on her conscience.

"We're done here." The glazier handed me a bill.

I slapped my pocket for my wallet only to remember the damn thing was upstairs on the dresser in Everett's spare bedroom. As I eyed the invoice, the realization I didn't have that much money on my credit card sank in.

"It's okay." The woman smiled. "We trust Everett will pay."

"You know him?" I knew about small towns, but that seemed a little much.

"My sister knows Gil. And yes, we all are friends around here." She smiled. "Like I'm pretty sure you're a stranger."

The way she said the word rankled a bit. Yes, I was a stranger to most of Mission City. But wasn't I getting to know people? Wasn't I setting down roots—however unintentional? "I'll see he pays this tomorrow." Because I wanted her to know I was more than just the guy caught up in this mess.

"Hey, is everything done?"

To my dismay, Denali descended the stairs.

The glazier gestured toward Everett's sister. "Heard what you did. Well done."

Denali's dark-brown eyes flashed triumph. "Yeah, I'm pretty awesome."

"I didn't know Everett had a sister. Do you live in Mission City?"

*Oh my God, is she flirting with Denali?* I'd witnessed men and women doing it frequently while we'd been in the hospital. Everett's sister attracted all kinds of attention.

Denali grabbed a lock of her hair. "No, I'm from New West. But I plan to visit frequently—"

"Which makes you a great sister." I pivoted to glazier. "So that's all?"

She blinked. "Uh, yeah."

"Great. Because I need to see to Everett." Denali had said he was fast asleep, but if this little untruth got the woman going faster, I was okay with that. If Denali was really serious about possible flirting, we had the woman's contact information on the invoice.

I escorted the woman out the door and breathed a sigh of relief when she left. If not for the glass and the shards of pottery—and the constant stream of men and women coming in and out of the place—I would've brought Champ down to stay by me. He was safe with Everett, but I needed his reassurance as much as I was certain he needed mine.

Someone knocked at the door moments after it'd closed.

Denali was there before I could blink. She opened it.

Three people carrying equipment and wearing hazmat suits stood at the door.

I sighed.

"Come on in." Denali opened the door wider for them, then motioned for me to shoo.

For once, I didn't feel like arguing.

I trudged up the stairs feeling the weight of a million stressors on me.

The cops had the thumb drive.

Everett still had his two as the cops hadn't, to my infinite relief, searched the house.

They'd also taken my broken phone and had tried to confiscate my new one. Since the damn thing was so simple and I hadn't installed any aps, I was able to show the investigator the thing literally had nothing on it.

She'd agreed to let me keep it.

That had felt like a monumental victory in a night when very few things had gone right.

I made it to the kitchen, stood for a moment to consider if I needed anything, but then decided I was good. I'd had a coffee—lovingly made by Denali—when the cops had first arrived.

Organized chaos had ensued, and every time I tried to get to Everett, the investigator had pointed out we might have to go down to the detachment where I'd be less distracted.

Yeah, like taking me farther away from my boyfriend was going to focus me in any way.

*Whatever.*

I tiptoed up the stairs, and was relieved to find Everett's door closed. I checked my room, but Champ's crate was empty. Which meant he was hunkered down in Everett's room. That realization brought me comfort. That Champ had been able to settle—at least enough that he wasn't fussing—and that Everett was hopefully asleep.

*Am I welcome there? He did welcome me earlier...except I left. I should've stuck around, because now I don't know what he's thinking. What he's feeling. I abandoned him. Yes, just so I could think...but he doesn't know that.*

Except if I hadn't been downstairs with Champ, then Sonny would've come upstairs. Might've gone into Denali's room first.

*Whatever. In the past.*

Now, the pull to Everett was too strong to resist. I followed my heart and made my way over to his room.

I opened the door quietly.

A low growl came from the corner where Champ's bed was.

"It's me." I whispered the words, vaguely reassured when Everett kept snoring. He didn't normally, but sleeping on his back turned him into a low-key cement mixer. Dialed his vibrations up to eleven. Was definitely not his silent mode.

I found it endearing.

Champ came to greet me as I shut the door quietly behind me. I hadn't told Denali that I was coming up here, but she seemed like a pretty swift person. She'd see the open spare bedroom door, with Champ's empty crate, and she'd know. Hopefully she'd leave us in peace.

Unless another emergency arose. *Please, not tonight.*

"Let's get you into bed." I scratched Champ's neck. "You're such a good boy."

He snuffed and allowed me to guide him over. Without being prompted, he lay on his bed.

"Bingo." I handed him a treat. "You're the bravest boy. The best boy." He wouldn't understand my words, of course, but he'd damn well understand the tone behind them.

After a moment's hesitation, I decided that *carpe diem* was the order of the day and shucked my clothes, leaving them on Everett's reading chair. Using the low light of the bedside lamp, I crawled into bed. I ensured I stayed well away from him, though. I was frozen solid and didn't want—

He reached out to me, vaguely patting the space between us.

I advanced.

"Cold." He mumbled the word.

"Yeah. So I'll just—"

"I'll warm you up, baby."

Okay, not what I'd been expecting. Still, I could deny him nothing. I inched over to him.

He sucked in a breath when I snuggled against him. He was newly out of the hospital—and this was all kinds of a bad idea. Except he'd invited me to his bed earlier, and I'd gone without hesitation then.

*After a mind-blowing orgasm.*

Well, that was true.

"Sleep." He murmured the word and, within moments, his breathing deepened.

Denali had said he'd taken his pills a while back, so I was relieved when he slipped back into sleep.

That same sleep was a long time coming for me, but eventually it overtook me.

When I came back to consciousness, I was aware of both daylight and Everett's gaze on me. I felt his focus, even though my eyelids were still closed

Warmth enveloped me—and not just from the human furnace I'd slept beside. I cracked an eye. "Time?"

"Eight-twenty. I've even managed to piss, but that about did me in."

"Are you okay?"

He pressed a hand to my cheek. "I am now."

I hesitated before turning in to the touch and pressing a kiss to his palm. "Is this real?"

"Did you almost get shot last night? Did your dog and my sister save the day?"

"Champ—"

"Fast asleep. I know you'll need to run him out at some point, but he's dozing. He barely stirred when I got up."

"I should've helped you."

"No, you should've kept sleeping. You were right out."

"I guess I needed it."

He chuckled softly. "Yeah, I'd say you did." His eyes were hard to read in the diffuse light coming from behind the closed blinds, but they appeared to soften. "Cuddle against me? I can't spoon—"

I was flush against him in an instant. "Did you take your pills?"

"The lighter ones, yeah. But baby, I'd endure a damn sight more than pain if it means having you close."

I blinked. "You shouldn't have to."

"But I would. You..." He swallowed, appearing to collect himself. "You almost died last night, Rayne."

"So did Champ and Denali."

"Both deaths that would've devastated me. But losing you? I wouldn't have been able to come back from this. I mean, losing my sister would just about kill me, don't get me wrong. And Champ?" He swallowed again. "I've kind of grown fond of the guy."

"Admit it, you love him."

"I do love him. Almost as much as I love you."

My breath caught. *It's the drugs. They're making him loopy. Because no way did he just—*

"I said it, Rayne. I meant it. I've never loved someone the way I love you. I have my family. I have Gil and his Cullen and their kids. I have August and his Julian—"

"The piece of work."

He grinned. "Yeah, they're so suited. But you're not derailing me."

I swallowed. "You don't know what you're saying."

"I do, Rayne. And I don't expect you to reciprocate. From what you've told me, you've had a rough go of it."

"I've done okay." I didn't want his sympathy.

"You have." Slowly he nodded. "But I've never gotten the sense there's been a lot of love in your life. I mean, we barely know each other."

"A couple of weeks."

"Almost three months." He countered that with a smile.

I laughed. "Nice try. January first to the fourteenth is not, according to any math, *almost three months*." Then I sobered. "You think I'm being silly." I was pretty sure he wasn't making fun of me, but I couldn't be entirely certain.

"No." he said the word with force. "I'd never think that of you." He let out a breath. "I get the feeling no one ever told you that you're smart. That you can accomplish things—"

"That I'm not a waste of space?"

My breath seized. "Your grandparents said that?"

"Yeah. After I came out. They said they wished my mother'd just had an abortion. Five years later, they were both dead. That felt...like karmic retribution. Which made me feel awful because, like, they were my grandparents. And I was supposed to care about them, right?"

"Some people are just...they shouldn't be parents. Like your mom. And they certainly shouldn't have the honor of being grandparents—like yours." He blinked. "If I could tell you...my grandparents were so amazing. They would've loved you..." He pressed a hand to my chest.

"It's okay." I shrugged as if I didn't have a care.

I read the pain in his eyes. Or sympathy.

"Well, I can promise you that I don't see you like that. Hell, we've barely talked about...I don't even really know everything about you. I want to know all of it. I want to hear whatever you want to share—your pains, your joys...your desires and what drives you nuts."

"Toothpaste in the sink."

He blinked. "Sorry."

"I hate toothpaste in the sink. Drives me nuts. If you happen to drop some of that crap on the bowl then you fucking clean it off."

Slowly, he grinned. "Yeah, I can agree with that." He tilted his head. "Is that it?"

I considered. "I'm an easygoing guy. Now, I don't know if that means I'm easy to live with—" *Oops. I probably shouldn't have said that out loud.*

"I wouldn't care." He cleared his throat. "And I might be a difficult person to live with. No one's done it since I left home. And I'm certain Denali would tell you I'm a challenge."

"Yeah, she probably would." I laughed. "And we should probably get up."

Something flickered in his eyes. "Oh."

I sighed. "You've just dropped a bombshell on me. Yes, I love you too. But I don't understand the ramifications of that. What it means in my life."

"You almost died last night. I don't want that to ever happen again." He said the words with force, then pressed a hand to his chest.

My heart squeezed. "You need to take it easy, okay? Let me walk Champ, and then I'll bring you breakfast. Any preference?"

"I want whatever gets you back to me faster. I should come downstairs—"

Even as he said the words, I spotted the fatigue in his face. "No. You've pissed and that wore you out. So why don't you nap a bit while I get everything ready? I'm certain Denali can help me."

"Yeah, she probably can." His eyes shut for a long time before he opened them with clear effort. "Just a quick nap."

I pressed a kiss to his lips. "I'll be back, I promise."

"Please do." He closed his eyes. This time, apparently, for real.

He needed the rest.

I slid from the bed and made my way over to Champ. "I just need to shower, get dressed, and then I'm all yours."

He nuzzled my hand.

I petted his neck. "I love you. As much as I love the big lug over there."

"Heard that." Sleepy and slurred.

I grinned and leaned closer to Champ. "That was the plan."

He yawned.

On that note, I hustled my ass into the shower and, fifteen minutes later, with still-damp hair, I guided Champ downstairs.

He hesitated on the bottom step when he spotted Denali in the kitchen.

"We're just running outside." I encouraged Champ to stick close to me.

"Great." She offered me a wide smile. "I'm making waffles. Everett's favorite."

"And mine as well. I'm amazed he eats something so unhealthy." I was only half kidding. Admittedly, I'd thought we might have to eat cold pizza for breakfast because I didn't want to delay in getting back to him.

"He'll survive." She bit her lower lip. "He lost weight in the hospital."

"You noticed too, eh?"

"Yeah. So a waffle with butter and real Canadian maple syrup is just what he needs."

"Sounds great."

Champ and I made our way downstairs.

I came up short.

In my head, I'd understood we'd hired people to fix things. To repair the glass and to clean up the blood and dirt as well as the shards of pottery and glass.

I just hadn't realized how no trace of last night would be left. In my mind, I knew exactly where the blood had been.

The tile was pristine.

I remembered how some of the dirt had coated the walls.

Not a trace remained.

Champ whined.

"Right. Sorry." I grabbed my coat from the closet, and we headed out into the bitterly cold January morning with its brilliant sunshine.

Twenty-five minutes later, I sat propped next to Everett on the bed, chowing down on the delicious waffles Denali had prepared.

She sat on the chair by the door, far enough from Champ for him to settle in his bed with his chew bone, eating with the same fervor. Finally, she sighed.

The sigh of the well-sated. "Okay, so I have to share my news."

Evertt and I glanced at each other.

He cleared his throat. "News? It's nine-thirty in the morning."

"Yeah. No rest for the wicked." She grinned. "I meant to tell you last night after pizza dinner, but then Rayne had these videos and, you know..."

"And you forgot?" Everett squinted. "You never forget news when it's about yourself."

"Hey."

Denali and I said the word at the same time, although hers was louder.

"Don't speak to your sister that way." I pointed my fork at Everett. I liked the idea of moving the discussion off the videos and focusing the attention on Denali.

He scowled back as Denali speared a strawberry and contemplated it. "Okay, maybe I won't share my news."

Given how much she was vibrating, I doubted that very much.

"You can be..." Everett shut his mouth. Then, "What's the news?"

"My walk-on role on *Vigilante Justice* has been upgraded to fifteen lines of dialogue." She pursed her lips. "No, I need to clarify. I've been upgraded to an entirely different role. From a coffee girl—my description, not theirs—to a badass businesswoman. I'm taking Montogomery Daley to task over some shady shit he's been up to."

Everett yet again blinked. "Who's Montgomery Daley?"

"Justice." She popped the strawberry slice in her mouth.

He shook his head.

"The Justice in *Vigilante Justice.*" I sighed. "Don't you watch the show? Huge ratings and massive following. They shoot in Vancouver. Have for years..."

He continued to stare at me blankly.

"Okay." I forked the last piece of waffle and considered it.

"Okay what?" Everett eyed his sister and then, in turn, me.

"Okay, tonight we're going to start watching the series. Twenty-four episodes a season times five seasons..." I cocked my head toward Denali. "Or four?"

"We're shooting season five. And we have to hurry up because Cole Hamilton's partner, Caressa, is very pregnant."

"Who is Cole Hamilton?" Everett, evidently finished, put his plate on the nightstand.

Champ, who'd been quietly chewing on his cheese bone after having consumed a massive breakfast, came to attention.

"Bingo." I tossed him a treat.

He ate it, gave one last look at Everett's plate, then continued to gnaw on his bone. After the chaos of last night, I expected him to be...more upset than just his wariness about Denali. Although maybe it would show up in other ways.

God knew, I was doing my best to get past mine.

"Cole is Justice." I sat a little straighter. *See? I know shit. I can pretend nothing's wrong.*

Denali snickered, but didn't stop eating.

"So who is Montgomery?" Everett's exasperation was showing.

I laughed. "Cole Hamilton is the actor. The role is Montogomery Daley. He's a corporate raider by day. At night, he's Justice. The seeker of...well, justice." I glanced over at Denali.

She swallowed, then nodded. "And his nemesis is Lyric. Played by the most amazing Julie Reyes."

"She's so hot."

"She so is." Denali fanned herself. "Although Cole's damn good-looking as well."

"But not single."

"No, not single." She sighed dramatically. "He's in a triad relationship with his best friends Caressa and Michael. And they're having a baby."

Everett cleared his throat.

We both turned to him.

"So we're watching this...tonight?"

"Yeah. Why not? Unless you're too—"

"Don't say it. I'm fucking tired of being in bed."

Denali grinned toward me. "If Rayne were my man, and I loved him as much as you do, I'd never want to leave bed." She rose. "I'll take the plates downstairs and clean up the kitchen. Now that I have lines to learn, are you guys going to be okay?"

"Of course." Everett said the words, clearly on automatic.

I gave her a smile. "Are you going to be okay?"

She nodded. "I want to get home to tell the fam in person. I don't think anyone here would've called them, but if they heard anything on the news, then they'll likely need to be reassured." Slowly, she made her way over to me.

Champ's ears flattened, but he didn't growl.

*Progress.*

I handed her my very empty plate.

She made her way over to Everett's side and grabbed his plate as well.

To my relief, he'd eaten most of the waffle and had drunk most of the decaf coffee. He was to avoid caffeine while he recovered.

Denali kissed his cheek, gave me a wink, and headed out of the room.

"My sister." Everett sighed.

"Yeah. She saved my life. Our lives." I glanced over at Champ.

He continued to devour his treat.

I gazed over at Everett. "So what do you want to do now?"

# Chapter Thirty-One

Everett

"Uh..." I tried to think of something. Anything that would keep Rayne close. "So we can watch an episode of..." I flailed my hand around, desperately trying to remember the fragments of the conversation.

"*Vigilante Justice*."

"Right."

"Everett, you'll love it." Rayne nearly bounced on the bed. "Even if you're not into superhero movies... Well, it's just so damn good. The storylines totally suck you in. I've been caught since day one. I don't think I've missed an episode. Well, when we're watching, I guess I'll find out."

"Rayne."

"Yep?"

"Four seasons?"

"Yep."

"Twenty-some-odd episodes a season?"

"Yep."

"Have you done the math?"

He blinked.

"An episode a night..."

"Oh, right." He yanked his phone out of his back pocket.

I was about to suggest that we could just call it one hundred and be done, but he was already tapping and scrolling and tapping and—

"There are one-hundred-and-three episodes. So, I figure we can watch six or seven episodes while you're, like, convalescing—"

I stared.

He kept tapping. "So let's say six—in case you get tired—although I've done like thirteen or fourteen in a day. But Champ needs his walks and training...so we'll say six." He worried his lower lip. "So that's seventeen days." He squinted.

"Rayne."

"Yep?"

"Don't you have a job to get back to?"

He shrugged. "My only two paying clients were the guy who set me up to get killed—so I'm going to say he's not likely to pay—and the person who hired me to get the dirt on Sonny. They were paying installments, but I'm suspecting that'll dry up oh, like, today? So I need to hustle to find new clients, but no...not anything that needs me right now."

My heart ached for him. He had a strong drive to succeed in a profession where the work wasn't always consistent. The pay wasn't steady. The hours weren't reliable. My analytical brain rebelled against all of it. "Okay." Finding courage, I reached out to him.

He grasped my hand.

"I'm asking you to stay with me. I'm asking you to stay. With Champ. For as long as you need. We can arrange to maybe sublet your—"

"I don't want to go back to that apartment. I'm on a month-to-month lease. If I walk away, nothing's going to happen. It came furnished, so it's just my portable stuff I want to keep." He blinked those stunning tawny-brown eyes. "Colton says it won't be safe to go back to my place without an escort. He's asked Constable Seth Jacobs to take me. He asked if I could wait until tomorrow, though, as they're kind of busy today taking down all the, uh, bad guys."

"I'm glad you told him you could wait a day. That was very considerate of you." *And I get to keep you close that much longer.*

"So Seth will help you pick up your stuff tomorrow."

"Yeah. Oh, Colton said he's confirmed my car's in the city impound lot." He snapped his fingers. "That's how they found me."

"What?" I couldn't figure out the non sequitur.

"They traced your call to the bylaw office. That's what Colton said. Or what he thinks. But it's also possible someone saw me in Mission City and let him know and then he followed me up here." He furrowed his brow. "I'm tired." Then he met my gaze.

"I'm asking you to stay with me, Rayne. I'm saying collect your stuff tomorrow, put it in the spare room, and we'll figure out the rest. If you want to hang around and watch six episodes of..." I cringed.

"*Vigilante Justice,*" he prompted.

"Right. Especially because Denali's going to be on it, and I'd better know what the hell is going on."

"Sure, because of that. Not because Cole Hamilton is the sexiest man around and queer to boot. And Julie Reyes is a feast for the eyes—even if you're very gay." He grinned.

Maybe him teasing me was okay. Because he hadn't answered my question. Teasing back felt like the way to protect myself.

To safeguard my heart.

"I am. Unlike you, the bisexual. And I'm not sure I like the objectification of women." I arched an eyebrow.

"Oh, but the objectification of men is okay?" He tried for mock seriousness.

I frowned. My head was starting to hurt.

He chuckled. "I'm kidding. They're a handsome couple. Their love-hate dynamic—and the sexual tension—just makes things all the more fun. Every show, audiences are left wondering...*will they or won't they*? Everyone wants to know if they'll get together in the end. Oh!" Excitement seemed to grow within him. "Maybe Denali will find out, and she'll share."

"The people who make the show—"

"The executive producers—"

"Yes, them. If they're smart, they won't tell my sister anything. Even with an NDA." Despite myself, I smiled.

"I suspect she's on the phone right now telling your parents how she's sure we're in love... What?"

"What?" I scowled.

"I know you love your sister. Hell, I love your sister. And if she wants to tell your parents, I'd be totally down with that."

"Sharing that we might be in love?" I squeaked that "Two weeks," I reminded him.

"Almost three months," he countered repeating my words back to me. "I certainly wasn't with anyone else during that time."

I blinked. "Really?" Doubt laced my voice. *No one? A sexy guy like him and he'd been celibate for two months while we were apart?* That didn't make sense to me. *Oh, except I was as well...* Not that I was a huge dater anyway, but I certainly had only been looking for one man.

Him.

"Really." He gripped my hand. "I know it defies reason—certainly I can't explain it—but leaving you that Halloween night was one of the hardest things I've ever done. I wanted to stay and...talk to you. Kiss you. Make you—"

I cleared his throat. "Maybe not at the moment?" Because the last thing I needed was to get riled up. My cock wasn't very interested and frankly, I was okay with that. I was truly dog-tired.

"But later?"

I sighed. "Much later. I'm exhausted."

"It's because of me. I exhaust you."

"Only in a good way. You keep me on my toes."

"Do you need a nap?"

"I'm fucking tired of napping."

"Because you've been doing that a lot in the hospital." He offered a sympathetic smile. "Tell you what. You rest your eyes for twenty minutes, and then we'll go downstairs and start watching *VJ.*"

"Sure." Slowly, I settled so I lay on his back. "Twenty minutes."

"I'm going to take Champ out so we can do some training."

Champ stood on his bed, leaning forward. He knew *training* meant treats. And I knew he'd be working hard. Which didn't seem to bother him in the least.

"Yeah, okay." I yawned.

He grinned.

I was out for a lot longer than twenty minutes.

# Chapter Thirty-Two

Rayne

Fifties diner was a hoot. With the décor, fifties memorabilia, and just rockin' vibe. I hadn't had a chance to take it all in the last time I'd been here, but today I got my fill. Dawn had barely broken on this cold winter day.

Everett's cabin fever had hit a new pitch this morning.

I'd coaxed Champ into his crate, with a squeaky toy and a Kong full of frozen peanut butter, and had brought my man out for some breakfast excitement.

Well, as exciting as Fifties could be.

"Glad to see you're looking better." Sarabeth grinned at me. Clearly she wasn't concerned if Everett overheard her comment.

"Yes, his bruises healed nicely." My *boyfriend's* dry tone didn't fool me—he was happy I wasn't black, blue, yellow, purple, and green anymore.

Just like I'd be happier when he was fully recovered.

Wait. Boyfriend? He'd asked me to move my stuff in. I had. Beyond that, I'd been dodging Everett's hints. My entire world still felt upside down. How could he be so certain this was real? I hadn't had a lot of luck with love in my life. Could I give up everything that had come before? Could I start a new life with him? Was it really as simple as saying *yes*?

Yeah. Yeah, I could. He'd proven his love for me over and over. In words and in deeds. I needed to give up my fear of rejection and move forward.

With him.

"What can I get you folks? Something to drink to start?"

"An espresso milkshake. Heavy on the espresso." I offered my winningest smile.

Everett shuddered. "Herbal tea for me." He pursed his lips. "I'm supposed to avoid caffeine. I really want some—"

"But you're going to follow the doctor's orders." I stared at him.

"Doctor? Have you been unwell?" Sarabeth's brow furrowed.

"He was in a wreck. I'm surprised you didn't hear about it." I propped my elbows on the table, put my hands under my chin, and grinned up at her.

She tapped the edge of my nose with her pen. "You're cute."

"Too much for his own good." Everett. Grumbling.

Sarabeth and I both burst out laughing.

"I'll grab those drinks."

"Actually, I know what I'd like, and I'm so hungry that I don't want to wait." I pointed to the menu. *Maybe I should've waited to see if Everett was ready. Oh well, he's got thirty seconds.* "I'll start with deep fried pickles and mac-n-cheese bites. Then I want the meatloaf with extra fries and gravy—"

"For breakfast?" Everett's expression was horrified.

"Yes. I've had several days of all-healthy food. I'm allowed to treat myself." I turned to Sarabeth. "No mushrooms."

"They're extra." She smiled.

"I know, but someone might hear I'm with Everett and think, I don't know, that mushrooms aren't gross fungi—"

"Keep it up and I won't pay." He offered a wicked grin.

I sat straighter. "I have room on my credit card." My bank account was empty, but I wasn't maxed out on the card.

Yet.

He frowned.

*Ha. I'm not destitute anymore.* Seth had taken me home, and I'd retrieved all my things. Which wasn't much.

Frankly, he'd been surprised no one had broken into my place. He hypothesized Sonny'd had it under surveillance.

Now that the crooked cop and all his goons had been arrested, I could breathe a little easier. I grinned at Sarabeth. "And I'll order dessert as well, but I need to see how much room I have before I decide."

"You bet." She pivoted her attention to Everett.

"I'll have the mushroom-and-cheese omelet. Instead of hash browns, can I get fresh fruit? I don't mind paying an upcharge."

"Which you know I'll never charge you." Sarabeth snagged the menus. "I'll be right back with your drinks."

I wagged my finger at him. "You ordered that just so I can't steal from you."

"I ordered that because it's my favorite. I love this place, but it isn't known for healthy food."

"It's a diner." I snickered. "Check your cholesterol count at the door."

"Something like that." He pressed a hand to his chest.

I seized the other one. "I was joking. Are you okay?"

"Just a twinge. And Dr. Leopold says my heart's in excellent shape. He did extensive heart diagnostics when he was fixing other stuff."

I winced. Even the thought of there being *other stuff* to fix upset me. We hadn't talked specifics because my gut clenched every time I thought of how close I'd come to losing him.

"Hey, Everett." A voice came from behind me.

Before I could turn, two men stood beside our table. One was a striking older Black man while the younger was of South Asian heritage. They held hands, and both had goofy grins.

"Arnav, Foster." Everett glanced at me. "Apologies, Rayne. Let me do proper introductions. Foster is the construction foreman on a local housing project—"

The Black man waved.

"And Arnav is a formidable attorney I've had the pleasure of sparring with a couple of times."

Arnav straightened and looked quite pleased with himself.

"They got engaged New Year's Eve at Quinton's Out of This World party."

"As opposed to the Epic Halloween gathering." I grinned.

Foster eyed me. Then glanced toward Everett. Then back at me. Clearly he was making some kind of calculation. Some kind of connection.

Arnav's cheeks pinkened. "Yes, well, that was also an epic party." He nudged his shoulder to Foster's. "Good memories."

The other man coughed. "Right."

*Okay, there's a story I want to hear. Just...another time.*

*Wait. When will there be* another time?

"Oh." Arnav snapped his fingers. "Have you responded yet? I know we gave guests almost no time, but who's busy the last week of January anyway?"

Everett blinked. "Responded?"

"To the invitation." Arnav nodded enthusiastically.

"By mail or by email?" My man still looked confused.

"Well, both. My mother insisted on engraved invitations, but I was like, you know how the mail can be—"

"I haven't opened my mail in two weeks—"

"Right. Which was why I sent an email invite last week—just to make sure we have all our bases covered."

Everett blinked.

I smothered a smile with my hand.

"Our wedding invitation." Foster's voice was just a touch softer. "We'd really like for you to come." He pivoted to me. "And you, if you're available."

"You don't know me." This felt super obvious. And a huge assumption if he thought I was with Everett.

*Oh, wait, we're holding hands.* I tried to pull my hand back.

Everett tightened his grip. "I can't speak for Rayne, but I'll be there."

"You don't even know—" Foster began.

"Doesn't matter. I'll clear my schedule." Everett glanced at me. Meaningfully.

"Oh yes. I'll be there as well." *Because that means another couple of weeks together. So...* I couldn't do the calculations. Couldn't figure out what this might mean for us. We hadn't even made it through the first season of *VJ* yet. He'd asked me to stay. We were sort of engaged. Or not. Hard to tell.

"That's great." Arnav nearly vibrated with excitement. "No gifts, okay? If you want to make a donation to Lissa's House, that would be great."

Everett met my confused gaze. "A shelter for domestic abuse survivors."

"Ah."

"Make way folks, I've got a milkshake and an herbal tea."

At Sarabeth's comment, Arnav and Foster shuffled to the side.

Our server put the glass and mug on the table and then skedaddled out of there. She again seemed run off her feet.

"I know why *we* left the house at the break of day, but you two are out early. Or is this your routine?" Everett gazed between the two men.

Foster cleared his throat.

Arnav laughed. "We were in a club in Vancouver until early this morning. We didn't feel like going home, so we came here. We're just leaving."

The men exchanged a look rife with meaning, yet clearly not something they were going to share.

"I promise to open both my mail and my email when I get home." Everett squeezed my hand again. "I'm way behind."

Arnav's eyes widened. "Oh shit, I totally forgot you were in that crash. How the hell are you?"

And they spent the next five minutes conversing about Everett's medical condition—which drove him nuts. I wanted to shoo the men along, but that wasn't my call.

Plus, Foster kept glancing at me.

*He knows something. I don't know what...*

Oh shit.

Hadn't Everett suggested one of the bedrooms at Quinton's party had been occupied?

By these two?

Okay, that definitely was something I wanted to explore further. But that risked giving away how I'd met Everett, and clearly his friends weren't in on that.

Or at least Arnav wasn't.

I met Foster's gaze head-on.

He offered a shy smile.

*Yep. He knows.*

"Okay, folks, I've got food. Do you want to move to a bigger booth so you can all keep talking?"

Sarabeth held a large tray aloft.

"No, thanks." Arnav squeezed Foster's hand. "My fiancé and I really are leaving this time." He pressed a hand to Everett's shoulder. "Take care."

"I will."

We waved them off as Sarabeth laid the most amazing-smelling food before us. We might've consumed Nanny's homemade lasagna that Simeon and Ryan had dropped off last night, but we now descended on our food like locusts and had devoured a good portion of the everything we saw before we came up for air.

At some point Sarabeth came to check on us.

While our mouths were full—of course.

We gave thumbs-ups.

She headed back to the front of the diner, happily greeting yet another family.

The place was filling nicely. Getting noisier, too.

"This is possibly the best meatloaf ever." I wiped a bit of gravy off the corner of my mouth. "Although don't tell my grandmother's former chef. He rarely made it, but he did a good job. This—" I pointed. "—is better."

"I'm certain the chef here would be appreciative of the comment." Everett forked a mushroom and popped it in his mouth.

I did my best not to wince.

He laughed.

*Okay, apparently not as discreet as I'd hoped.*

He eyed my meatloaf. "How can you eat such a heavy meal for breakfast?"

"Did you see the trucker's breakfast?

"Uh..."

"I've already put Champ through his paces." He enjoyed the early morning training sessions.

As did I.

Everett cocked his head. "What?"

"Does this...?" I waved my fork around. "Feel so...normal?"

A laugh escaped. "Baby, nothing is ever *normal* with you. If you're not escaping rogue cops wanting to kill you, you're rescuing German Shepherds in need of good homes, or charming the pants off wayward sisters."

"Hey." I frowned.

"What?" He blinked.

"She's not wayward. She's...artistic. And I want nothing to do with her pants."

He cleared his throat. "She also pointed out we were in love with each other.

I put down my fork.

"Oh, are you guys done? You ready for dessert?" Sarabeth organized the plates and held them as she waited for our response.

Part of me wondered who ate dessert at seven a.m. and the part of my brain that had put Champ through his workout said, "Banana split. Two spoons."

I watched Sarabeth leave with our dirty—but empty plates. "If you don't like banana splits—"

"Who doesn't like banana splits?"

"Well, uh, people who don't, I dunno, like bananas? I had a friend in high school..." My voice trailed off. "Okay, so we're in agreement about bananas, ice cream, strawberry and chocolate sauce, as well as whipped cream."

"Whipped cream..." He frowned.

"You know, I'm aware of some pretty creative things you can do with whipped—"

"Rayne?"

I shut my mouth. And nodded.

"Maybe now's not the time?"

I nodded.

"But..." He shrugged. "Maybe later?"

I grinned. "Oh man, when you're healed, we're going to have so much fun."

"Rayne?"

"Yep?"

"Are you..." He swallowed. "Are you going to be around after I've healed? I mean, I know you've moved your stuff in. I know we've talked about watching all one hundred and three episodes..."

I frowned. "You're overtired. I should ask Sarabeth to get the banana split to go? They can do that, right? I'm sure they can. I mean they must, because everything on the menu is to go, and wow, this was the best milkshake ever, and I'd get one every day, but then I'd have to work out twice as much, and—"

"Rayne?"

I squinted.

"We can eat the banana split here. Although you're going to wind up eating most of it since I'm pretty full."

"So you're okay?"

"I'm getting tired, but I can hang on long enough for us to have this conversation."

"Ah." I sat a little straighter. "Right."

"So you're staying?"

"For however long you'll have me."

We were interrupted by, "One banana split with two spoons."

We gazed up at Sarabeth.

Asking her to box up the dessert was on the tip of my tongue, but Everett snagged his spoon and dug it deep into the scoop of vanilla ice cream with the chocolate sauce.

"Hey."

"You snooze, you lose." He put the spoon into his mouth and moaned in bliss.

My cock twitched.

*Seriously? Now you're interested? When he's still recovering?*

Sarabeth met my gaze and gestured to the spoon with her chin. Then she hustled away.

Again, we consumed half the split before we slowed down.

"I didn't know I was that hungry." Was I going to get an ice cream headache? Nah. I took another bite.

"Right? That omelet was amazing. But this? Pure heaven."

I couldn't disagree.

In the end, we finished the entire dish.

I leaned back with a satisfied moan.

He snickered.

I winked. Then sobered.

"What?" Concern laced his voice.

"Something Denali said."

"My sister said a lot of things."

"Yeah…" I scratched my belly through my T-shirt.

"What? Talk to me."

"She said she thought we loved each other."

"Yeah." He tucked the spoon onto the plate holding the bowl. "That."

"We were about to discuss this before the split arrived. I'm wondering what she sees."

"I think sometimes Denali has brain-to-mouth filter issues. She lost a modeling job because she accused the photography director of being racist. Of course, the guy actually was. She was standing up for all the women who might follow her. But she risked future jobs. People don't want to work with difficult people."

"But she was right."

"Well, yeah. We dug up some photos of the guy, and he was really horrible with women who had darker—"

"I mean she's right that I love you."

"Oh."

"Yeah, *oh.*" I reached out my hand.

He met me halfway.

His gaze held mine. "I'm just trying to figure out how I got so lucky."

"Well, a criminal hired you as her lawyer, and—"

"I mean you."

"So do I. If not for Allyson getting mixed up with Sonny and hiring you, we never would've met."

He laughed.

As did I.

"I guess I'll have to give her zealous representation."

"I explained to Colton about her innocence in the robbery. It'll be up to the police to figure out why she was interacting with Sonny."

"Blackmail?"

"I don't know. She might tell you, though."

He pressed a hand to his chest. "Yeah. I should be—"

"It'll keep. Why don't you call Gil? He can cover for you, right? Dr. Leo said a couple more weeks off work."

"I want to get my laptop out soon."

I pursed my lips. "Okay. Today's Sunday."

"Is it? I thought today was Saturday."

I waved him off.

He grinned.

"So how about Monday, I make you breakfast in bed, and you can, I don't know, check your email? Reply to Arnav and Foster. When you're tired, we'll cuddle. While you nap, I'll put Champ through his paces."

His smile took on a dreamy quality. "You know, I can't think of a better way to spend my time."

I squeezed his hand. "This is a forever thing, right?"

He blinked. "Uh, yeah. I think it could be."

"Then let's settle up the bill and head home."

The smile that broke across his face was radiant. "Yeah, let's do that."

And we did.

# Epilogue

Everett

Quinton's Absolutely Amazing Valentine's Shindig was *the* place to be on the second Saturday in February.

We were experiencing a mild thaw. The weather felt spring-like—but the temperatures were expected to drop precipitously tomorrow with snow in the forecast the day after that. So, tonight, we wore light jackets, but we'd be back to winter coats by Monday.

Such was the Pacific Northwest during the winter.

Before we could knock, Quinton's door swung open.

"Everett. Rayne." My friend, Dean, grinned. His Aussie accent had diminished a bit over his nearly yearlong stay in Canada. The visit that had turned into love, a permanent job, and marriage.

I grinned. "Married life looks like it's been good to you."

He grinned back. "Mate, you have no idea. I didn't know I could be this happy. Come in before the heat escapes." He grinned at Rayne. "I like the choice of shirt—very à propos."

Rayne laughed. He'd chosen a white dress shirt covered in red hearts.

I'd opted for a simple black satin dress shirt.

Dean had gone even more casual with a green-and-blue plaid.

We shucked our shoes, hung up our coats, and followed him into the main room.

I spotted more than a dozen people I knew.

Rayne snagged my hand and dragged me over to Dean's husband, Adam. "How's it going?"

Adam smiled. Something he did more and more. When he did, his facial scar was less prominent. His happiness came to the fore. "It goes well. My boss offered me a promotion. They want me in the office more. I think Chip and Maurice will survive."

Just like Adam to shift the concern to his dog and cat. I wondered if he was hesitant about appearing in public more, but loving Dean had really given him new confidence.

"A promotion's great." Rayne swung his arm around Adam's shoulder. "I'm so proud of you."

Adam rolled his eyes.

"I'm going to get us drinks." I'd leave them to it. They'd formed an odd friendship over the past month. Both had been spoiled children of privilege, and both had been desperately unhappy. For Adam, that had resulted in destructive behavior which led to the death of his twin brother. For Rayne, rejection had sent him down some tough paths before finding his way home.

To me.

In the kitchen, I found Quinton organizing a tray of hors d'oeuvres.

I snagged a pig in the blanket before he could slap my hand away.

He grinned. "You're incorrigible. What happened to the man who always follows the rules?"

"Uh...I met a man who likes to break them and fell in love with him?"

"When's the wedding?"

"May. Dad's coordinated with Isaac, the harbormaster here in Mission City. We're marrying in the Maritime Hall."

"I'm invited, right?" Quinton angled his cheek.

I kissed it. "You bet. Wouldn't have it any other way." When he'd visited me as I convalesced, Rayne and I had come clean about defiling his office.

Quinton had laughed for a good five minutes, sworn he'd never tell another soul, and then had teased us mercilessly ever since.

"Food?" Rainbow poked her head into the kitchen. She grinned as Quinton handed her the tray.

I noticed a couple standing by the window in the breakfast nook that overlooked an adorable backyard. "I don't know them." The taller man had long, shaggy blond hair and the other man—slightly shorter with brown hair—had a look of concentration on his face. Not unhappy...just very serious.

"We'll leave them to it. I'll explain later." Quinton handed me a couple of cans of ginger ale and shoved me out the kitchen door and back into the living room.

Rayne was surrounded by a bunch of my friends. All laughing uproariously at something he'd just said.

I approached.

He moved to my side, grabbed his drink, and kissed me on the lips.

When he pulled back, I gazed into his eyes. "Do I want to know?"

Arnav snickered. "We were just reminiscing about Halloween." He gazed at Foster and grasped his husband's hand.

Rayne and I had attended their wedding at the end of January. I'd been exhausted, but the effort had been worth it. I still had days where fatigue hit me, but I was back to work full time.

With an exonerated and grateful client. Allyson had, in fact, been blackmailed by Sonny the scumbag ex-cop. Who apparently was pleading guilty to a bunch of charges including first-degree murder. He wanted a chance at parole before he turned ninety.

Zach, the crown prosecutor, intended for that to never happen.

We'd see.

Dean guffawed. "Yeah, Halloween."

Heat suffused my cheeks. "Repeat?" I might've squeaked that. *Do they know what we'd been up to?*

Maddox laughed. My friend had a great sense of humor, although, thank goodness, he'd failed in his attempt to set me up with our friend Simeon. Since Simeon was happily living with Ryan and their rescue dog Chia. My mind spun at how much had changed in just a few months.

Including my love for Rayne. And his, finally, clearly, without hesitation, for me.

"Quinton is not known for discretion." This time, Foster spoke. Despite his dark skin, the tips of his ears appeared to be reddening. He was so shy, but his marriage to Arnav, and apparently therapy at the ranch, had him becoming stronger. Bolder.

I wished him all the happiness in the world. Although not via jokes at my expense. I mock-glared.

Rayne grinned. "I might've whetted their appetites."

*Oh dear God. Please save me.*

Yet I didn't want to be saved.

Rainbow arrived with the tray.

My friends all nabbed something.

While they were busy, Rainbow nudged me. "So, Champ's entering Torah's agility dog training with Rayne."

"Yes. She thinks he can handle being around the other owners and dogs, even women, if he's focused on a defined task."

Champ had sailed through obedience training. He didn't need to be crated when we left him alone. Although he had access to his crate if he felt the need for safety.

Oh, and he'd saved our lives by barking that night at Sonny. He'd not barked at a person since. He still seemed anxious about using his voice, but as he calmed down, he was showing a more playful side.

He slept on his own bed every night. He was still reserved around women, but he no longer cowered or whined, as long as they respected his personal space. He loved to fetch a ball. Somehow, he'd transformed into the dog he was meant to be. Such a good boy.

That said, if either Rayne or I left the bed to leave early, Champ would take the spot on our bed and keep the other company.

Torah said that was okay now he clearly trusted us, as long as we only let him on the bed on command, not on his whims. The "Up!" command was now one of his favorites.

Rayne's reputation had been enhanced when word got around he'd helped bring down a dirty cop. And ten thousand dollars—from his apparently legitimate client who'd never identified themself—had appeared in his bank account almost the moment Sonny was arrested. Rayne could've told the police, and they could've traced the payment. But he hadn't wanted to expose someone who was clearly on the right side. He'd earned the money. He kept it.

Now he was using that money to pay his tuition to take cybersecurity courses. He had a knack for computers and wanted to dig into forensics. Being able to dig deeper into people's digital footprints would be a boost to his PI business.

And, in his spare time, he was working for a bunch of lawyers, doing investigations for them. As well as tracking down the odd cheating spouse.

He had a full plate.

And I couldn't have been prouder.

Of both of my loves. Because yeah, I loved Champ too.

Suddenly, Rayne stepped up onto the fireplace hearth.

Heat shot to my face. He wasn't...was he...?

Because, at the New Year's Eve party, Foster had stood in that exact spot and had proposed to Arnav—to everyone's shock.

Obviously someone had shared that story with Rayne.

"Everett?" He held out his hand. He had that cocky grin on his face I loved so much. His playful side called to me in a way nothing else ever had. Anyone who might've come before was a distant memory.

Still, his eyes held uncertainty.

Part of me wanted to make him wait, and the rest of me wanted to put him out of his misery.

I handed my ginger ale to Dean. I fingered the harlequin mask in my pocket, and then I took his hand and allowed him to pull me up. I glanced out to find everyone watching us.

"Okay. Now everyone's clearly wondering what I'm doing up here." Rayne spoke loudly enough that if someone was hanging out in the kitchen—or upstairs—they'd have likely heard.

"Get on with it." Quinton tapped his foot. "I have more pigs in the blanket in the oven."

"I brought curry puffs too." Dean's contribution.

"Right." Rayne turned to face me, gripping my hands. "We've only known each other just over three months—"

I arched an eyebrow.

"Work with me, here." He whispered the words.

"Right. Three months. We met at Quinton's Halloween party." I said that so everyone could hear.

Hoots and hollers went up. The loudest being our group of friends who apparently knew—or would eventually know—about our half-a-night stand.

"And I just..." Rayne swallowed. "It's presumptuous of me to propose. I moved into your house. I inserted myself into your life. I invited my dog to shed all over the place—"

"I love Champ—"

"Well, that's good to know." His tawny brown eyes still showed...wariness? Fear?

*Put him out of his misery.* I grinned. "Will you marry me?"

Those stunning eyes widened.

Quinton hooted.

A huge cheer went up in the room. Clearly Rayne had been trying to find the courage to propose. Since I'd just done it, obviously we were...getting married.

He threw his arms around me and pulled me into a huge hug. Then he planted a kiss on my lips.

"Okay...now?" Quinton's voice broke through the cheers.

Rayne turned to him. "Yeah, now."

Quinton sprinted up the stairs.

"What the hell...?"

"Don't be mad—"

A squeal had us turning. Before I knew what was happening, Denali had joined us on the fireplace hearth and was hugging Rayne.

"Hey, *I'm* your brother."

"Yeah, but he asked the family's permission first. And he proposed—"

"Actually, Everett beat me to it."

Denali turned to face me. "Always the dark horse."

"Yeah, something like that."

"Oh, my darling boys." Mom was there, a huge grin on her face. With Ursula and my dad next to her.

Laila was nursing a sick child, so I didn't worry about not seeing her.

Rayne, Denali, and I stepped off the ledge, and my family exchanged hugs and, from my dad, a tear or two.

Then everyone else wanted in, and the next thing I knew, I'd been hugged by about thirty people.

I'd never been happier.

The celebrations went on long into the night, and only after my family had headed back to New West, did Rayne and I finally take our leave.

I was completely wiped when we got home, but I managed to stay awake while Rayne walked Champ.

They entered our bedroom quietly, but Rayne's face lit when he spotted me in bed and awake.

I grinned. "Dr. Leopold gave me the green light."

Rayne's grin grew. "Tonight?"

"If we're gentle, then yeah, tonight."

"Woohoo." He hotfooted into the bathroom.

Champ nuzzled my hand before heading over to his bed. He turned three times, dropped, and was out almost immediately.

I liked the idea of high-energy agility training for him.

Rayne exited the bathroom naked.

I was waiting for him naked as well—for the first time since coming home from the hospital.

He slid into bed.

We came together.

Gently.

Passionately.

In a way to seal our lives together.

Forever.

Afterward, as I lay replete in his arms, he pressed a kiss to my temple. "Thank you."

"For?"

"For taking me in. For giving me a home. For giving me a family."

"For giving you love?"

"Yeah."

"Easiest decision I've ever made. Right up there with following a certain hot harlequin up to a home office and fucking him."

Rayne giggled. "What a story."

"Epic."

"Yeah." Another kiss. "I love you."

"Me too." I ran my hand along his cheek. "Thank you for bringing happiness and love into my life." I had a wonderful family, of course, but sharing my body, my heart, and my life with Rayne was teaching me what love really meant and had brought a joy I never imagined I'd find to my life.

His eyes drifted shut.

I pressed a kiss to his nose.

And thanked my lucky stars I'd taken a chance that fateful Halloween night.

Want to know the mysterious couple in Quinton's kitchen?
Check out the next story in the Love in Mission City series!

Archer's Awakening

Other Love in Mission City stories available:
Ginger Snapping All the Way (Love in Mission City Book 1)
Stanley's Christmas Redemption (Love in Mission City Book 2)
The Beauty of the Beast (Love in Mission City Book 2.5)
Sleigh Bells and Second Chances (Love in Mission City Book 3)
Rayne's Return (Love in Mission City Book 4)
Gideon's Gratitude (Love in Mission City Book 5)
Quinton's Quest (Love in Mission City Book 6)
Ulysses's Ultimatum (Love in Mission City Book 7)
Love in Mission City: The Boyfriend Gamble
Love in Mission City: The Four Seasons
Love in Mission City: The Boyfriends Duet
Love in Mission City: The Shorts
Love in Mission City: The Wedding Duet
Rayne Check
Archer's Awakening
Leo's Lust
Finn's Find
Styx's Storm
A Daddy for Christmas 2: Foster
Puppy Pride
A Daddy for Christmas 3: Lorcan
Pup, Pup, and Away
A Daddy for Christmas 4: Raphael
Anderson's Reinvention
Thought You Were the One
Love Without Reservations
Page Against the Machine

The Lightkeeper's Love Affair

Ace's Place

Marcus's Cadence

Not in it for the Money

Also:

Edging Coach (co-written with L.A. Witt)

Hugh (Single Dads of Gaynor Beach)

Anthony (Single Dads of Gaynor Beach)

Xavier (Single Dads of Gaynor Beach)

Love Furever (Friends of Gaynor Beach Animal Rescue)

Husky Love (Friends of Gaynor Beach Animal Rescue)

Yorkie to My Heart (Friends of Gaynor Beach Animal Rescue)

A Furever Home (co-written with Kaje Harper – Friends of Gaynor

Beach Animal Rescue)

Axe to Grind(Road to Rocktoberfest 2023)

Grindstone's Edge(Road to Rocktoberfest 2024)

Voice to Raise (Rocktoberfest 2025)

Drums and Lullabies (Rocktoberfest 2026)

My Past, Your Future

If Only for Today

Catch a Tiger by the Tail

Solstice Surprise

Valentino in Vancouver

You See Me

Sun, Surf, and Surprises

Ginger in the City

Caressa's Homecoming (Bound by LoveBook 1)

Cole's Reckoning (Bound by Love Book 2)

Donovan's Men (Bound by Love Book 3)

A Little Christmas: Tobias

An Uncommon Gentleman

A Sensible Gentleman

A Wounded Gentleman

Sizzling Sydney Nights

Didn't See You Coming

Finding Noah (Foggy Basin Season 2)

Noah's Holiday (A Foggy Basin Short Story)

Dancing Through Pride (A Foggy Basin Short Story)

Keystrokes and Kittens (Foggy Basin Season 3)

Hot Rucking Canadian

Big Rucking Disaster

Unlocked and Unlost

Audiobooks

Ginger Snapping All the Way

Stanley's Christmas Redemption

Sleigh Bells and Second Chances

Rayne's Return

Gideon's Gratitude

Quinton's Quest

Ulysses's Ultimatum

Rayne Check

Archer's Awakening

Leo's Lust

Finn's Find

A Daddy for Christmas 2: Foster

Puppy Pride

A Daddy for Christmas 3: Lorcan

Thought You Were the One

Love in Mission City: The Shorts

Page Against the Machine

The Lightkeeper's Love Affair

Ace's Place

Marcus's Cadence

Not in it for the Money

Hugh (Single Dads of Gaynor Beach)

Anthony (Single Dads of Gaynor Beach)

Love Furever (Friends of Gaynor Beach Animal Rescue)

Husky Love (Friends of Gaynor Beach Animal Rescue)

A Furever Home (co-written with Kaje Harper – Friends of Gaynor Beach Animal Rescue)

My Past, Your Future

If Only for Today

Catch a Tiger by the Tail

Solstice Surprise

An Uncommon Gentleman

A Sensible Gentleman

A Wounded Gentleman

Didn't See You Coming

Unlocked and Unlost

Want a free short story? The story is set in Gaynor Beach, California where there are plenty of single dads and puppy rescues! You can sign up for my newsletter so you can keep up with all the great stuff I'm doing as well as pictures of my own pooches, Ally and Finnegan.

Hemingway's Happy Day

Love contemporary MF romances? What's better than love in the beautiful Cedar Valley in British Columbia, Canada? Find small town romances with a touch of angst, a bit of heat, and a lot of heart...

The Absolution of Abigail Reardon (prequel)
The Luminosity of Loriana Harper (Book 1)
The Making of Marnie Jones (Book 2)
The Redemption of Remy St. Claire (Book 3)

# Interested in knowing more about Gabbi?

Sign up for her newsletter

Follow her on Bookbub

Follow her on Instagram

USA Today Bestselling author Gabbi Grey lives in beautiful British Columbia where her fur baby chin-poo keeps her safe from the nasty neighborhood squirrels. Working for the government by day, she spends her early mornings writing contemporary, gay, sweet, and dark erotic BDSM romances. While she firmly believes in happy endings, she also believes in making her characters suffer before finding their true love. She also writes m/f romances as Gabbi Black and Gabbi Powell.